THE
VILLAGE

Also by Lisa Rookes

The Empty Cradle

THE
VILLAGE

LISA ROOKES

ORION

An Orion paperback

First published in Great Britain in 2024 by Orion Fiction,
under the former title *The Vanishing of Joni Blackwood*
This edition published in 2025
an imprint of The Orion Publishing Group Ltd.,
Carmelite House, 50 Victoria Embankment
London EC4Y 0DZ

An Hachette UK Company

The authorised representative in the EEA is Hachette Ireland,
8 Castlecourt Centre, Dublin 15, D15 XTP3,
Ireland (email: info@hbgi.ie)

3 5 7 9 10 8 6 4 2

A CIP catalogue record for this book is
available from the British Library.

ISBN (Paperback) 978 1 3987 1649 0
ISBN (eBook) 978 1 3987 1650 6
ISBN (Audio) 978 1 3987 1651 3

Typeset at The Spartan Press Ltd,
Lymington, Hants

Printed and bound in Great Britain by Clays Ltd,
Elcograf S.p.A.

www.orionbooks.co.uk

For my girls ... all of you

I

All Gallows' Eve

Now

Joni's breath is heady and sweet as she pulls me to her. The crook of her arm hooks the back of my neck and my face is pressed into her shoulder. She still smells of The Body Shop's jasmine oil, twenty-five-odd years on.

Rogue embers from the fireworks lie dying on the ground and the promise of tomorrow's regret begins to lay gently on the eyelashes and crowns of the village throng.

The cobbles are packed for All Gallows' Eve and it's always now, just as dusk is melting into night, that I look around our little Yorkshire village and wonder why anyone would want to be anywhere else. Thistleswaite isn't chocolate-boxy by any means. I always joke that it's a good thing we live in the North because the rain is the only thing that washes the grime from the steelworks away. But there's something about this place.

I've been at every All Gallows' Eve since I was born. There's always a drama of some kind. It's almost like the village needs it to keep going. I wonder what tonight will bring. I have a very strong feeling I'm going to be at the epicentre.

I feel eyes on me, but I don't know if they are his.

'You were meant to keep me off the red wine tonight. I'm

drunk!' I snake my arm around the small of Joni's back. My face is warm and I smell the ashes and her perfume together.

'Don't bother with the fake laugh,' she whispers, so close to my ear, I can feel the dampness in her breath. 'He's not watching.'

I feel crestfallen for a second. I both love and hate that she knows me so well. Just for once, I would love to keep a secret from her. When we were kids, she said she could tell when I was keeping secrets because the freckles on my nose went black. I believed her. I had no one to tell me otherwise.

'Where's Millie?' I straighten up and scout the village square for her red hair. I'd wanted to call her Scarlett as soon as I saw those locks. She was born with a frosted ginger halo. But Kit said I was hanging onto our grunge days and needed something less slutty-sounding. He looked at Joni when he said that.

'I think I saw her headed up the rec.' Joni unscrews the cap of the bottle of red wedged under her arm. 'Top-up.'

It's a statement, not a question, and I hold my plastic glass out.

'I don't want her up there. It's too dark.' I look over my shoulder and down Gallowsgate. The children are running up and down, throwing firecrackers at the cobbles, and the gunfire noise of it makes me shudder. Whatever ends up happening tonight, I don't want Millie anywhere near it.

'She's always there after dark.' Joni empties the rest of the bottle between our plastic glasses. 'Getting fingered, I should imagine, like we were at fifteen.'

'Jesus, Joni! *You*, you mean.' I swat her arm before realising my drink is in my hands and the wine sloshes all over her kimono. 'Shit, sorry.'

'Ah, it'll wash. Anyway, you can't really tell with this pattern.'

'She's not getting fingered. Anyway, by who? In this village? I mean, I may be middle-aged, but even I can see it's slim pickings.'

'True.' Joni sniffs and looks up at the sky. 'The stars are out. It's really clear. Have you seen?'

'I thought it was meant to rain tonight? They've covered the bonfire up in plastic sheeting for tomorrow.'

I crane my neck and realise how stiff my joints are, how high my shoulders are to my ears. There's a loud and satisfying crack at the top of my spine that makes me feel sick and relieved in equal measure.

'Ooh, I heard that,' Joni winces at me. 'Feeling tense, love?'

'Can you blame me?' I have another sip of wine. Joni's right. The sky is like Perspex. The stars seem almost too low.

'Remember when we used to climb out of your bedroom window and lie on the roof?' Joni pulls me down to the kerb and starts rummaging in her bag for her cigs. Little Oscar from next-door-but-one runs past with hollow, black eyes and purplish-green cheeks, his ghoulish make-up streaked with sweat.

'*You* did. I sat on the windowsill.'

Firecrackers explode by our feet and we shriek obligingly as the little ones, dressed up in hessian sacks and rags, laugh and jump up and down. Joni smiles at them. No one has a smile like Joni. It almost splits her face in two. White teeth and huge crimson lips, even without make-up. Not unlike a shark when you think about it.

'Now off you fuck,' she says quietly. Never the one for kids. Millie excepted.

'God, I'm pissed.' I rub my eyes. 'I'm going to need that hog roast tomorrow.'

'Could do with it now.' Joni blows her cheeks out. 'What time is the bonfire again? Two? Or three?'

'Three for the food. Fire getting lit at two. God, I said I'd help collect all the scarecrows and take them up on Kit's trailer. I'm really regretting that now.'

'That sounds awkward,' Joni grimaces. 'Just get Millie to do it.'

'Speaking of, I'd better go and find her.' I make to get up, but Joni yanks me down.

'Let her have fun. It's All Gallows' Eve.'

'Yeah, that's what I'm afraid of.' My eyes track a sinister-looking clown on stilts, teetering down the gate towards the fields. You can really only make out his silhouette – gangly, elongated. Knives for legs.

On the edge of the clumps of people, I can see him. Just by Crazy Dave's Emporium van. He's holding a pint and talking to Andy Shepard, the landlord of the Noose and Bough. God, he really is beautiful. The strings of fairy lights are casting a glow over the side of his face and, for a second, I wonder if everything is going to be all right. That I've made the right decision. Then he catches my eye and smiles and everything inside me squirms and squelches, and all I can see and hear is the pain in Kit's eyes and his words.

Those words.

What have you done?

I take a long, long slug of my wine until it's gone. I poke the hole in the back of my gum with my tongue and wince.

'You OK?' Joni says.

'Yeah. Still hurts.'

'Your tooth? It will do for a couple of days. You've done

well not to get a black eye. I did when I had my wisdom tooth out, do you remember?'

'Well, it wouldn't be you if there wasn't a drama. Think if I put it under my pillow the tooth fairy might come? I'm so skint.'

'Worth a try.'

There's a horrible, head-splitting foghorn that makes us both drop our cups and clasp our hands to our ears. The smell of candyfloss and sausages is all around us. The sinister laughs of the Punch and Judy-style show stop abruptly, and everyone gets to their feet.

Andy is clambering on top of one of the outside pub tables, wearing a waistcoat like a complete dick.

'Ladies and gentlemen, boys and girls!' He doesn't need a megaphone with that gob. He was always a bit of a try-hard at school. That's what the lads used to call him anyway. The goalie. Useless up front apparently.

'God love him, but he does make me cringe.' Joni rolls her eyes and I smirk.

'It is approaching the witching hour of All Gallows' Eve,' Andy bellows. His parents used to own the pub when we were younger. He may have been a try-hard, but we'd always get the crisps for free when they went out of date. 'And as is tradition, our Gallows Queen is about to be crowned.'

A sleepy toddler rests his head on his dad's shoulder, arms around his neck, legs clamped around his waist. I ache for Millie. 'Koala, koala, koala,' she used to say, her pudgy hands reaching up for mine. I glance down the cobbles, but I can't see her. I can't see the spindly shadows of the clown either.

'I'm going to go and look for her,' I say to Joni. Even I notice my words are slurred.

'No, it's my big moment.' Joni slaps the top of my arm. 'Just ring her.'

We get to our feet and some of the school mums turn and raise their eyebrows and grin at Joni. Except the one who moved here recently, who can't due to the Botox.

'As is tradition ...' Andy booms.

I press my phone to my ear, but it's just ringing out. Millie is attached to that bastard thing every waking moment except for the one time I want to get hold of her.

Everyone is gathering together around the oak. The Gallows Tree. Centre of the village, a shoddy black metal fence circling it that tourists ignore and clamber over so they can have their picture taken next to it. The cobbles are uneven and ruptured under it. My mum used to say this village was built on its roots, that they are underneath the ground, under all of our houses. It used to scare me as a kid. Thick, waving, snaking roots squirming under me. No matter how far you ran, they could tunnel after you. I still shudder now.

Tom and Pete are plucking and twitching at their instruments on the makeshift stage. It may be about to turn midnight, but noise licence be damned. There's not a single resident of the village who isn't here.

Well. That's not *quite* true. There's one.

'Now, we all know the story, but just in case, for any comer-iners who may not know the legend of the Gallows Tree, the boughs of the oak are famous for more than just the folk song. The song is inspired by the legend that a sacrifice must be made for the village to prosper, for the crops to grow. And on All Gallows' Eve, traditionally, that sacrifice was hanged from the boughs. It was seen as a great honour to be chosen, and the young maidens would compete to be the Gallows Queen.'

'Did they? Or is he getting mixed up with *The Hunger Games*?' Joni looks at me, smirking.

Andy continues, 'The last girl standing after the maypole dancing would earn the crown. Legend has it, they'd dance all night.'

'Well, you'd make damn sure you didn't win the maypole dance,' Joni replies.

'When has there ever been a dancing competition you would willingly lose?' I point out.

'One that ends in me hanging.'

'Now, we're not hanging anyone tonight...' As if he heard, Andy pauses for dramatic effect and arches one brow in the same way he does every year, playing the villain in the village-hall pantomime. 'But our nominated queens have been selected by the village elders. In this case, my dad and the village-hall trustees. And you'll have seen in the village *Focus* newsletter, this year they are ...' Andy tugs on the noose nearest to him and reads out the tag. 'Helen Cartwright. Nominated for her walking-to-school buddy scheme. Means we can all get off to work that little bit quicker. All hail Helen!'

Everyone applauds and raises a glass to Helen, all pointy-faced and sharp elbows. She smiles thinly from the edge of the crowd. Everyone knows she hasn't won, so no one wastes too loud a clap.

'And next...' Andy tugs on the middle noose. 'For her tireless efforts and dealings with the devil – sorry – our fearless parish council leader' – sniggers ripple through the crowd – 'to turn the red phone box into a children's library, Ruth Walker.'

Again, more applause. Ruth's more popular than Helen, so a couple of other school mums cheer, the ones who win prizes for their lemon curd and nut-free rocky road, and who all fancy the head teacher. I catch her eye and smile. She smiles back, even though she knows she has lost and knows I know it too, so it's a pity smile. And we both hate me for it.

'And last...'

Please don't say 'but by no means least'.

'But by no means least! Nominated for leading the primary school in their victory at the Cross-Valley Choir Competition, Joni Blackwood.'

There are some catcalls and a wolf whistle. Joni laughs, flipping her middle finger at the noisy pack. She's about the only one who could get away with that. Andy is much more traditional than he likes to let on and doesn't usually tolerate profanities on his stage. But he has a thing for Joni. They all do.

I retry Millie. No answer.

'The nooses have been hanging all week, and the good pub-goers have been voting in their masses.'

One of Andy's glass collectors staggers up with a huge jar filled almost to the top with coppers and small silver pieces, the odd chunky pound. His fed-up-looking wife Emma follows out with another, and then a third is plonked next to it on the table.

'Whoever's jar contains the most money is declared our winner!' Andy announces. 'And before I announce our new Gallows Queen, can I just thank everyone who has chucked in their change. I can formally announce that in total we have raised over five hundred pounds for the playgroup's new outdoor kitchen!'

I nudge Joni so we can share our usual scathing eye rolls, but her cheeks are flushed and her green eyes are getting glassy. In fact, she is only looking out of one eye, which is appearing bigger and bigger, and this usually means it's time to leave.

Andy makes a big show of opening the envelope, but we all know what's inside. I can't be the only one to spot the odd note crumpled up in Joni's jar.

'And our Gallows Queen is ...' Everyone starts clapping and whooping before he gets to the end and Joni jumps up and down, wringing her hands like a little girl. She's at the side of the stage before her name is even read out.

Even though I knew it was coming, I can't help but smile as Joni bends her head for her cheap plastic crown and pink sash. Normally, Andy reads out the amount in each jar first. He hasn't this time. So that must mean she's won by a land-slide and he doesn't want to embarrass the others.

'Well, this is kind of weird?' He's here. Suddenly. Right next to me. Jamie. 'Aren't May Queens usually kids?'

'Not in this village.' I glance up. He is so tall. Taller than me. I'm not used to it. 'It seems wrong to vote for children to be sacrificed.'

'Ah OK. Just spinster virgins then? Bit *Wicker Man*?' He puts his arm around me and I feel all the eyes of the village on us, as if we are in some Ira Levin novel.

'I think we both know Joni is no virgin. And does she count as a spinster when she is voluntarily single? I can't believe you don't remember this,' I say.

'Hey, I only lived here for two years. And, erm, we were otherwise occupied for one of those All Gallows' Eves if I remember rightly?'

He must feel me stiffen because he lets his arm drop. I

want to say something, apologise, but, as usual, I don't need to.

'It's OK,' he says quietly. 'Maybe it was a bit soon for our first public outing.'

'I'm sorry,' I say as Joni catches my eye from the front of the crowd and raises an eyebrow.

'You OK?' she mouths. I nod and give her a discreet thumbs up.

'I just feel so awful Kit isn't here. I shouldn't have come. He always loved All Gallows' Eve. I mean, he took the piss, of course. But he liked this kind of thing. The band. I should have just stayed at home. It's just so awkward to know what to do now. Is this going to be my life? Only one of us at parents' evenings? People having to choose between us all the time...'

'Well, I guess it's me that shouldn't have come. Too raw. Sorry. I was being selfish.'

I can hear the hurt in his voice and I want to take it away. I want to get up on my tiptoes and pull him to me, his huge hands on my waist, his stubble sandpapering my cheek. But instead I look back over my shoulder for Millie. When I turn back, he bends down and kisses the top of my head.

'I'll call you in the morning, Cass.'

'You're leaving?' I shiver, but I have no idea why, when the air is close and muggy.

'It's best, I think.' The crinkles around his eyes deepen. 'You've still got my phone, though.'

'Oh yeah.' I fish it out my back pocket and the intimacy of the fact I've been looking after it while his team lost in the tug of war is not lost on either of us. 'I'm sorry,' I whisper. 'It's just... I have no idea how to behave.'

'We'll work it out.' He lifts my chin and I think he is

going to kiss me and immediately I feel the little hairs all over me rise.

But instead he strokes my cheek, then turns and walks away, past the field I hope Millie is in. Towards the mills, where he left his car. Not outside mine. I watch him walk until he becomes part of the purple shadows. Drama averted. I breathe a sigh of relief. I hadn't realised how tense I'd been all night.

Joni is laughing while she readjusts the mic, mouthing something at one of the mums at the back of the crowd.

I catch Tom's eye and offer a tentative smile, but he doesn't return it. He just stares. For a few seconds, everything goes a bit cold. Then I feel warm hands snake over my shoulders and everything feels upside down until I see the fingernails are electric blue.

'Where have you been?' I turn around and Millie is grinning that mischievous smile she's been offering up since she was a toddler, especially when she used to do a secret poo in a variety of unusual locations and watch me with Machiavellian eyes as I tried to hunt down the source of the stench. 'What have you been up to?' I try to block out Joni's earlier comment as I see a grey-hooded youth who looks a lot like Andy's son shoulder-barge his way through the groups of parents and friends with a sense of entitlement his dad never had. 'Is that Chris?'

'Dunno,' Millie shrugs. 'I'm starving, can we go yet?' I stare at her pupils as she looks towards the stage. Joni is adjusting her silver plastic crown. 'Ah, she won!'

'Again.' I put my arm around her and I am shocked when she doesn't try to hiss and spit at me.

'Never any doubt.' Millie looks at me and smiles. Her freckles have started to come out. I can always tell because her nose is caked in concealer and looks three shades darker than the rest of her face. I wish she wouldn't cake her face in so much crap.

Her eyes start to follow the boy in the hoodie, and we both watch as he walks round the back of the pub and hear the fire door open and slam. It *is* Chris. And it's blatant that's who she has been with. I decide it's not worth poking the beast, though.

'I really am tired.' Millie lays her head on my shoulder and I smell the sickly notes of B-list celebrity body spray and weed.

Now is not the time.

'Go home.' I kiss the top of her head. 'I'm going to watch the band and then ...' I have to mouth the rest of the words as Tom drops the bassline to Fleetwood Mac's 'The Chain' and everyone cheers. 'I'll be straight home.'

'OK.' Millie yawns. I can see our house from here.

From the top of the village, the terraced houses lie squat, like a guard, in a circle around the bottom of Gallows Hill. 'Flash your bedroom light when you get in,' I say and she looks at me oddly.

'Can I not just text you like a normal person?'

'No, because you could be texting from anywhere,' I point out.

'I'll send you a pic then.' Millie shakes her head, climbs over a fence in the gap between two houses and drops into the field. It's the shortest way home and I see her phone torch bobbing as she goes.

The short fear. That's what I used to call it. On the way back from Joni's when we were kids. No phones then and I never had batteries in my torch. But running over the fields in the dark, the moon swaying in the black smoky clouds over the treetops, listening out for the howls of the were-wolves that I was always convinced were hot on my heels. Never rapists. I long for the days when the only monsters around were the ones in my dreams.

I smell rain in the air and feel as if the clouds are dropping down. I look up, but the sky is just black and thick and I can't sense what is going to happen. But it feels as if thunder is gathering. The stars are shutting off one by one.

I watch for a few minutes before turning my eyes back to Joni at the microphone. Even with the faint red wine moustache, she is so beautiful. Her nose is slightly crooked. Her mouth hangs wide. It reminds me of the picture I took of her at last year's street party. She is wearing the same kimono. The bird print one. The curve of her breasts in the black satin top underneath. The beads on her wrists. The friendship bracelets I have made for her. One every year. Until they wear thin and fray open. The Tanglewood midnight-blue parlour guitar across her middle.

This is the picture they use in the papers.

Because the next morning, the noose with Joni's name on it sways in the wind, her plastic crown tied to it with the scarf from her hair.

The debris from the night before is scattered underneath the tree, across the cobbles, the uneven pavement. Crushed plastic cups. Red wine stains the flags like blood. Candyfloss sticks are strewn among the trailing bunting that has plunged from the trees in last night's unexpected hailstorm.

And Joni has vanished.

2

It's me who sounds the alarm. She always used to say no one would notice if she fell down the stairs, broke both legs and died staring at the cream cracker under the sofa. I pointed out that she messages me about twelve times a day. If I don't know what she's had for breakfast or what day of her menstrual cycle she's on, I fear she's been abducted by aliens.

So, as usual, I send her a WhatsApp when I wake up. We always do an autopsy of the night, before we've even got out of bed. It's still early, though. And I'm not expecting a reply.

I lie in bed for a bit, stretching my fingers and toes to each corner of it. I haven't got used to sleeping on my own yet. It's been a few weeks now, but I'm still sleeping on the left side, although I must have rolled over in the night because Kit's side is crumpled.

Outside the window, the blackbirds are gathering in the treetops and I watch for a while as they sway in the breeze; their nests look so fragile in the boughs but stay firm. I always loved leaving the curtains open, letting the moon be my night light, but Kit hated it and would close them tight with a flourish, as if he was making a point. No light cracking the thick dark anywhere. I used to lie awake, my eyes trying to make out the shapes against the walls, otherwise I'd feel like I was being swallowed up in a dark, inky abyss.

Now I lie and watch the night turn to day. It's only when the sky starts to soften that I let my swollen eyelids close and drift away.

I check my phone again, but still no blue ticks. Not that I was expecting any. So I climb out of bed and don't bother to straighten the sheets. What's the point? It's only me in here, seeing it. Kit wants to see Millie tonight. We still haven't figured out how it's all working. At the moment, he is still crashing with Tom. I guess I should offer to leave for the night so he can be here with Millie. On familiar ground. Not fair to hang around and make it painful for everyone.

But then he'll ask where I'm going and that makes it all feel worse somehow. I could lie and say I'm going to Joni's. Or I could really just go to Joni's. But the need for him is so strong. It's almost strange now I'm allowed to see him. It still feels shady.

I think about him. Jamie. His fingers in the small of my back. The way he looks into my eyes. I know that sounds like a line from a book, but he really does. First one, then the other. Then back again. Like he is trying to memorise every line in my iris.

He wants me to leave the village. I know he does, deep down. The way he always did when we were kids. When he moved here with his dad, he was already seventeen. It wasn't inbuilt, the pull to this place. He isn't part of its roots, not the way I am.

I think about his flat in Leeds. At least, the pictures I've seen on Facebook. I've never actually been there. His wall-mounted TV. Granite worktops. Appliances I don't understand; vegetable spiralizers, I should think. Coffee pods. His shiny life. I picture him, lying on the sofa. His usual crash position, he tells me. *Match of the Day* on mute. Smiling as he types back to me on his phone. Making promises we never thought we would keep.

My ancient filter coffee machine fizzes and splutters and when my phone buzzes, I snatch it up eagerly. I used to live for these notifications, seeing Jamie's name on the screen. Now I just feel sick, like it's some horrible reminder of what I've done. To Kit. To him. To me. But the want is still there; it's so real, it's all-encompassing ... I can't understand it. I can't understand me.

I have done a terrible, terrible thing.

My fingers grasp the wooden counter and my chest heaves a little. It's not a bad one. I know it will pass. Sometimes I feel so much emotion, it's like there isn't enough room in my body to contain it, like it will eat me from the inside out, like the rot that has set into the wood beneath my palms.

'Mum?' Millie is ruffled and puffy at the bottom of the stairs, her joggers hitched up over one knee and her vest top back to front.

'Hi, love.' I stand tall and make a show of getting the milk. 'Do you want a coffee?'

'Why would I want a coffee?' Millie scratches the back of her bird's nest. Her hair is so thick, nothing like my fine strands. I wish she wouldn't iron out the curls, though.

'Sorry, I'm ...' I pinch the bridge of my nose and shake my head.

'Is Dad coming over tonight?'

'Yeah, is that OK?'

'Are you going to be here?' she asks without meeting my eyes.

'It's probably best I'm not, sweets. He really wants to spend time with you, and definitely doesn't want another

row with me, so I'd better stay clear.' I sip my coffee and feel
like my chest is bursting. Must keep my voice steady. Calm.

'Is this how it's going to be now?' Millie slams the fridge
door, a bottle of something green in her hand. 'Am I from
a broken home?'

'Millie ...'

'Because if I am, that means I can go out, get wankered,
do some class As and stuff and blame it all on you.'

'So basically you want to have a reckless night out without
any responsibility?'

'Pretty much. That's what you did, right?'

Millie slurps from the bottle and wipes the green, snot-
like sludge from the top of her lip, her eyes on me. My
stomach churns and I wonder if I am more hung-over than
I thought.

I can't bring myself to reply.

Half an hour later, my ticks remain grey, so I pull on my
jeans and hoodie, scrape my hair into a ponytail and wander
up into the village for the clean-up. The air smells wet and
the hailstorm from the night before has painted the tarmac
dark grey, the sun breaking through as I walk up Maingate.
The cobbles shine like conkers.

'Tom,' I call out as I see him up ahead pulling parapher-
nalia out of the back of his van. I almost immediately regret
it, remembering the hard stare he gave me last night.

He looks over and nods. I feel embarrassed as he starts
packing his amp up, the rear of his battered red Transit
backed up to the makeshift stage. As he bends over, I notice
his builder's bum over the fallen, baggy waist of his jeans and
realise how much weight he's gained again. Not that he was

ever a waif. But it's noticeable he's not taking care of himself No one to keep an eye on his diet. Or his drinking.

'Cass!' Andy is unplugging stuff and ripping bits of gaffer tape from the floor. 'Come to join in?'

'I said I'd collect the scarecrows and take them up for the bonfire,' I say. 'But I need Kit's trailer. Is he around?' I look at Tom and his face stiffens.

'He's not up yet. Drank himself into a coma last night, I think.'

I can't meet his eyes.

'Sounds like your mate,' Andy laughs. 'Take it Joni's still in bed too?'

'She was wasted last night as well.' Tom slams the back of the van shut. 'Pete had to get her home.' He looks at me accusingly, as if I should have been looking after her. As if I am not always looking after her.

'I had to get back for Millie,' I remind him. 'She didn't look that bad when I left.'

'Yeah, well. She was. Just give me a minute and I'll hook the trailer up for you.'

'Thanks,' I say and busy myself helping to clean up.

Andy and Tom chat about the lack of gigs. Joni and the Slaughterhouse Boys are due to play again on Friday, an acoustic set at the pub. For free, of course. I wonder if I will ever be able to go and watch them again. They had to get a stand-in for Kit last night. Johnny Hinchliffe, a plumber from the next village. Nowhere near as good, mind. Or so I kept getting told.

I'm anxious to crack on with the collection. The rain last night will make the scarecrows hard to burn, even though the weather has cleared a little now. The Gallows bonfire will still go on, though. Even if they have to pour petrol over it. No one will miss the hog roast and hair of the dog.

Up and down the Gallowsgate and the houses surrounding, the jaded-looking scarecrows are hanging, less plumped and pinned together. Arms have fallen off and heads are lolling. This year's theme is horror classics. There's a wolfman hanging outside the pub with ripped jeans and a lumberjack shirt, a plastic Halloween mask over his sacked head. I've seen at least four ghost faces from *Scream* – probably the easiest to make. Joni went all out, of course. Hers was Britt Ekland from *The Wicker Man*. I had to convince her to put a dress on and not make boobs and pubic hair from straw, although she was convinced she would have won if she had. That honour went to little Albie Tucker who made Foxy from *Five Nights at Freddy's*. Whatever that is.

'OK, I'm going to start bringing these scarecrows up.' I prop the litter-picker stick against one of the outside beer-garden tables.

'OK,' Tom says. 'I'll come back with the trailer.' He only lives round the corner, where Kit is right now, so I unhook the Wolfman, who falls to the ground with a thud, and begin dragging the others so I've got a pile to start with.

My phone buzzes in my back pocket and I wrench it out to see it's Jamie, asking if I'm OK. Do I want to come over tonight since Kit is going to be at my place? Do I want to eat out? Or can he cook? Stay in together? Little dreams.

Strange really, to think that we can do all these things normally. Date. When I thought about how our relationship was going to be, all I felt was excitement at making pasta together. Watching a box set on Netflix. My head in his lap. His hand stroking my hair. I told Joni this once and she screwed up her face and reminded me that Kit used to do that and I hated it. I tried to explain that it wouldn't be the same, but my tongue couldn't wrap around the words.

Tom is back within minutes and helps me chuck the scarecrows on the trailer before handing me the keys to Kit's beaten-up Ford.

'You OK driving it?' he asks. 'Do you want some help?'

I want to shout yes, yes, yes. But I know I can't. So I just thank him and shake my head.

It's thankless work, and by the time I've reached Fargate I'm covered in straw and mush. Some people are helpful, bringing their scarecrows out to the trailer for me. I almost feel like grabbing Andy's megaphone and driving slowly up and down, shouting, 'Bring out your dead!'

Even though the sun is still breaking through the clouds, I shiver a little as I head up towards the rec, thinking about the creepy stilt clown last night. I turn right, up Fargate Lane. Joni's cottage is right up at the top, next to the football pitch and backing onto Morton Woods. As I pass the terraces, and the spaces between the houses become wider, I see that her pygmy goat, Carlos, is wandering around her small field at the side. I say field, Joni calls it her paddock. It's basically a garden with a shed that she calls the barn. It's open, though, and Carlos comes trotting to the fence when he sees me.

I hold out my palms for his nose and he pushes his little, wiry face in my hands. 'Hi, boy. Who let you out? Not your mum ...' I hold up my other hand to wave at Stella, her neighbour, who is power-washing her drive.

She waves back, and I climb over the fence to go to the back door. The chickens are out too, scratting in the dirt in the corner. I notice their food bowl is empty, so I quickly scoop some feed from the bucket and they flock around me, pecking the plastic container like tiny machine guns.

Thelma and Louise, the two Gloucester Old Spot pigs, are spark out in the barn, looking full and content. Thelma flicks her curly tail as a fly lands on her belly. There's a bit of a stench coming from them and I wonder when they were last cleaned out.

The back patio door is locked. I give it another wiggle and frown, then knock. There's no reply, so I walk round the path to the front.

'Have you seen Joni this morning?' I call over to Stella. 'Back door is locked and there's no answer.'

'No, love. Early for her, though, isn't it? Especially after last night.'

I nod in agreement.

Joni's scarecrow is sat stiffly against the front door. I bob down and admire it. The blonde wig. The crown of flowers. It's exquisite.

'Come on, beautiful,' I whisper and drag her to the trailer. It takes me a while to make room for her. The pile of effigies looks like bodies and I shudder.

I go to knock one more time on Joni's front door, but still no answer, so, shrugging at Stella, I get back in the Transit and drive onto the back field to the bonfire. It's already half built with discarded furniture and rubbish jammed in everywhere. MDF and nails sticking out. Crap that people just fling on in the hope it will burn because they can't be arsed to take it to the tip. If Billy was here, he'd be rummaging through it for treasure, I think, and my heart pangs so much, I bury the thought.

I roll on the scarecrows one by one. Joni's was last in, so is now first on the pile. When I'm happy I've done my village duty, I ditch the van and now-empty trailer and walk back up to Joni's. I knock on the front door, then try the handle without waiting for a reply. It's open. But when I walk in, I know straight away that something is off. *The energy is all wrong*, as Joni would say. I would scoff and roll my eyes, but this time I get what she means.

'Joni?' I call, and look back onto the path through the open front door.

Stella cranes her head to look, but I head straight for the stairs, stepping over Sausage, Joni's massive ginger Lionhead house rabbit, who looks at me in disgust and stamps her foot. She hates me.

'Where's your mum?' I ask loudly, but she just stamps again and then hops off to the kitchen, where her litter tray is. She nudges something metal, and I hear a scrape and clang of her empty water bowl.

Jogging up the stairs quickly, I hear the sound of the shower running, and I pause when I get to Joni's bedroom door. On the wall of the landing, on the exposed brick, there is the picture of me and her when we were kids. The same one I have in my living room. Sat on the stacks, me with my torn jeans and a baggy Levellers T-shirt. No shape to me. Just folds of material and my dark hair loose, with little butterfly clips holding back the front bits. Joni is wearing a long tie-dyed purple dress, a holey crochet jumper over the top because she was always cold. Still is. Each of us wearing one black Dr. Martens boot and one purple. Her hair is so red, the setting sun catches it on fire. She is all you can see in that picture. My head is on her shoulder, her arm is around mine and she is laughing so hard, her eyes are wrinkled and completely crinkled up. Neither of us can remember what the joke was now.

'Joni?' I call as I push open her bedroom door slowly. Her bed covers are wrinkled, and there is the smell of something in the room. Something damp. Sour. Her kimono from last night is on the floor in a puddle, and the sound of water is coming from the adjacent bathroom. The door is wide open, though, and there's no steam. The water is cold.

Walking into the bathroom, I pull open the shower door and jump back as the water hits my shoes and the spray from the shower head soaks the arm of my jumper.

Reaching in, I pull the handle, getting the other arm wet. The sudden silence is spooky.

'JONI!' I shout, marching back into her room. Yanking open her curtains, I see her battered black Land Rover on the street. I go back downstairs and check, and yes, her keys are hung on the peg in the kitchen. Sausage is making that awful scraping noise with the bowl, so I snatch it up and fill it with water.

There's a knock on the open door, and I go back into the hall to see Stella, looking concerned. Her white hair is tied up in a seventies scarf that I'm pretty sure I've seen on Joni. She looks how I imagine a seventy-five-year-old Felicity Kendal would look if she'd never left *The Good Life*.

'Everything OK, love?' She peers round the frame.

'Yeah. Just, bit weird. I don't know where Joni is. The shower was running, but she's nowhere to be seen,' I frown.

'Oh God. Do you think she's all right?' Stella's bony hand flutters to her chest and I remember about her angina.

'Oh, don't worry. I'm sure she's out for one of her walks in the woods or something.'

But in my bones, I already know otherwise.

3

Then – 1996

'There are ghost children down there,' I said.

We were standing at the cavernous mouth of the old railway tunnel, behind the abandoned steelworks, its brown tracks split and woven through the moss-like tree roots. The nettles had snaked and spread. Brambles were withered but hostile.

'Bullshit.' Tom turned and spat into the bushes and I wrinkled my nose as he wiped his mouth with the sleeve of his blue lumberjack shirt.

'That's gross.'

'I know. That's why I don't want it in my mouth,' he shrugged.

'That's what she said,' Joni said drily and Pete held up his bony arm for a high five.

Kit didn't say anything. As usual. He was perched on the Big Stone in the scraggy overgrown field and picking away at his guitar. The shit one school had given him. I couldn't imagine our music teacher being best pleased when he eventually returned it at the end of fifth form, not with the vast array of stickers he'd plastered it in.

It was midsummer and funds were low. There was no work anywhere. Maybe if we could have got the bus into town ... but most of us were too skint even to afford that, and hardly anyone took on sixteen-year-olds. Only Pete looked the part enough to get a job at the music counter at Woolworths, but he got fired after labelling up the new Faith No More tapes as 99p in the bargain bin so we could all get it without having to fork out £5.99 for the record.

The pub was closed: boarded windows, paint peeling from the sills, potted plants withered and crumpled. Andy, from our school, and his family still lived there. Three doors up, the butchers had shut down and moved to the nearest town. The building was empty, offers of lamb livers and brisket still spray-painted on the inside of the window in red, like some ghoulish reminder.

So the days were spent on the streets, in the fields, climbing up to the cliff. The 'cliff' was one of our favourite spots, but it was just a crag and a bit of banking, really. Sit on the top, get the backs of your thighs bitten by the red ants and look out over the village. The steeple of the church and the steel factory lay beyond, like a spider crouching over the hill, the web of the cottages below.

'It's not bullshit. My grandad told me. He used to drive the train when the steelworks were still open. Did you know that's why the station was built? It was for the workers. It's true. I'm not making it up.' I tried to make myself sound confident.

'Like the time you said Joni could play the violin just like in "Welcome to the Cheap Seats", just so Kit would talk to you?' Tom raised his eyebrows and I furrowed mine.

'Oh, fuck off,' I said.

'I *can* play.' Joni put her arm around me. 'She just bigged me up a bit because she loves me.'

'Anyway,' I now said pointedly at Tom, 'my grandad said whenever the train broke down or something happened in this tunnel, the conductors would refuse to walk down it.

Apparently, this guy, I don't know his name, some guy he used to work with, well, the train was going through to Leeds and it was almost midnight. Apparently, the train was pretty quiet, but there was, like, twenty, maybe thirty, people on it. Anyway, something happened, and it broke down in the middle of the tunnel.'

'Hang on, when was this?' Tom asked. His eyes were glued back down the tunnel and, standing next to him, I realised his blonde hair wasn't the only thing that had grown over the summer. His curtains seemed to make his cheeks that little bit more hamster-like, and it was like he'd swelled an extra twenty per cent in all directions. He bit down on an own-brand chocolate bar and I was tempted to yank it out of his hands. I hated it when the lads teased him about his gut. He always took it like a champ, but I could tell it hurt. Sometimes you just can't change the things you hate about yourself. But it's always worth a try.

'I suppose the seventies,' I shrugged. 'Anyway, because there were no phones or anything on board back then, if the train broke down, the conductor had to walk down the tunnel. It's about three miles in total. Can you imagine that? Walking in the pitch-black to get to the phone thingy at the other side?

'Anyway, my grandad said that the guy had to go, so he took the torch and started off down the tunnel. My grandad said they must have been sat there for about twenty minutes before he heard this really freaky laugh. He said it was so loud and so clear, he jumped because he thought a kid had come into the driver's cabin.

'And he couldn't see anything out the window. I mean, you know what trains are like when they go through a tunnel. You can't see shit. Anyway, he said he heard this laugh again. And then this weird squeaky scraping thing. Like a bike or a tricycle or something on the tracks.

'So he got closer to the windscreen and started peering through, but he couldn't see anything. Not really. Just, he said, the air was thicker, even blacker. And it was like it was moving. Well, not, like, *moving* – I know that sounds weird. More like, you know when you turn the TV off and the air is fizzy? Like static? Like that.'

The boys nodded. Joni smiled with encouragement at me. It wasn't often I had their ear. Even Kit was listening. He wasn't looking up, of course. But I could tell because the plucking had paused.

'So he climbs up out of the driver's seat, and leans into the screen to see if he can see better. But there's nothing. Just the long dark. That's how he described it. Then he said he saw something again. Like the air was clumping together and forming something. And just as he was trying to work out if it was just his eyes, there was an almighty BANG.' I clapped my hands together and Joni had the good grace to jump, even though she'd heard this story a million times.

Tom took a hurried step back, but Pete hunched forward and peered into the gloom. The afternoon sun cast his shadow against the crumbling bricks, all gangly and insect-like – a tall Nosferatu. But with spiky hair. You never saw Pete or Tom without each other. Pete looked like Tom's elongated shadow. His dark side.

'It was just another guard. The train hadn't come into Leeds, so they'd sent someone out to look. But get this ... it had been *two* hours. And Grandad said it felt like five minutes at most. And the guy? The other guy that went to make the call?' I paused for effect. 'He never got there. I mean, he never made it out the tunnel.'

'That's bollocks!' Pete shook his head and mooched over to Kit on the Big Stone. 'Have you heard this shit?'

Kit didn't say anything, but he looked up and turned his head towards me. His fresh undercut made his scalp pale, like his skull was on display.

'No, wait,' I stammered on. 'They found him, like only a few metres away. He was shaking, and crouched on the floor. But he couldn't remember anything. He, like, quit his job and everything.'

It was the most I had ever said in one go.

'We'd have heard about it,' Tom said, digging his hands deeper down into his pocket. His curtains were beginning to plaster to his dampening forehead.

A bead of sweat trickled down from the nape of my neck between my shoulder blades. I shook myself like a terrier. Joni, of course, remained glowing as if the sun reflected off her.

'Nah. People don't tell the truth about stuff like that, do they? Makes them sound nuts.' Joni took a step forward, ahead of us all, as Kit picked out the bassline to 'Something in the Way'. The notes were unnerving.

A branch broke under Pete's foot and he scuttled away from the stone, towards the mouth of the tunnel. Towards Joni.

'He said he heard a baby crying,' I said.

'Who? Your grandad?' Pete asked.

'No. The other guy.'

'You said he couldn't remember anything?' Kit placed his guitar down gently against the rock and stood up, brushing the muck of his combats off. So he had been listening.

'Yeah, but, well, I don't know,' I blushed, tripping over my words. 'That's just what he told me.'

Kit laughed quietly, and came and stood next to Joni,

draping his arm around her neck. 'What are you doing then? Going in?'

'How deep is it?' Joni tried to get closer, but the nettles blocked her path. 'I mean, how far along does it go?'

'A couple of miles, I reckon,' Tom said. 'It comes out near the Gardeners pub, doesn't it?'

I shrugged. 'I don't know. I've only ever seen this end.'

'Come on. Dare you.' Joni looked over her shoulder at me and winked. 'Shall we, Cass?'

I glared back and shook my chin in a tiny, jutting motion. I have always been, and still am, terrified of that tunnel.

'Two miles isn't long. We can walk it in half an hour,' Pete said, at Joni's side, as he always was. He reminded me of John Cusack in his weird beige trench coat thing that really should have been chucked, along with the rest of the eighties.

'It's full of brambles and shit.' Tom kicked at the exposed, jutting track. 'We won't be able to see a thing.'

'Get a torch then.' Joni turned around. Her green eyes were sparkling and startling against the darkness of the mouth of the tunnel. 'You came on your bike, didn't you?'

'Why do I want to walk down a tunnel in the dark?' Tom said.

'What else are we going to do?' Pete looked back over his shoulder. 'Kit, skin up first. Be a laugh. Let's freak ourselves out.'

'No way.' I shook my head. 'I'm not going in there.'

'Come on, Cass.' Joni nodded very unsubtly at Kit and I clenched my jaw and looked away. 'It'll be fun. Like Pete said, what else are we going to do?'

'I'll just wait here for you,' I said.

'I'm with you, Cass,' Tom agreed. 'I'm not going in. There's that warning sign as well.' He nodded towards the

LISA ROOKES

bright yellow metal triangle depicting a stick figure and some falling rocks. 'We're not meant to.'

'Then you're not having a toke on this.' Pete held up the spliff he had been busy working on.

'Come on...' Tom held his hand out to me.

'Only if you go and get your torch. Come on, you're only round the corner,' Pete said.

Tom grunted and glanced at me, then at Pete.

Tom lived with his grandma only a couple of streets away. His mum was in prison. None of us really knew why. She had been for as long as we'd known him, which was almost ten years. He used to shrug and say it was because she didn't pay her poll tax. Seemed like a long sentence for tax fraud. But what did we know?

''Sake. All right.' Hands shoved deep in his pockets, he headed over to the path where his bike was discarded next to the drystone wall. No locks. No one stole anything here. No point. Everyone knew what belonged to whom. You didn't do that to one of your own, and apart from the tourists who came to the village to have their picture with the Gallows Tree in their cagoules and with damp sandwiches, there wasn't much in the village to attract outsiders. Just the folk enthusiasts. And even they looked sorely disappointed when they arrived to see the village was not, in fact, full of flower-headdress-wearing pagans banging drums and erecting giant wicker men on the green.

The spliff was passed round and I stared into the tunnel. I knew the smell. Damp weeds. The moistness of the bricks. The long cold. The sliminess of the inside, like intestines festering.

After all, I'd been in it before.

'Do you really believe in ghosts?' Kit asked and I jumped. I hadn't realised he was so close.

'Yeah, I do actually.' I suddenly was very aware of my arms. They felt too long. Apeish. I didn't know what to do with them and all the saliva in my mouth dried up, so my mouth felt claggy. 'If you had seen my grandad... He's the toughest man ever. I once saw him cut his arm open on a lawnmower and just carry on cutting the grass even though it was about three inches deep.'

'Sure, he's a cool guy, but that doesn't justify the existence of the undead.' Kit did a little smirk and I felt stupid.

I could see Joni widening her eyes at me. I knew they were saying 'don't back down'. I crossed my arms over my chest and did a little shrug.

We heard the whirr of tyres signalling Tom's return. He was a big lad, but his paper round meant he was as fast as Speedy Gonzales on his bike.

'OK, I got one.' He held it up and rattled it by Pete's ear, shaking the batteries. 'Gimme that now.'

Pete passed him the end of the spliff, all cardboard roach and not much else.

'We're going to go all the way, then? All the way through?'

'Absolutely.' Joni nodded, linking arms with me and stepping through into the graffiti-donned mouth.

'I still say it's bullshit,' Kit said and Joni linked his arm, too.

'Come on, misery guts. Open your mind just one little fraction?'

'Besides,' I added, 'you don't have to believe it. Just believe that I believe it.'

Tom held up his torch and took a deep breath. 'I've got a bad feeling about this.'

We walked into the stale breath of the tunnel.

There are many ghosts in there. I know that now.

Just not the kind I thought.

4
Now

I fish out my phone and call Pete — he answers almost straight away. I don't even give him a chance to say hello.

'Pete, it's Cass,' I say pointlessly as he has had my number since we first got mobile phones. 'Did Joni get in all right last night? Tom said you took her home?'

There's a pause. A pause that makes me bite my lip. Stella looks at me, her eyes wide.

'Are you trying to make a point?' Pete says.

'No, what do you mean?' I reply.

'Have you spoken to her?'

'No, that's why I'm ringing you.'

'Well, call her. Ask her.' Pete is sharp, and for a minute I think it's because of me. Because of Kit.

'Pete, I can't call her. She isn't here. She's not at the house. I'm ...' I look at Stella and stop myself, '...just wondering where she could be.'

There is a sigh and a cough. 'I wanted to walk her home; it was her that started getting all freaked out.' There's a tone in Pete's voice.

'Pete, what do you mean?'

'I've told you. Ask her.'

'And I've told you I *can't*. I'm at Joni's now and she's not here. But the front door is open and the animals have been let out.'

'Well, she's probably out then. She never locks her door.'

'The shower's running. I think … I think it's been running for a while. And I think the animals have been out all night. I don't think they ever got put away. Pete, what happened last night?'

'Jesus, nothing. She could barely walk, so I was just trying to get her up the hill. She said she didn't need help and then made me go back to the party.'

'And you *let* her? Go off in that state?' I raise my voice and my blood starts thundering in my ears. I turn and walk back into the house so Stella can't hear.

'Hey, I tried. She fucking slapped me. What was I supposed to do?' Pete says and I go very quiet.

'Why did she slap you, Pete?'

'You know what she's like when she's drunk.' Pete's voice is getting higher and I feel sick.

The thing is, I do. She's a liability. Especially when she's been on the village-hall wine. She could have slapped Pete because he was trying it on. Or because he wasn't. It could go either way.

'Look, Pete. No one is accusing you of anything here.' I try a calmer approach, but it has the opposite effect.

'Accusing? I should think not. I was trying to do the right thing. She was all over me.'

I wrinkle my nose in disgust. I hate it when men describe women like that.

'Just … when did you last see her? What time was it?'

'About quarter to two. Something like that. Tom'll know. He saw us leave. She just ended up staggering up the hill.

I left her on the bend. Are you sure she's not on the bench in the field?'

'Why would she be on the bench?'

'Why would she slap me?'

I can think of a few reasons.

'Well, can you help me look? Pete, I'm really worried. *Really* worried.'

There's a pause. He hates me right now. He's probably not that fond of Joni either. But there's also thirty years of history. And I know he can be a dickhead, but he's not a complete twat. 'Yeah. Of course. Where are you now?'

'At hers.'

'I'll come up.'

I think about calling Kit, but even the thought of his voice on the other end of the line makes me tremble. Instead, I go back out, placate Stella and send her home with promises I'll let her know when Joni turns up, and climb onto the bottom rung of the fence and peer over the field. I don't know what I'm expecting to see, exactly. A glimpse of her coming out of the woods? Carlos nibbles at the beginning of a rip in the knee of my jeans. I can feel Stella looking over. She may even have called something, but I can't fake a smile. My ribs are too tight. The air is too thick. I look up at the sky. The little ribbons of sun have all been stripped away and the clouds have engulfed themselves into one giant ball.

Tom's Transit starts up the hill. Lazy bastards. I should have known Pete would bring his best buddy. Scared of what big bad Cass is going to say to him? Anyway, it's not like Tom's exactly Mr Tough Guy. If he tries squaring up to me, I'll remind him of the time he wet his pants in reception class when a thunderstorm caused a power outage in the school. It's not like anyone else let him forget it.

I jump back down and stand in the road for them. Pete is looking hung-over. But then he always looks dishevelled, a bit like he has fallen out of a tumble dryer. His skin is grey. Matches the way his hair is going. Always so proud of those black spikes. Now he just looks like a boom mic. When he gets out, I see his New Model Army tattoo on his bicep, poking out from underneath his T-shirt, and I can hear Joni sniggering about it, as if she is right here next to me. She always said she loved a man with a shit tattoo. The shitter, the better. She said it gave her the fanny gallops. Even Tom's boss-eyed eagle, which he only got because Pete got one and he wanted to look hard. It got infected and made it look more like a deformed pigeon. We took the piss for weeks.

I'm already talking about her in the past tense, and I want to yank a fistful of hair from my scalp to punish myself. A squall of coffee rises in my throat and it's all I can do to swallow it back down. The acid burns my windpipe.

'What's gone on then? Can't you find her?' Tom slams the door of the van and actually looks at me. In some tiny way, I am grateful for the drama.

'I don't think she came home last night,' I tell them both. Pete's blue eyes look oddly bright.

Tom runs his hand over his buzz cut.

'She wasn't on the bench,' Pete says. 'We checked.'

'Of course she's not on the bench.' Scorn drips from my voice. 'She's a forty-three-year-old woman. We're past passing out drunk on benches.'

Pete doesn't reply and I cringe inwardly, remembering last month when Tom found him out cold on the pub bench in the early hours.

'Come on then, let's have a look.' Tom is clearly trying

to take the heat off Pete; it's not like him to take charge. I follow him into the house.

'I'm telling you, she's not there,' I say as I follow, feeling irritated. I let them go upstairs and go to the kitchen to see to Sausage. She has a right face on her and she's shat all over the rug. Joni swears she is litter-trained, but I've yet to be convinced. I bob down and stroke her velvety ears. Her fur smells of jasmine oil.

I can hear the lads making banging noises and what have you in the bathroom, so I start riffling through the drawers. Her passport is here. Her driving licence. A bit of weed.

Pete comes down the stairs and into the hall.

'Yeah, it's weird that, innit? But she must have come home because the shower was on? I mean, she wouldn't have left it running before she went out, would she?'

'I don't know. Do you think it's from last night or this morning?'

'I'd say last night.' Tom has appeared in the hall and pokes his head around the living-room door. 'Yeah, look.' He bobs his head back out and motions to Pete. 'It's come through the ceiling.'

'Shit.' I go and look and he's right. Beads of water are oozing through a tiny grey line near the jam-jar light hanging she made at some arts festival last year.

'It'll stop. It's OK.' Tom and Pete glance at each other and I know they are worried.

'Have you called Kit?' Pete asks quietly. I look down and shake my head.

'I think I'd better ring the police,' I say, half expecting one of them to laugh, to tell me it's all in my head, that she's just staggered to someone else's house and passed out on their sofa. But they don't.

'Come on,' Tom says. 'Let's do it back at yours. We probably shouldn't touch anything. In case ... you know.'

The last bit of his sentence hangs there. They both look at me as if I am about to start sobbing. But I don't. I feel numb. Dazed, I follow them into the van.

The sky is now dark. Darker than before we went into the house and the weight of the rain is swelling in the air. As I slam the door to the van, thunder cracks.

We drive silently through the village. It's quiet. Most people are up at the hog roast on the field, but Joni's definitely not there, according to Millie's texts. There's still litter lying on the cobbles; discarded bags of rubbish that I thought I'd be back to finish. The noose is still swaying on the Gallows Tree.

'Wait!' I slam my hand on the dashboard and Tom swears and brakes. The tyres squeal, but I am already halfway out by the time the van comes to a standstill. 'Was she wearing her crown?' I grab Pete's sleeve. 'Was she wearing her crown when you started walking home?'

'Er, yeah, I think so. She was wearing it all night.'

I'm out of the van before they start shouting at me, but I run as fast as I can to the tree and grab the noose.

'It's her crown,' I shout back to the lads. 'Her Gallows Queen crown. It's here.' I try to untie the ribbon, but my fingers feel swollen and fat.

I feel Pete behind me. 'She was wearing this.' He nods over at Tom, who is getting out of the van shakily. 'She had it on when we started walking home.'

'Someone's tied it here.' I yank too hard and the plastic snaps in my fingers. And then I really do start to cry.

'Hey, hey.' Tom puts his arm around me awkwardly. 'Come on. Someone probably just found it and left it here for her or something. But let's call the police anyway. Back at yours. It's the right thing to do.'

The broken bit of plastic is still in my hands. I've been gripping it so tight, it has pierced the skin. When I look down, spots of my blood are on the stones.

The van won't make it down my winding road, so we leave it wordlessly and head through Gallowsgate, down the hill towards the terraces that squat, eyeing us suspiciously. Beyond them is the purple peak that isn't quite tall enough to be a mountain, no matter how much it tries to stretch and scrape the sky. The cloud has rolled into a tumescent growth and there are no shadows now.

On the left is the side entrance to St Peter's Church. The church Kit and I got married in. Where Millie was christened. It's small, like the rest of the village, and sits on a little hill, the cemetery surrounding it like a moat. There's a wooden gate and an archway, with the names of the fallen village soldiers engraved on a well-polished plaque. The red poppies in the bricks, fired and glazed by the primary school children, are fading now. Petals missing. Stems cracked.

There's a light coming from the graveyard. At first, I think it's lightning, but it can't be because it's blue and rhythmic. As we walk past, I crane my neck and see it's a police car, parked in the main drive.

I stop still and stare. There's a handful of people and someone in white is putting up a screen. I see Reverend Cooper standing there in his Barbour jacket and Hunters.

'What's going on?' I reach out and try to grab at Tom or Pete's sleeve. Either. Anything. But my fingers just tickle the air. 'Oh my God. They've found something. Is it Joni?'

I don't even look for traffic; I run across the road and

fling open the gate. A man in uniform looks up at me and gestures to a woman in grey trousers and a shirt. Reverend Cooper turns to look at me and his face seems to be almost caved in.

The lads are calling me back, I hear their footsteps behind me, but I carry on running. That's when the policeman and the woman come towards me, palms outstretched, signalling for me to stop.

'Is it Joni?' I shout. 'Is she OK?'

'Cass, just wait.' Pete grabs the top of my arm, but his voice is hesitant. I try to shake him off, but he holds onto me strongly, and I pull and yank like a defiant toddler trying to escape being marched from the swings.

'They've found something!' I plead.

'Cass.' There's a gentle voice, and Reverend Cooper appears at the other side of me. 'Cass, it's OK.'

'Then what? What is it?' I stop wriggling and turn my head.

The man in white is working fast and I realise it's not a screen, it's some kind of tent. But I catch a glimpse of something small on the ground. On a mound of fresh earth.

I hear some words. Something comes out of the reverend's mouth. *Human remains.*

The church bell strikes, but I don't hear it. I feel it in the ground. Everything has moved.

5

Then — 1996

There was no noise. No air. Like a bell jar. Just the scrunch under our feet and the drip, drip, drip of something squalid. I imagined green, sloppy tentacles and weeds hanging down, brushing my cheek, like stalactites.

Kit was the other side of Joni. Of course. Tom behind us, flanked by Pete. Joni held the torch. In a way, the beam was worse. I imagined what sunken faces could be caught in the light, black-eyed children. Dirty dresses. I wanted to turn and run back, but being alone was so much worse.

I tried to check my watch, but it was too dark. Joni shone the torch on my wrist and winked at me.

'Are you timing us?'

'Two miles should be a half-an-hour walk right?' My heart was hammering in my chest.

'What time is it now?' Tom asked.

'Five past three,' I replied. The words ricocheted off the walls.

'Fucking hell,' he said. 'I'm shitting bricks.'

'Mate, we're only a few yards in.' Kit turned his head. I wondered what we looked like from the outside. If the tunnel was a mouth, we were the tonsils.

'What do you think we're walking on?' Pete kicked the ground and we all heard the rattle.

40

'Bones.' Joni held the torch under her chin and sucked in her cheeks.

'Pack that in.' Tom swatted her back.

'Don't, Joni.' I shuddered and hung back a little bit, nestling myself between Pete and Tom.

'Hey, no, I don't want to be at the end.' Tom darted back into the middle and elbowed his way in.

'Me neither.' I tried to bury myself back into the centre spot, but I tripped and stumbled into the back of Kit.

'Watch it!' he shouted and we all jumped. His voice seemed to roll around the tunnel.

'Sorry, sorry.' I wrapped my arms around myself, now in the middle of a huddle. The light was getting further and further away, but we carried on.

'So where do these ghosts come from then? How come there are ghost kids in here? How did they die?' Pete said.

'Playing in here and got hit by the train apparently,' I answered quietly. 'Though why you'd be playing in here is beyond me.'

'Maybe it was a dare gone wrong?' Tom suggested.

'Jesus, why do I feel like we're at the beginning of an episode of *ER*?' Kit joked and we all sniggered a bit.

'Yeah, like the tunnel is about to collapse,' Tom said. 'Don't do drugs, kids. Just say no ... I'm getting a bit worried about that warning sign. What if there's, like, an avalanche?'

'An avalanche?' we chorused, and for a minute there, the tension broke as we all started to laugh. We stopped fast, though, as the sounds echoed like howls.

Our breathing was slowly becoming in sync as we walked tighter together, all a writhing black mass of arms and legs.

'This weed is turning on me, man,' Pete said. 'I'm beginning to freak out a bit.'

41

'Don't,' Tom said and threaded his arm through mine. 'I think I want to go back – I really don't like this. Like, at all. It feels wrong. The air is … weird.'

'What did you say about the air again, Cass?' Joni asked. 'What did your grandad say? That it was what?'

'Static,' I whispered. We all stopped at once and I glanced back. The tunnel had curved somewhat and there was no longer any light. I raised my hand to my face, but I couldn't see it. Just inky swirls of black.

A tumbling of little rocks ahead made us all jump. Joni shone the torch to the ground and swept the light across the floor. Just crumbling bricks. Dirt. The tinkling of debris scattering.

'Jesus. That was a scuttle,' Pete said. 'That was a definite scuttle.'

'Oh God.' Tom stepped back, then jumped back into the huddle again. 'I hate rats. My gran hates rats. She said they scream at you when you accidentally disturb them in hay. They fucking fly at you. Let's go back. Please.'

'It was probably a mouse. We're hardly in the sewers,' Kit said.

'I don't know, it is feeling a bit James Herbert,' I pointed out. 'I'm up for going back.'

'Wait.' Joni tugged my sleeve. '*Wait.*' She turned round and flashed the torch on our faces so we all squinted and recoiled. 'Can you hear something?'

'Joni, shut up!' Tom shouted, but Pete shushed him.

'Hang on. Listen …' Pete cocked his head like a spaniel and we all stood as still as we could. Frowning to hear, as if that would make it clearer.

But just silence. Not even the scurry of vermin or the tumble of gravel underfoot.

'I can't hear anything,' I said. 'What did you hear?'

'Just, like, a cat or something. Like a meow,' Joni whispered. 'Or a screech.'

'Fox maybe?' Kit said.

'Fuck, man. Seriously, can we go?' Tom pleaded. 'Either way. I don't care. I just don't want to stay still. I feel like something is … circling us.'

'You've watched too much *American Werewolf*,' Pete said.

'No, he's right,' I said. 'I think we should keep moving.'

We were silent as we moved forward. Even Kit and Joni were moving a little quicker, shoulders tense. There had been a change in the air. Suddenly, I understood what my grandad had meant about the static.

Then we all heard it. A low, guttural cry. We all halted and scrabbled over each other so as not to fall down.

'Fuck, what was that?' Joni said, raising the torch.

'No!' I reached forward and batted her arm down. 'I don't want to see.'

'It's a fox, right, or like a badger?' Pete whispered. None of us had moved even one toe.

'I don't think so,' Kit replied.

Then we heard it again. This time, a sharper cry. A squeal. Then a series of choked sobs.

'What … the … fuck … is … that?' Joni reached out and grabbed Kit's arm.

'Give. Me. The. Torch.' He held out his hand, but Joni let go too soon and it fell to the floor, its light flickered and then we were plunged into complete darkness.

'Shit,' I whispered. The cries were becoming louder. Then, all of a sudden, they stopped. 'Maybe, I mean, do you think that's a kid? Is someone actually hurt?'

Kit bent down slowly, his fingers tracing the rubble for the torch.

Then we heard it. A high-pitched giggle. Unmistakable.

'Fuck this!' Tom turned and, dragging Pete with him, they started to run through the darkness.

'Wait, don't leave us!' Joni bent down, helping Kit look for the torch.

'Just leave it, Joni!' I screamed. Then I looked up. And froze. 'Oh God. What is that? What actually is that?'

Kit jumped up and started to run. 'We need to get out of here. NOW. Come on.'

He had only staggered a few steps before the darkness swallowed him. Joni and I stood. Unmoving. We heard his footsteps stop and a yell further down the tunnel, followed by a bang.

'Think someone's fallen over.' Joni looked at me and giggled.

I bent down and picked up the torch from under my foot where I'd been hiding it.

'I thought we were busted then,' I whispered.

'JONI! CASS!' The shouts of the boys drifted towards us.

'Shine it over there,' Joni said, and I flicked the torch back on and shone it over her tape recorder, lodged on a jutting-out brick.

'That was impeccable timing.' I held up my wrist. 'You were right.'

'Told you. Although I did shit myself over that rat.' She pressed stop on the tape.

We set off down the tunnel.

'One last scare?' she asked and I nodded.

We both took deep breaths. And let out two blood-curdling screams.

6

Now

'You don't have to believe me? Just believe that I believe it? Yeah, I've heard that bullshit before.'

Of course Pete called Kit. I became a bit hysterical in the churchyard. I don't think they knew what to do with me. The vicar and the police tried to explain that what they had found were bones, nothing fresh. They bundled me out of there fast. In all fairness, I wasn't helping their situation.

Kit's got a face like thunder. I look up from the kitchen table. I cannot believe that he is being like this now. Of all times.

'Kit, stop it.' I pull my knees up to my chest and lower my forehead to rest on them.

'It's probably just another prank,' he says, then turns and starts filling the kettle. As if he still lives here. He looks tired still. There's a stain on his T-shirt. I wonder if he's washed it and it's not come out or whether everything is still screwed up in his holdall. I'm surprised his mum hasn't sent him round with it all.

Just because you've separated doesn't mean you should stop looking after him. That's what his mother said to me. My hackles are rising already. Like she looked after him when he was a kid? We all seemed to be cursed with absent mothers.

'A prank?' I look up and my voice is so high only dogs can hear me. 'Jesus, Kit, it's not like we are fifteen.'

'Mate.' Tom looks at him and shakes his head. 'Don't, man.'

Tom seems so hulking in my tiny kitchen. He's not tall, but, still, he reminds me of John Goodman in his early *Roseanne* days. There's even a fold at the back of his neck that his now-shaven head makes all the more prominent. Kit just looks gaunt and miserable next to him. No change really, for the past few years.

'So what exactly did the police say?' Millie is picking the gel from her nails. She always does this when she is nervous. There's a tiny pile of blue ash-like remnants on the kitchen table.

'She shouldn't be here.' Kit slams the kettle down, nods at Millie and looks accusingly at me.

'I'm not a kid, Dad,' Millie says.

'Joni is her godmother,' I remind him quietly. 'And they've not said much yet, honey. They said they will come out and see me if we've not heard anything by the morning.'

'And no one at the hog roast has seen her?' Pete asks.

'No,' Millie says. 'I asked everyone. Mum did too.'

'I thought you weren't going?' Kit frowns at me.

'I needed to do something. I was going crazy just pacing up and down. And I thought she might turn up.' I hate it when he makes me account for exactly where I've been and when. Even more so now it's no longer his business.

'Everyone was just talking about the police at the church anyway,' Millie says. 'It fizzled out pretty fast. It's like no one cared.'

'It's not that. Joni's a bit of a flight risk. They probably just think she's taken off somewhere on a whim.' Pete reaches out and tries to rub Millie's head and she ducks away from him. He looks crestfallen at his empty palm. He used to do that when she was little all the time.

'I wish someone would tell us what's in the churchyard.' Tom digs his hands deep down in his pockets and looks out the kitchen window. 'Those blue lights have been going all day. Someone from the paper was here, did you see? Some snapper.'

'Fucking reporters,' Kit sniffs. 'No respect.'

'Well, we wouldn't find out about anything if there were no reporters,' Tom points out.

'We would. We'd see it on Facebook,' I chip in.

'Yeah, with a link to a story. Written by a reporter.' Tom looks back over his shoulder at Millie.

'Why have you got a hard-on for reporters all of a sudden?' Millie screws her face up and neither Kit nor I bother to tell her off. I'd quite like to know the answer myself.

Instead, I get up and join Tom at the window. You can just see the edge of the grounds from here. The wall that wraps around the graveyard from over the field. It's dark now, but there's still the blue flash of the police car that's been left behind. The crime-scene tape covering the entrance, over the arch. The dogs in this village have never been walked so much.

'If it was anything that could be related to Joni, they'd be all over it. Are you sure she's not just knocking someone off in the next village? She could have called a taxi pissed last night, or got picked up.' Kit pours out the tea. I notice he has given me my least favourite mug. His *Game of Thrones* one. Black inside so the tea tastes weird and metallic.

'And *is* there anything on Facebook yet?' Tom asks Millie, but she just shrugs.

'I dunno. Facebook is for old people.'

'Well, snaptok or whatever then.'

'Actually, I should make a TikTok, that's a really good idea.' Millie sits up straighter.

I open Facebook again and scroll down the comments on my phone.

'You shouldn't have put it on that bloody community group.' Kit shakes his head. 'You've just wound everyone up now.'

'Kit, what else am I meant to do?' I notice I'm talking with my hands.

'Leave it to the police.'

'They're not doing anything, though.' I go back to the kitchen table and curl back up in the chair, bringing my feet up towards me. My head falls to my knees and my phone buzzes. I snatch it up and Kit's lip curls.

'Where's your boyfriend then? In your hour of need. That him?'

I ignore it. But he's right. I don't open the message and turn my phone over. As if that is going to help anything. It's obvious it's him. I've probably just made it all worse.

'Kit.' Pete sniffs and nods to the back door, holding up a packet of cigarettes. Kit hasn't smoked since we were in our twenties. Since we started trying. But he has clearly started up again. He follows Pete outside and I watch the orange tips glow through the back-door window. The muted hum, up and down octaves, cigarettes like the conductor's baton. I strain to hear, but Pete must sense the silence that has settled like dust over the kitchen, as he reaches out and pulls the door to.

'Where is he then?' Tom nods towards my turned-over phone on the kitchen table. 'Not having a go, like,' he adds a little quieter.

'At home, I think,' I say. 'It's not … He shouldn't be here.'

'Oh my God, it's a baby.' Millie replays a video on her phone. 'Look at this. It's on the *Sheffield Star* TikTok. Human remains. Of a child.'

Tom and I lean over and watch a young reporter at the church gates, talking to the camera with police behind her. She can't be much older than Millie. Good God. I can't hear it properly, but it's captioned. Millie is right. They've described the remains as bones belonging to a baby. When I exhale, it's shaky.

'Jesus.' Tom looks at me. 'See then, it's nowt.'

'It's a baby!' My mouth falls open. 'That's *not* nowt.'

'Nowt to do with Joni. You know what I mean.'

The door opens. 'What's that? What's happened?' Pete's head almost skims the frame.

'The thing at the church.' Millie holds up her screen, as if we can read it. 'It's human remains. It's a baby.'

'How long has it been there? Does it say any more?' I ask Millie, but she just does a tiny shoulder shrug that tells me absolutely nothing.

'It'll be too early,' Tom says. 'There'll be tests and stuff. Probably really old. There will be loads of unmarked graves there.'

'A dog probably dug it up,' Pete says.

I wince at the sheer brutality of the thought and Kit shoots him a look. I am grateful and for a moment all I want to do is wrap my arms around his neck and nuzzle into his chest, and feel the gentle beat of his heart. I'll never stop loving him.

'A dog isn't going to dig that deep,' Tom says. 'Has someone dumped them there?'

'No, they were … what's the word again?' Millie looks at me.

'Exhumed,' I say.

'Dug up,' Kit adds unhelpfully.

'From a grave?' Tom asks and I shake my head.

'I think the police said it was an unmarked grave. So I guess, yeah. A grave. But not one with a headstone.'

'There must be loads of bodies that no one knows about in that graveyard,' Pete says.

'I think it's an offence? To bury someone on hallowed ground or something? If it's not a proper burial,' Tom says.

'They might date back to Victorian times. Maybe the headstone just rotted away,' I suggest.

'Not sure police would get involved with that?' Kit stubs his cigarette out on the outside wall. I want to rub Savlon on the bricks.

This house is hardly a cottage in the shabby-chic, exposed-beams way. It's a true cottage. Rising damp. Cold, concrete floors under the carpet. Poky stairs and condensation on the mullions. I hated it when we bought it. Well, Kit bought it really. His plasterer's wages were more than my florist's assistant wages. A project, Kit called it. Work on it over time. The sink had a curtain underneath it to hide the pipes. The wallpaper was flocked. I would sit at night picking at it until it looked diseased. Every time I walked through the back door, I would smell the wetness of the walls and the coldness from the floor and would have to remind myself that this, that anything, was better than living at home. With Mum.

As with most of his ideas, Kit soon lost interest. Like the oil painting. The boxing. Moving to Sheffield after a trip to the Leadmill to see if the Slaughterhouse Boys could get signed. Drugs. Festivals. Writing a book on the history of London punk. Me.

He'd plastered the living room, and that seemed to be it.

So it was me who painted. Who pulled up the red carpet with the gold diamonds and hand-sanded the floorboards until my palms were red and sore. Scoured the charity shops and eBay for the battered old leather sofa. Sally Army in the end. Pete put the fire in for us. There most nights. Eating cheap meals. Pasta. Shepherd's pie. So grown-up.

I tended to that house like it was the child I longed for but couldn't afford. Dusted the skirting boards. Made Joni paint jam jars in bright colours for candles. Burned nag champa so you couldn't smell the damp. Scrubbed the old, scuffed enamel bath daily, the one that the water would never stay warm in.

Those floorboards are covered now with carpet. The walls smooth. The kitchen sink nestled into a duck egg blue cupboard to match the rest of it. The water stays hot in the bath. The shower is on the wall, not a plastic attachment to the taps.

And still I tend to it. There's washing on the stairs. Dishes in the sink. But I still dust the skirting boards. I run my fingers along the bricks. I feel the hum and the vibrations in the walls. I felt the house undulate when Millie was born; breathe out almost, creating room.

And now, as Pete and Kit come back in, the dirty scent of nicotine clinging to them, I feel it contract.

'You going to be OK, Cass?' Pete says. 'I mean ...' He looks at Kit and back at me. 'Here alone?'

'I'm not alone.' I reach over and squeeze Millie's hand and she lets me.

My phone buzzes again and I know it's Jamie. For a brief second, I let myself remember the way he kissed me on the bench and the way I watched the moon hang over the world on the water and felt as if we were fifteen and none of it had happened. Like I could fix it all. But then I see Kit looking away and I know he's got half an eye on the road for the headlights of Jamie's car. Even though I promised him I wouldn't let him in the house. It feels like all the rules are broken somehow. I've kept to it. Apart from All Gallows' Eve, he's pretty much barred from the village. I know Jamie thinks it's ridiculous, that even when there is no chance of bumping into Kit, he still has to keep his distance. I can't explain that it's not just Kit. It's the village. It's Thistleswaite. It's a treachery. I shouldn't have let him come last night, but I couldn't find the words.

'I'll try the police again in the morning,' I say. 'I can't think of anyone left to call. Can anybody else?'

The lads all shake their heads. No surprise really. Men don't understand the complexity of female networks.

I turn my phone back over. 'Do you know she's said goodnight to me every night. Every single night since we first got phones.' I look at Kit and his eyes have softened slightly. 'You know that. And you know this isn't some kind of prank. I'm not that cruel.'

I regret the words instantly. The house seems to shrink even more as his eyes darken.

'Come on then. Let's all get some sleep,' Pete says. 'We'll call the police first thing. And then ...'

'Yeah. We'll start looking.' Tom nods.

They leave quietly and I get up to lock the door behind them. Through the glass panel, I see them all walking down the lane. Hands in pockets, hoodies. Like the boys they were. Tom puts his hand on the back of Kit's neck. He lets him.

The cobbles shine under the street lights.

7

Then – 1991

There were only fifteen kids in our school year. These days, they'd combine classes. Or shut it down. Until Joni moved here, there was only me and two other girls. They were the whispering sort and never came to call for me, so I ended up playing on the streets with the boys. Tom lived opposite. Pete round the corner. Kit was the furthest away, two streets up, but Pete always made us knock for him because he had a SodaStream.

That day it was me, Tom, Pete and a kid called Luke Jacobs, who ended up getting kicked out of school for telling the deputy head to go and fuck a gum tree after they made a comment about his pierced ear.

That day, as usual, there was little else to do. *Honey, I Shrunk the Kids* was on in town, but none of us had any money, even for the bus there. So we made our own entertainment. The Miles's house, which could only be described as a shack, was up by the back fields, close to the railway tunnel. The cottage was on its own, way down the track after Joni's house. Maybe a mile. They owned some of the land, and could have sold it for a decent amount apparently. There was no real reason for them to live the way they did. But Billy Miles and his dad Terence lived in that cottage that looked as if it was sprouting in the way a soft and old potato does if you leave it in the back of the cupboard for too long. Slightly nightmarish. Tentacles. Weeds knitted into masses in the garden, swallowing car engines and old mangles whole. Foliage bursting through tiles. Broken toilets in the yard. No electricity, but for no good reason. They cooked off a gas camping stove, someone told me once. No one saw much of his dad really. He worked in the fields, but no one knew what he was doing. Tinkering.

Billy must have been in his mid-twenties back then, although no one really remembered him ever going to school, or playing out as a kid. It was as if he had been born that age, in his long black dirty coat that flapped around him as he rode around the village on an old black iron bike with a basket full of weird things. Rags and bones, Tom's gran said. I once saw him riding through the village with a sheep skull and a pint of milk.

We peered over the drystone wall. Chubby little hands mushed into the gaps.

'My gran says you've got to hold your breath when you walk past it, or the devil will get you,' Tom whispered.

'I dare you to look through the window,' Pete said. Even at eleven years old, his hair made him feel a foot taller than the rest of us. It peeped over the wall like some kind of carnivorous plant.

We all stared through that window, marvelling at what kind of horrors could lie within. We'd been ghoulishly fascinated by this house since we were five years old.

Pete was the only one who had made it past the wall. Kit once dared him to go to the door and knock and pretend to be collecting milk-bottle tops for Guide Dogs for the Blind. His gangly legs were almost knocking at the knees as he opened the rusty gates and it almost fell off its hinges. The clatter was enough to send us all running.

'*Double* dare,' Pete said with relish.

'No way.' Tom shook his head vehemently. 'I'm not.'

No one even expected me to reply. It was a given. I was even more chicken shit than Tom. We looked over at Luke. It was the first time he'd been playing out for a while. Rumour had it he'd nicked some tombola money from the village hall and got caught. He didn't come to school for a week and when he turned up, his head had been shaved and his left ear pierced. Just like his dad and brother.

'Nah, mate.' Luke didn't move his head, but his eyes were like steel. I suspected he didn't dare get into more trouble. His ear looked sore. Red and inflamed around the gold stud.

'OK, what'll you give me if I do it?' Pete looked at the boys. There was nothing in my possession that would interest him. A headless My Little Pony or Annie, my slightly creepy but much-loved glass-eyed doll.

'What do you want?' Tom asked.

'A quid.'

How we laughed.

'I'll give you my frogspawn,' Luke offered. 'They've got legs and tails now.'

'Deal.' Pete began to stand.

'I don't think this is a good idea.' Tom ran his hands through his hair. 'I can't run as fast as you. What if he chases us? What if he tells my gran?'

We all knew Luke's dad had threatened to pour bleach in that frogspawn unless he got rid of it.

'It looks empty,' I said, trying to be helpful.

'It always looks empty,' Tom added, less so.

We stared as Pete walked to the gate. It was open this time. Hanging off one hinge. It squeaked as he pushed it, squeezed past and along what was once a path, past the innards of a tumble dryer and a headless gnome. Turning his head, he glanced back at us.

Luke gave him a short, sharp nod and Tom grabbed my hand. It felt soft, like Play-Doh. Damp. We didn't look at each other. Not once.

Pete raised his knuckles to the door and we recoiled at the light tap, tap, tap.

The hairs went up on the back of my neck. It made me think of Beatrix Potter and her little black rabbit. Tappit tappit. That rabbit used to give me nightmares.

Three pairs of wide eyes stared over the wall. He rapped again. Slightly louder this time. Not loud enough that you wouldn't be forgiven for thinking it was a banging pipe or a cat on the corrugated iron roof.

'Look in the window,' Luke hissed through his hands.

'No, no, no,' Tom mouthed and I shook my head in support.

I mean, after all, it was the first time a boy had ever held my hand.

Never one to welch, Pete ran his hand through his spiky hair and stepped back from the door.

'Tell us what you can see!' Luke stage-whispered.

Pete sidestepped to the left and pressed himself like a lizard against the wall. If you looked closely, his tongue was even darting out of his mouth, between his teeth.

'Tom,' I muttered breathlessly, like I'd seen the women do in *Baywatch* on Saturday at 6 p.m. He just squeezed my hand harder.

Pete pulled himself up onto his tiptoes and pressed his nose against the grimy glass. We all stopped breathing simultaneously. Then we heard it. The creak, creak, creak of the wheels of Billy Miles's push iron. Tom looked at me in horror and I leapt to my feet.

'RUN, PETE!' Luke shouted, and we turned and started pounding up the track. We were almost at Dead Man's Bend before I realised Pete wasn't behind us.

I stopped. My skinny legs were shaking in my jogging shorts. I turned, fully expecting to see Billy Miles, creak, creak, creaking, holding Pete's head in one hand by the hair, cycling slowly towards us, his yellow teeth exposed by his curled-back lips.

'Pete.' I yanked Tom back by his arm. He was the same height as me back then. Still as stocky as he would always be. But his eyes looked straight into mine. The whites were as round as moons. I could feel the fear seeping from him, like it did that day in the railway tunnel. Like it did the night everything changed.

He didn't say anything, but he didn't run either. We both turned and looked down the track, hearing the ever-decreasing thud of Luke's dirty white trainers. Used to legging it.

'We've got to go back,' I pleaded but Tom just stood there, frozen.

I thought about every night when I locked the back door by myself. The ghouls, the werewolves, the clown from *Poltergeist*, all in the backyard. Faces at the glass, licking the window. How I would yank the curtain across and run upstairs, leaping into my bed, pulling the covers over my head, the big light blazing, the sound of my breath and my heart thumping together like some kind of obnoxious brass band, filling the room, until I could swear everything evil out there could hear it. Hear me. While my mum slept in the dark. There was a beacon all over my room. They could see me. They could hear me. They could taste my fear.

'We can't leave him alone,' Tom agreed. 'He ... he'd never leave me.'

He was right. The previous year, Pete had punched Luke in the face for dragging Tom off his bike. Tom had only just started his paper round and Luke was after his 50p pittance of a daily wage. He gave Luke a black eye, and then some Hubba Bubba gum as a peace offering. He was a man of light and shade, even aged eleven. Always loved the underdogs.

We began back, slowly, ensuring there were no cracks of twigs underfoot or loose gravel to give us away. Tappit tappit.

The tree boughs knitted together overhead, and the hawthorn bushes puffed themselves out. I could smell the cow parsley. Bad luck to bring in the house. I once picked a bunch for my mum and she pulled it out of the mug with such violence I was afraid I had tried to poison her. Mother-die, I later learned it was called.

We reached Dead Man's Bend and Tom's fingers found mine. Together we craned our necks around the chestnut tree that always rained the best conkers that we could soak in vinegar and cause some serious casualties with. Nunchucks be damned. You try getting a knuckle-whipping from one of those bad boys on a yo-yo string.

'Shit,' Tom said and I followed his gaze, ready to see Pete's corpse pinned to a makeshift scarecrow stand. But he wasn't.

There, on the front steps of the cottage that we believed to be the holiday caravan of the devil himself, sat Pete and Billy. Both sucking happily on raspberry Mr Freezes.

'What the hell ...?' Tom spluttered.

Pete waved happily to us and on Billy's face there was a gentle smile.

Whenever I think about Billy, which I always try not to, I see him just like that. With Pete. In the stale sun. But then the screams in my head become too loud. And the clouds sit too low.

8

Now

The next morning, I call the police as soon as I'm awake, even though I feel like I haven't been to sleep at all. They are neither helpful nor unhelpful. Someone reads out a list of questions like when they ask you if you understand what gift aid is, then, eventually, computer says yes, and someone apparently is coming out to see me and they'll call me back.

I'm up at the field in my wellies scraping up the bonfire before Andy and the committee turn up. Kit says I've always been this way. When I'm anxious, I clean. The embers have cooled to ash now and I shovel it into garden-waste bags, while repeatedly checking my phone and calling the boys, who eventually stagger up to meet me along with the few volunteers I have recruited to help search.

We decide to start in the woods by Joni's house. The more I think about it, the more plausible it sounds that she staggered off in a mood to lie in the bluebells or some shit like that. She could have hit her head. Broken her leg. Rolled into the water. So that's where we go first.

The leaves are wet and claggy underfoot and the mud squelches under my hiking boots and we all comb different sections. The shreds of sky I can see between the partings in the branches of the trees are pearl grey and the woods feel unusually grim and unwelcoming.

There's a few more of us now. Andy from the pub. A couple of Joni's friends from the am-dram group. We ripple out. The woods are not that deep; as Pete and I walk along the edge of the stream, he's already down on the idea.

'There're so many dog walkers in here, someone would have found her by now if she was here.' Pete slings his arm round my shoulders and gives me a squeeze. I close my eyes and welcome the affection, even though he drops it again pretty quickly.

'I went up this morning to see to the animals,' I say. 'It all feels so wrong. Like, all the energy is off. The goat is anxious. The rabbit is pulling its fur out.'

'Yeah. Maybe we need to ... I don't know, you can't really put them in kennels, can you?' Pete says.

'No. I'll bring Sausage back to mine. I'll just keep going up for the other animals, I guess.' I shake my head. 'I mean, hopefully I won't have to. I'm sure we'll find her soon. Just, for tonight.'

There is a swoosh of branches being pushed back, the crackle of bushes being intruded.

She's not here. I know it. Of course I know it. I can't feel her. I can't sense her. But I can't give up. I can't explain it to the others, and what would they think? Her best friend walking away. Back to her squat little terrace. Not turning over every stone, scraping every leaf. There's a black hole inside me that is slowly getting bigger and bigger. Soon, it will overtake my guts, shadow my lungs, absorb my heart. Still, we search for the next hour until we all end up back in a circle with drawn faces.

'Well, this is a good thing,' I say. 'At least we know she's not hurt, or had an accident.' I surprise myself with how upbeat I sound.

'Should we call the police again then?' Kit pulls his collar up. It's not cold, but for some reason we have all wrapped up.

'I have. About five o'clock this morning. That twenty-four-hour thing is a myth, by the way,' I say. 'They are treating it as "concerned for her welfare".' I make little bunny air quotes.

'So, what now?'

'Just waiting for a call.'

'Yeah, they've already called me. I'm going in this afternoon,' Pete says and I look at him in surprise.

'You didn't say.'

'Didn't think I needed to. Obvious, isn't it? I guess it's you who told them she was last seen with me?'

There's an awkward silence. Everyone starts looking away, sneaking furtive glances at each other, self-consciously rubbing temples and raising eyebrows ever so slightly, but ears are pricking.

'Well, yeah. I mean, I had to tell them where she was last seen. That we know of.' I try to make it sound light. Nothing to see here. Move on with your day.

I glance over to the others, the ones outside our inner circle, and wait until they make soft noises and platitudes and start to excuse themselves. Back to their latte machines and playgroups and the giant landmine of gossip that has just landed in their laps.

'I'll come with you, mate,' Tom sniffs. 'Do you, I don't know, need a lawyer or anything?' He lowers his voice at that bit and cocks his head.

'No? What for? Why would I need a lawyer?' Pete rubs the back of his hand against his nose and sniffs unattractively. God, what was Joni thinking? The long coat and arty hair are long gone now. The eccentric charm has vanished. Now

Pete is a spindly, skinny odd-job man with a shit tattoo and yellow-stained fingertips. His eyes are still fiery, though.

'You've been watching too much Netflix, mate,' Kit says loudly. 'No one thinks he's done owt. He was just the last one to see her. That's all.'

'Was she upset then, Pete?' I venture. 'I mean, I know you said you argued, and I'm not accusing anyone of anything. I just...You know how she is when she's drunk. If she was angry, she might have just staggered off somewhere.'

'Like she used to, you mean?' Tom says. There are trees behind each of us, as if they are our tall, thick shadows.

'Yeah. You know how she used to go walkabout at parties? Or, like, when we were wasted? She always wanted to go to the reservoir or just be outside. Anywhere. Where else could she have gone? I mean, we live in the middle of the countryside. There aren't just these woods.'

'What about the steelworks?' Kit's voice is low.

'She wouldn't have gone there,' I say coldly. 'She hated it there. Why would she have gone there?' There's more aggression in my voice than I intended. 'And that doesn't explain the shower, does it?' I point out. 'Or the crown. If she just wandered off randomly. Who does that, just decide, oh actually I'll not have a shower and leave it running, I'll go for a walk and tie my crown to a noose on the way.'

'Calm down.' Scorn drips from Kit's lips. He hates it when I'm sarcastic. He says it makes him feel stupid. 'I still think someone just tied it up there,' Kit says. 'Found it and just put it there so it didn't get lost.'

'Everyone knows where Joni lives,' I point out. 'They'd have just taken it round.'

'Unless you're right and she put it there herself,' Pete says. 'Big dramatic gesture. I don't want to be your Gallows

Queen, or some kind of political feminist statement. I mean, that's very Joni.'

'She did want to be the queen, though. She always does.' I feel my eyes start to fill. 'You know what's awful? When I was giving my statement. They asked me about close family members. She didn't have anyone. She only had me. I failed her.'

Kit shakes his head and opens his mouth, but I hold my palm up fast.

'Please don't, Kit,' I beg.

I think of all the times he sat on the sofa. Shaking his head, just as he is doing now, as my phone buzzed and buzzed and buzzed. Coming in from the pub or from band practice to find us there, sloped on the couch, her head in my lap. Laughing. Sometimes crying. Often both. Subtle eye rolls.

'I'm the only family she has.'

No one argues.

I feel as if the clocks should have stopped. There should be crows on the gate. Why is the world still turning?

I stare at my phone as if somehow it's going to ring, and it's going to be her, laughing about what a state she was in, that she woke up in Manchester with one shoe and accidentally found herself on a tour bus singing back-up to some almost-famous indie band.

The lads are talking of secret boyfriends and I want to laugh. There have never been any secrets between Joni and me. Literally none. She even inserted my first tampon for me when I got all confused about the holes. I held her hand when she had her pre-cancerous cervical cells scraped.

I know the face Pete makes when he orgasms. I know Tom cries after sex.

She poured my mother's vodka down the sink with me

when we were nine and didn't even really know what it was. She bandaged my broken finger with her doll's first-aid kit and didn't tell anyone. It's still wonky now. Sometimes she kisses it, when she is feeling that way. There's nothing we don't know about each other. Sometimes I don't even know where she ends and I begin. Even though we shouldn't fit. Our edges don't meet up.

She wasn't born here. Not like me. But it didn't matter. She was exotic from day one. No mum. Living with her dad. It was unheard of. She came into the last year of infants with a Rainbow Brite lunch box and an off-centre ponytail. The teacher redid it for her at break. I watched with envious eyes through the playground window as she brushed through her curls and French plaited it. I touched my own lacklustre, brown mane and longed for the fingers of a woman's hand, smoothing it. Stroking it. Taking the time to tie it out of my way.

Her dad picked her up after school. Again, I hid and watched. She ran out to him and he folded her up into his arms until her feet lifted off the floor. Then, he reached out his hand and took her lunch box. Carried her Rainbow Brite lunch box. Even though he was a man. And it was *Rainbow* Brite. Her eyes lit up as he put his hand in hers. I ducked behind the bike shed and watched as they walked away, through the gates and past the sign. Thistleswaite Primary School, 1988. I hid and watched for two years.

'Come on then.' I turn my head and look over my shoulder. 'No point just hanging about here.'

I make out as if I am heading home, but I don't, of course. The police said I could go to Joni's and for some reason I want to go alone. I don't want them following me, criticising me. I need to get Sausage and her things.

I have no idea how to carry her. Joni used to take her to the vets in a cat carrier. I manage to find it under the stairs, but I can't convince her to get in it and the more I try to push and squeeze, the more she bucks and stamps until I give up and stick her harness and lead on. I am surprised there's no crime-scene tape here. No people in white suits. I can just walk right in. This worries me. Are they taking this seriously or not?

I walk around the house, looking for any signs. Anything out of place. The police say they are going door-to-door this afternoon after they call in. But there's no sign of them yet. No missed calls on my phone declaring their arrival. There's a gnawing sensation in my chest. I feel like my lungs are about to explode, like I haven't taken a breath in minutes.

Where are you, where you are you, where are you? I can't picture her. I can't see her. The house is so quiet. It's never quiet here. Ever. There's music. Always music. Coffee machines spitting. Animals muttering. TV blaring. Joni's guttural belly laugh. Pings of phones. Chimes. Hums of knackered fridges and the whoosh of the Aga.

She may live alone, but it's the fullest, most alive house you've ever been in. The smells are wrong now. It's all so wrong. I feel so wrong here.

I pick up Sausage and close the door behind me gently.

And three days later, they come.

9
Now

It starts with a press release, whatever that is. A notification about Joni. An appeal. Her picture.

When they tell me they are doing this and I see it appear on the local paper website and start getting shared on Facebook, I feel like I am going to be sick. This is happening. This is real. Jamie comes and I have no will or want to stop him. I long for comfort. I want to sob into his chest and not care if anyone sees us or not.

The tears come then too. I sit outside the pub and sob into his chest and I don't care if anyone sees us or not. I don't care about the hard eyes of Tom. The wince in Pete's frown. The absence of Kit. I just need someone to cuddle me, to tell me it's going to be all right. That she is somewhere. That she still exists.

I can't do this on my own.

More and more people are out searching. There are torches in the dusk bobbing like fireflies across the skyscape. Someone has taken down the nooses on the Gallows Tree ... silently. Joni's crown has been taken by the police. They don't think she's here. I can tell they think she's just done one. No mental health issues. Not considered vulnerable. Give her a chance to come back. That's what they said. But she has still been registered as a missing person.

Joni is a missing person. I can't get my head around it. She is the opposite of missing. She is here. So *here*. So present. I feel her shadow everywhere.

Every time I look out of my kitchen window, I see a solitary magpie on the guttering of the village hall. If the little bastard doesn't find a friend soon, I'm going to take Tom's air rifle and shoot the fucker. Moons and goochers bullshit, Joni used to say.

I see omens everywhere. I always have.

'Have you seen it?' I don't even wait for Tom to speak when he answers the phone that morning.

'Yeah,' Tom says. 'We've seen it.'

'Is it in print too or just online?' I walk up and down the kitchen, my hands shaking.

Millie isn't up yet. She went to sleep last night still holding her phone; the bluish glare made her look otherworldly. I tried to prise it gently out of her hands, but she pulled it with her as she turned on her side. I think about Chris, the boy from All Gallows' Eve, and Joni's jokes, and it seems impossible to me that it was only two days ago. But as I pulled the duvet up to her chin, it was not an app she was on, but some site about missing people. This is so hard on her too. Joni taught her eyeliner flicks and how to down a pint as fast as a boy. This is the kind of wisdom that is invaluable at her age.

'Print too. Page five. Kit went to the newsagent's first thing.'

'They make us sound like lunatics.' I sink to the chair by the kitchen table and tap on Millie's knackered school laptop to bring it up.

Woman missing in South Yorkshire after Pagan festival crowns her Gallows Queen.

I read it out again in disgust. 'I mean. It's not a pagan festival, it's just a song. Just a ... local myth. We were raising money for the church hall for crying out loud.'

The picture they have used just adds to it. It's the one from the band webpage, she's all flowing red locks and a mix between Stevie Nicks and Britt, Ekland. They may as well have photoshopped a twig and berry crown on her and superimposed her in front of a giant maypole.

'Yeah, they explain it further down,' Tom says. 'In a way, it could be good. Gives it more ... what's the word?' He goes quiet for a second and there's a muffled noise in the background. 'Yeah, no, not attention, exposure. That's the one.'

'It makes us sound like we killed her in some weird ritual to the tree gods or something.'

'It'll make people read ...'

'Or not bother looking because they assume we ate her like some kind of hog roast.' I turn on the tap to fill the kettle far too aggressively and cold water splashes onto my T-shirt, making me yelp.

'Cass. Come on. It's good. No such thing as bad publicity.' It's Kit saying that. He is in his ear. I can tell.

'Please don't talk in clichés,' I sniff.

'Clichés are clichés for a reason.' Definitely Kit.

'Is the print version any different? I mean, what do they say? There's a whole link to the history of the song online.'

'Nah, it just mentions it. That's all. Who do you reckon talked to them?'

'What do you mean? The neighbour who didn't want to be named?' I scroll down the screen. 'This bullshit about the village being obsessed with folklore and tradition. We're a steelwork community. It's just ... it's so cheap. Who on earth

68

would …? Unless it's that new couple? The ones who bought the conversion?'

'Yeah maybe. Can't see Stella spouting off, can you? But they're not going to want to make enemies. It's probably not anyone. That's why they've no name,' Tom says.

'They know about the crown, though. And All Gallows' Eve. That wasn't in the press-release appeal,' I reply.

'Yeah, but some copper probably told them that. They are all as dodgy as each other.'

'Will you tell Kit to stop talking through you?'

'Look, let's just see what happens after this. We still think it's good.'

I make some kind of noise that passes for goodbye and then hang up, resting my forehead on the table. We. We indeed. What he has always wanted, I suppose. Tom always hated being alone. First Pete. Now Kit. He really is getting his band back together. My eyes feel soothed somehow when closed and I stay there for a while, palms either side of my face.

I wonder if the police have started trawling Joni's social media accounts and phone records yet? Maybe that's where I could start, although I could do with Millie's help. I want to get up, move quickly, start bringing up her bookmarks on her laptop, but my head feels like lead, as if my neck will snap if I try to force it off the table. I don't remember when I last slept. Actually slept, not napped.

I open my eyes and the grain of the table so close to my eyes reminds me of the woods. My breathing becomes deeper and the browns and blacks begin to swirl like a kaleidoscope.

There's no noise anywhere. Just the breath of me and the house. I stay just like that until a sharp knock at the door makes me raise my head and there's a pain that flashes across my eyes. I envisage reporters, like when Hugh Grant opens the door in *Notting Hill*, or Kit maybe, come to make sure that when I yelped earlier it wasn't for some untoward sexual reason. Stella. Ruth. The mum brigade. I don't have the energy. My hair hasn't been washed for three days. It wasn't even as if I forgot. Just didn't have the energy. There's a cluster of spots by my chin. I consider not opening it, but it could be the police, so I smooth the strands of my hair back and snap the laptop shut.

Yanking open the door, I curse myself for not peering through the blind first. Because he is there. Jamie. So tall. Hunched slightly. Adidas zip-up and bright white trainers. He stands out like a sore thumb with his expensive sunglasses and air of discomfort.

'Jamie.' I open the door widely. I haven't seen him since that night. We agreed the timings were bad. That Kit needed to be around. Not him. It would be insensitive. Optics. That's the word he used. I didn't really understand what he meant, and thought he was on about measures from spirit bottles in the pub until I googled it. And Kit used to moan I made him feel thick. But here he was. His dark hair all styled, his blue eyes like the break after the storm.

I can't help it. I stand on the step and throw my arms around him and I don't even care who sees. If Kit is walking past. Or Tom. Or Pete. It still matters. Of course it matters. But right this second, I just have nothing left in me to care.

'Baby.' He kisses the top of my head and his hands stroke down the back of my hair and I want to warn him about the grease. But he doesn't even seem to notice. He tightens his arms around me and rocks me to and fro. I think about the lullaby. When the cradle will fall. 'I know that we said I should stay away. But I can't. I can't leave you to face all of this alone.'

He smells both comforting and unfamiliar. Not of dirt and sweat and plaster, or soap and steam. But musky. Like a shower gel that comes free with a fancy aftershave gift set from Boots at Christmas. His top smells washing-machine clean. Even if I wrench the clothes out of the drum the second the last spin stops, I can't achieve that smell.

I nestle into his chest and breathe deeply. Jamie. Jamie. Jamie.

'I'm sorry,' I murmur. He feels right. I fit here. In the nook of his shoulder and arm. In a way I never quite fitted into Kit's.

'I'm here. I'm here.' He kisses me again and then uses his fingers to tilt up my chin in the way I have only ever seen on television. 'When was the last time you ate?' He puts his hands on my waist and they feel amazing. We talked so many times about how this would feel. When he could touch me, kiss me, when we could go to bed together and wake up together and he could move inside me. When there would be no guilt, and in a world where Kit didn't love me in the dark way that he does. And he would let me go.

'God, can't you just fuck him and get it out of your system?' Joni said once, slurping spaghetti so violently, strands were flying upwards and smacking her on the nose.

And I would shake my head sadly, because I knew, she knew, Jamie knew, that I could never do that. I could never live with the guilt. I'd confess and that would be my marriage over anyway. So what would be the point?

'Kit wouldn't leave you,' Joni said, sloshing more red wine into our glasses. 'No one else would have him and we both know he can't be alone. I mean, he'd break Jamie's face, like, and he would probably chain you up in the basement. But he wouldn't leave you. He would also want to save face. Think how that would look? His wife shagging Jamie fucking Copland. Oh do it, please, the drama! The drama!'

But there were some lines I couldn't cross. At the start, there had been loads of lines. Hundreds. No kisses at the end of messages. Just emojis. No messages late at night. No talking about the past. No talking about regret. Or longing. And we slowly began to rub them out. Line by line.

It all started as an innocent friend request. That's how it all begins. Always begins. If you read Mumsnet. I never thought of myself as a cliché. I was scornful when I heard stories like it. As if you can fall in love online. As if you can make that kind of connection. It's just the fantasy. The romance. It's not the person. It's desire for something more. A spark in the darkness.

And now I'm here. My best friend is a missing person, and I've given up on my marriage for, according to Joni, the massive risk of being with a man who's penis I have never seen.

'Leave for you, Cass. Not for him. I mean, great, you can shag him now and that's a bonus. But don't leave for another man. You don't need one. You don't need Jamie. You don't need Kit either.'

Didn't I? We sat by her fire and finished off the pasta and drank all the wine. No. I didn't need a man. What I needed was something much, much more.

'I'm not unhappy though, Joni.' I rested my head on her shoulder and tried to pat Sausage, but she was having none of it and jumped off the sofa to stare at me stonily from the other side of the room. 'Kit, well, I know I moan, but ... I mean. Millie. And, after everything.'

We watched the flames of her fire lick the glass of the stove, leaving brown, smeary stains.

'It's not selfish to want to be loved.'

'I am loved, though,' I said and kissed her cheek.

Joni didn't reply. She didn't have to. We watched as the fire burned down to ashes.

'I can't remember when I last ate,' I say now to Jamie honestly. It's the most honest I have felt in the last forty-eight hours. It feels good to not be holding everyone together. Not to be putting on a brave face for Millie. Holding my head up under the watchful eyes of the village. I will not crumble. I will not fall apart. I've had so many years of practice. 'I'm not hungry, though. I can't stomach anything.'

'Yeah, well, that may be, but you're no help to anyone if you're not looking after yourself.'

Jamie kisses me again on the top of my head and moves me into the kitchen, shutting the door behind me. It's the first time he has ever been in the house and I am suddenly so conscious of the unwashed dishes in the sink and the slightly cheesy smell the fridge gives off when he opens the door. I want to slap his hand away. A woman's fridge is personal. Joni used to say having someone rummage through your fridge is the equivalent of having a smear test in public.

'OK, Goldilocks.' He slams the door shut again and I am relieved. 'No porridge in here.'

'We've been living off sandwiches.' I grimace. 'I know. I'm not normally like this. I do feed my child. Honest.'

'No judgement from me.' Jamie smiles, his eyes sparkle, and for a second I remember why. Why we're here. Why I'm here. 'There's nothing in my fridge apart from some BrewDog and a mega kebab.'

'What's a mega kebab?' I frown.

73

'An entire naan filled with mixed meats and chilli sauce. I got it to cheer myself up after the party. I mean ... God, sorry. That was insensitive. I mean ... Anyway, I couldn't take it down, so I'm chipping away at it day by day. I won't let it win.'

'Why are we talking about kebabs?' I shake my head, dazed.

'Go and have a shower, Cass. Get dressed. I'm taking you to the pub.'

'It's 9 a.m.'

'Cass,' Jamie puts his hands on my shoulders. 'It's almost 1 p.m.'

I dare not think how long I was sat at the kitchen table for.

I leave Jamie in the kitchen with the kettle and cheap Aldi coffee that you need to chisel out with the handle of a teaspoon, thinking how mortified I would be in the real world. Not this strange, foggy world that feels like mine, but is altogether something else. Like I'm watching from the outside, or having an out-of-body experience, like those people in ambulances or whatever who float up and see themselves in their bed from the corner of the room. Those stories always freaked me out. When I die, I hope that's it.

Millie is still in bed, but I can hear a tinny sound coming from her headphones as I pad past her door, so I pop my head round and she's all buried under the covers like a hamster.

'Sweetheart,' I call. The duvet ripples slightly, and I go to the edge of the bed. 'You awake? It's almost 1 p.m.'

Millie pulls down the covers and squints at me.

I gently remove the headphones from over her ears that remind me of the eighties. 'It's afternoon, sweetheart.'

'I didn't get to sleep until, like, 4 a.m.' She holds her hand out for the headphones, but I set them on the desk.

'Come on. You need to get up. We need to get our shit together. Who were you talking to until so late?'

Millie just shrugs.

'You don't know? Or you can't remember?'

Her hair is in clumps and stuck to the pillow as if it's made of chewing gum. When she moves her head, it stays there, tendrils stretching against her scalp.

'Chris for a bit. Jenna. Everyone's talking about it. Like, what's happened. Just, putting out fires. You know?'

Poor Millie. Joni's fiercest fan, defender and confidante. I haven't thought enough about her.

Leaning down, I kiss her forehead. It tastes salty.

'I made this, look.' Millie rubs her eyes and holds up her phone screen. There's a beautiful picture of Joni on a Facebook post, the picture Millie took of her just last week, sat at our kitchen table, laughing so much that wine had started to come out of her nose. That huge, wide smile. Millie talking to the camera with that bloody hood up, spliced with video she must have taken at All Gallows' Eve. Joni getting her crown. For a minute, I think I'm going to puke.

The page is called 'Please find Joni'. There are already 277 likes and shares.

'I know Facebook is for old people, but you're all old, so I figured it would be best. I've done a reel for Insta too.'

'Oh darling. That's brilliant. I'll share it in a second. Has anyone posted anything? I take it no sightings or anything?' I sit on the end of her bed.

'No, but I thought I'd tag some of the areas her band used

to play. The other band. You know. The one she was almost famous in.'

I tense, then smile. 'Yeah, well, it was your dad's band too. If you ask him, he might have some ideas.'

'Cool.' She buries back down and motions for her headphones again.

'Jamie's here. I'm going to go to the pub for some food. Do you want to come?'

'Ewww. No. What do you mean "here"?' She sits bolt upright, mascara under her eyes, her bony shoulder jutting out of the torn neck of Kit's CBGB T-shirt. 'Does Dad know he's here?'

'He's only just turned up. We're going to go and get some lunch. I need to get my head straight. There're crumpets in the bread bin. Or I can bring you something back?'

'I'm not hungry.' She lies back down and shrinks back under the duvet and I vow that tonight I'll cook a proper dinner and we will watch Netflix or something. Anything to bring back a bit of normality.

The shower revives me somewhat, even though all I can think about is Joni's water running and her naked body being snatched, manhandled. It's not true. It's not true. I've always been prone to bad thoughts.

I blow-dry my hair and see the silver peeping through at the wispy bits around my ears. I can't even remember when I last dyed it the reddish brown I've kept since I was fifteen. I look so pale, but the make-up I smear on makes me look even worse. I stare in the mirror and see the line of foundation on my jaw, the clumpiness of the mascara.

I look like a little girl who has got into her mother's make-up bag. The blusher is too bright against the sallowness of my cheeks, but I just give my hair one last brush and pull on some clean jeans and a pink silky top that clashes with my hair.

When I think about how I used to imagine my outfits, planning to meet Jamie, the drinks in the pub, first dates. The surge of excitement. The thrill. Now it's just … numb.

We walk up to the pub and I'm past caring who sees us together. I'm pretty sure it's done the rounds now. At least I can say I never cheated. Not in the way Kit thinks.

When we walk in, I automatically head to our usual table. Mine and Kit's. In the back corner, round near the fire. One side an old leather sofa, the other a rickety bar stool. I always got the sofa. When others arrived, usually Joni first, she would throw herself down next to me, Tom and Pete would end up perched on the arms. Andy would sometimes pull a stool over. A few waifs and strays threading themselves in-between. It never occurred to us to get a bigger table.

I stop short, then pull out the chair at the table next to me. Smack in the middle. It's not a huge pub. Dark wood and red beer mats. Bit of a smell of wet dog. Best chips in the world. About the only place in England that still sells Scampi Fries.

'What do you want?' Jamie asks me gently and even though I know this menu as well as my two times table, I just gaze at it blankly.

'I have no idea,' I admit eventually.

'OK. Don't worry.' He heads to the bar and I hear him ordering chips and sandwiches, and then he comes back carrying a pint for him, a large glass of red for me.

'Here, let me give you some money.' I look down for my bag and then realise I didn't even bring it with me.

'Shhh, don't be silly.' He leans forward and takes my hand. It's not altogether new. Holding hands. Edges of reservoirs.

Car parks. I have only seen him a handful of times since we got back in touch. Four at the most. He laces his fingers through mine and the familiarity of it makes me want to cry. Again. 'Right. Tell me everything.'

I do. From the moment I said goodbye to him that night to now. The way I'd had to take emergency leave from the florist. There was no way I could focus on arrangements for funerals. I could barely make Millie her tea, let alone fanny about with calla lilies and white, dreary, colourless, ghosts of flowers.

Then, just as I show him the article on the Mail Online, a van slam from outside makes us both look up. I think we expect it to be Kit. Or Tom. But it's not. It's a pristine white van with 'Sky News' in huge lettering on the side.

'Jesus, TV?' I look at Jamie in alarm.

'It's silly season. They're probably jumping on it because there's nothing else around. That's all.'

'Do you think they are here for Joni then?' I say, thinking about the ghoulish remains in the graveyard.

'Well ... looks like it.'

I look at Jamie and then back outside. The crew are setting up by the Gallows Tree. There's a man in a suit flipping through a notebook. I am up before I even realise it and the chair topples over so fast that Guinness, the pub cat, hisses and arches her back, before scrambling off the windowsill and away out the back.

'Cass,' Jamie stands up too, but I'm already halfway out the door, striding towards a fed-up-looking cameraman and a guy holding a boom mic.

'Excuse me, hi! Are you here about Joni?' I shout across the quad.

THE VILLAGE

The cameraman and the sound guy look at each other, then step to the side so the man in the suit can deal with us.

'Do you know her?' The man looks less impressive close up. His jacket is slung over his arm and there's the beginning of a sweat patch through his mauve shirt. There's something beady about his eyes.

'Yes I know her. I'm her best friend.'

I see the cameraman and sound guy exchange a glance and I wonder how many times they have heard this before.

'What are you reporting?' I crane my neck to make sure all traces of the crown and the nooses are gone. 'That stuff from the *Mail*? Making us all out to be some kind of cult?'

'Just the facts. I'm sorry. This must be incredibly distressing for you.' The man tosses his jacket over the railings to the tree and pulls out a pen from his back pocket. 'We're actually looking for Joni's friends, her family, to perhaps say a few words on camera. Drum up publicity for the search. How long have you known her for?'

'Since we were kids,' I say. 'I … I was the one who raised the alarm.'

There is a flash in his eyes. 'Well, if you feel able … we'd love to—'

'She's not going on camera.' I feel Jamie's hand on my shoulder. 'She's not in the right state of mind to consent to this.'

I shrug it off and turn my head sharply to him. 'I'm fine.'

'She's been drinking. I'm pretty sure that's against Ofcom codes.'

'I've had *one* sip of wine. Excuse me, sorry.' I pull Jamie away and lower my voice. 'What are you doing? What gives you the right to speak for me?'

'Baby, I'm just protecting you.'

'From what?'

'The fucking gutter press. Please.'

'You heard them! It might help. And I can clear up all those awful rumours.'

'Cass, I really don't think you should do this. It's your choice. But please remember how vulnerable you are at the moment. Appearing on Sky News really might not be the best thing for you right now.'

'I'm not thinking of me. I'm thinking of Joni.'

'Excuse me, sorry.' The man has sidled over and has a weird kind of bounce to his knees. 'Let me properly introduce myself. I'm Scott Chambers. I'm a reporter for Sky News. We really do want to do a sensitive piece here. Facts. The sort of person Joni was—'

'Is,' I interrupt.

'Absolutely. Sorry, that was clumsy. Hopefully put a bit of pressure on the police for a press conference. I mean, just because it didn't happen in London shouldn't mean your friend gets brushed under the carpet, right?'

'God. Yes.'

I hear Jamie sigh, but I don't care. He doesn't understand. I need the world to know about Joni. That's why I tipped off the press. That's why I gave them those quotes. And it's worked. They're here. And I'm going to do everything I can to make sure the media stay here. Joni's picture should be on the cover of every paper, on the bulletin of the six and nine o'clock news.

She will not be buried.

I turn to Scott Chambers. 'I'll do it.'

10

Then — 1996

I proudly sipped from the Newcastle Brown Ale bottle without grimacing and passed it to Joni. Kit was sat on the empty beer barrel in the alley behind the pub. The outside light shone down on him and me; he looked almost bird-like, angelic. He'd shaved the left side of his head and I thought it was the coolest thing I'd ever seen. Not that I could possibly tell him.

'Why do we have to hang out on the back steps?' Pete sniffed. His weird glasses were still pulled up over his fore-head even though it was night. 'I don't want to sit in the piss all night.'

'Cos we can't get served,' Joni pointed out.

'They need to get a decent band in there,' Kit said, knocking his paraboots against the metal tin, his blue and white lumberjack shirt tied round his waist. 'Karaoke is for losers.'

'Please don't say you think that should be us.' Tom shook his head. 'We're utter shite, man.'

'Nah, we're all right. Just need more practice.' Kit stubbed his cigarette out on the wall and I watched the little sparks fly.

'Need somewhere to practise first,' Pete sniffed. They'd been banned from the village hall after Alan from the church realised they were letting themselves in through the play-group door using Pete's mum's keys and not paying.

'I heard Shop Local is closing,' I volunteered. 'Gone bust. Maybe you could break in there.' I was joking, but for a minute I saw Pete's eyes light up, but Tom almost impercept-ibly shook his head at him.

'Another one. Jesus.' Kit shook his head. 'This place is fucking dying.'

'Yeah.' That's all I could come up with. God, I wanted to sound cooler. He never even looked at me and I wasn't surprised. What did I bring to the party? Nothing.

Well, Joni. That's why they put up with me.

Joni looked between me and Kit and narrowed her eyes, and I could tell she was about to open her mouth, but a stumble and a smash made us all jump. We craned our necks to see who could afford to be drunk and staggering out the front door.

'Oh, it's Billy,' Joni whispered and we all exchanged glances and tried not to smile. It was bad luck to laugh at Billy. Like walking under a ladder or forgetting to wave at a lone magpie.

And he was there, in his weird flappy coat and cargo trousers, black greasy hair all pushed to one side, like George McFly in *Back to the Future*. Billy put his hand on the frame to steady himself and glanced over at us. Whereas we norm-ally just used to blend into the wall for most people, he always noticed us. I saw his eyes search for Pete and then a tiny smile play across his rubbery lips. He raised his hand into a salute and Pete grazed his temple with two fingers and pointed back. Then we watched as he grabbed his iron bike from the wall and mounted it with a wobble.

'Night, captain. Bring her home steady,' Pete called. We

watched as Billy's knees buckled to try to keep the wheels in line, then he set off down the cobbles, his head wobbling like a nodding dog at the back of the car. 'There he goes. Off to do his rounds.'

'Why does he always ride around at night?' I asked. 'I mean, what's he doing?'

'He's checking up on the village. You know, unofficial protector,' Pete grinned.

'Where do you think he gets his money?' Joni pulled her floor-length checked shirt around her. 'Like, to get that pissed?'

'Probably had some tins before he came,' Tom said.

'I think, I mean, isn't he something to do with the steel-works? Not him, I mean. His family,' Kit asked.

'Yeah, I think old Terry has a few bob, you know,' Pete remarked. 'Billy said one of their relatives was one of the founders of the factory.'

'Nowt to brag about there,' Tom laughed. 'That place is as dead and dried up as Pete's sex life.'

'It's getting a transformation.'

'What, your sex life?' I got there first and everyone snig-gered and for a second I felt a burst of pride rattle behind my ribs.

'Summat in the paper. They've put in plans for it. Turn it into a leisure centre or something. I think it's a chain,' Pete shrugged.

'What kind of chain? Round here? God. Hardly prime location, is it?' Tom said. 'Kit's right. This place is going to the dogs.'

'Maybe that's why. Must be cheap,' I offered.

'Maybe that'll be good then. Give us somewhere to go? Bet we would get jobs?'

'These things take ages. It'll be a couple of years.'

'Oh my God. That's it.' Kit jumped down off the barrel. 'Isn't there still that old generator in there?'

'What?' Tom furrowed his brows.

'There's a generator. I'm sure of it,' Kit nodded. 'That's it. That's where we can practise.' He threw his bottle into the wall and it smashed into pieces, some of which tinkled into the bin. I wished he would not do that. It could hurt the foxes.

'Someone will have robbed that generator by now.' Joni shook her head. 'Or it'll be knackered.'

'Pete, you can fix it right?'

'Who do you think I am? The mice in *Bagpuss*?'

'We will fix it, we will fix it,' Joni and I squeaked along together.

'Billy would help you, I bet,' Kit said. 'I thought that was what the two of you did. Isn't that, like, your *thing*?'

'Don't be a dick,' Pete growled.

'Man, I'm not.' Kit threw his hands up. 'I just mean, I know you two like fixing up stuff. Be pretty sweet if one of your little projects actually benefitted us. That's all.'

'I don't reckon Billy would like us going in there,' Pete said.

'Come on, let's check it out.' It was as if Kit hadn't heard a word. The fag end of the summer sky was burning out on the hill and the clouds looked like smoke behind the factory. There was something about the ugliness, the intrusive Dickensian nightmare, against the blaze of the dying sun. Something in its shadows that beckoned us.

'Lads, we're not meant to be down there. We could get done for trespassing. I'm with Pete,' Tom said.

Kit and Joni looked at each other and rolled their eyes.

'Come on. There's nothing else to do,' Joni said and my hackles went up. I didn't like the little frisson that had just passed between them.

Kit jumped down from the barrel and started to head down the cobbles. Pete and Tom looked at each other with resigned expressions on their faces.

'The factory freaks me out, though,' I whispered to Joni and pulled her back by her arm. 'I don't want to go in there when it's dark.'

'Stay here then.' She pulled her arm back and trotted off after Kit. It was like taking a bullet.

Pete caught my eye and gave me a sympathetic smile. It made me feel even worse.

'Come on.' Pete nodded down the hill. 'Let them have their fun. We can come straight back up when they realise there's nothing to do there either.'

'Anything for an easy life,' Tom conceded.

I was torn. Half of me was so hurt Joni had just been like that with me. The other half was a raging jealous banshee. She couldn't be after Kit. She wouldn't do that to me. Would she?

II

Now

It's been a week since the Sky News report went out.

I sounded like a mental person. I couldn't stop watching it on YouTube. Me protesting far too much about the pagan undertones. It just spilled out of my mouth before he even asked me about it. It made everything worse. The next morning it was in the *Sun. Mirror. Express*. Facebooked. Tweeted. Comments. Comments. Comments.

'Yorkshire Village's twisted tradition'. 'Woman set for "sacrifice" vanishes without a trace'. 'Dark folk song predicts the disappearance of beautiful Yorkshire singer'. It went on. And on.

And then they got hold of the baby remains.

Since then, it's been a circus.

Millie and I sit in the kitchen. Blinds down. Millie is scrolling through her social media campaign and reading out the comments. There really are some sick people out there.

'There's absolutely no reason to connect them,' the DI assures me. The nice one. She's taken to dropping in.

'Why is no one saying that to the press?' I turn my laptop round so she can see the screen. 'Look at this. The bones, the noose. It's like ... it's like some kind of horror film. There's this theory here that we're all witches. And we've dug up baby bones for some kind of ritual. And that Joni is dead because we've killed her to make the crops grow. Jesus Christ. I'm on the PTA, for crying out loud. I go to sewing club. We won best small village in Sheffield in Bloom.'

'I know.' Jenny, the nice DI, shakes her perfectly smooth blonde head. She gets highlights. You can tell. It's not a bottle job. It's all glossy. She's got no lipstick on, but she's had something funny done to her eyelashes. They can't be a normal length. 'They'll settle down. It's silly season. Nothing else is happening, so they've jumped on it. I know it's awful seeing your friend get raked over the coals like this.'

Nice DI Jenny leaves her biscuit too long in the tea and it plops off with a little thunk.

'Shit!' She makes to grab it, but it's too late. I offer a new one, but she shakes her head. 'I'll just swill it around, it's OK. Look, Cass, I need to ask you a few more questions. Was Joni dating anyone new? Had she mentioned any dating sites? Or, you know ... even casual meet-ups?'

'No.' I shake my head. 'And, you know, she told me *everything*. Far too much sometimes. So I'm pretty sure she would tell me. Can we get into her apps? I mean, to see any conversations?'

'I'm afraid without a password we can't do that.'

'Not even for Facebook?' Millie asks. 'I mean, if you suspected her of a crime, surely you'd be allowed to hack in?'

'We don't have jurisdiction here in the UK for Meta. And no company will hand over passwords.'

'So you think "someone" has done something to her? For definite? Is this now a murder investigation?' I reach for Millie, and she pulls her chair closer to me and grabs my hand. I didn't even realise how much I was shaking. 'Because ... I'd know. I'd know if she was dead. I'd be able to feel it.' My voice cracks and I know my eyes will be wild, and rolling almost.

Jenny takes a deep breath.

'No, it's not. Joni is still being treated as a missing person.'

'For how long?'

'She's not what we could consider a vulnerable person, so we still are very hopeful that she will turn up.'

'What if she's been abducted? What if some lunatic has got her chained up somewhere? Why haven't we got police dogs out, or … Christ. What if she had gone out on a date? And I didn't know about it. What if she didn't tell me because … God, I don't know! Why wouldn't she tell me?'

I feel Millie's hand on the back of my neck and close my eyes. Joni, her eyes closed too, her mouth wrapped around the microphone. The smudge of mascara that was always under her left eye but, for some bizarre reason, never her right. Millie's hand feels like hers, her long fingers. The coolness of her palms.

'It'll be OK in the end,' she whispers. 'And if it's not OK, it's not the end.'

'What?' I look up sadly at Millie.

'That's what she used to say to you, isn't it?' Millie bites her bottom lip and I want to draw her close. But for some reason I can't. I just stare into those beautiful feline green eyes.

Jenny makes a few other bland comments and then takes her mug over to the draining board after her final swallow, which must have had all the bits bobbing around in it from the biscuit. She downed it anyway. Bless her.

After she leaves, which includes an awkward dither on the doorstep as she is clearly wondering whether to hug me or not, and thankfully chooses the latter, I go back to my laptop and pull open Facebook.

Millie looks at me and shakes her head. 'Mum ... no. Don't.'

I click on login ...

'Careful, you'll get locked out if you guess the password wrong too many times,' Millie says.

I drum my fingers on the table and then type in Joni's email address. That one is straightforward enough.

'If I can get her email right, then could I reset the password? And get in that way?' I ask Millie.

'Yeah probably, but you'd need to be able to get into her emails to click the reset link. Plus, what if Joni is out there and needs to access her account to get in touch?'

'Oh yeah.' I open Gmail and stare at it as if it is magically going to give me answers.

Millie chews on her thumbnail. Her bony knee is poking out of her artfully ripped jeans. She looks like I did in the nineties, with her baggy trousers and striped top. Except beautiful. And with grace. And much better applied make-up.

'Do you think the police will be able to see that someone has tried to access her account?' Millie ties her hair up into a messy topknot.

'Well, who cares if they do? It's only me. I'll tell them.'

'But is it illegal? Could we be tampering with the investigation?'

'What investigation?' I hover the cursor over the password again. 'I mean, they're not exactly getting very far, are they?'

'Mum, seriously, I think we should leave this to the police – I've got a bad feeling you'll get into trouble.'

I look up and Millie's eyes are filling up. Poor kid. She's going through enough.

'OK, honey. You're probably right. I'm sorry.' I pull down the laptop screen and it shuts with a decisive click. 'Go on. Go out and do something. You can't sit around here moping with me all the time. It's not healthy.'

'I don't want to leave you alone.' Millie tries to pull her hood up, but the topknot gets in the way. She makes a face and we both manage a small smile.

'I'm not alone,' I say. 'Jamie is coming round. And even if he wasn't, I'm the mum. I can look after myself.'

'We both know that's not true.' Millie kisses me on the top of the head. 'OK, I'll be back for tea then.'

I don't ask where she is going and she doesn't tell me. I assume it's to meet Chris. There's nothing else to do round here and she hasn't asked for a lift anywhere. I stand as I watch her walk up the main road, hands shoved in her pockets, hair down loose again, her cheap earbuds nestled in. Stunning, agile, cat-like Millie. She deserves better than this world. Sometimes I really do hope she leaves. Gets to uni. Gets away from Thistleswaite. From me. From Kit. This curse. She's never really belonged here.

I go back to the laptop and open it back up. I check Joni's social media pages, even though I know there'll be nothing there. The police aren't that inept. It's weird not getting the constant alerts. She hasn't been this quiet on socials since she fell off the table at the school quiz fundraiser and told the deputy head she sometimes thinks about her husband when she masturbates.

I go back to the Facebook login and before I can think about it, I type in joniandcass.

Invalid username or password.

Ouch.

There's a knock at the window on the back door. Jamie is

there, all expensive navy wool jumper and two-day stubble. I beckon him in.

'Hey.' He looks down softly at me and the empty feeling in my stomach for a second is replaced by something else.

'Hi,' I say and stand up. And for no reason at all, I take a fast step towards him, put my arms around his neck and pull his face down to my lips.

His tongue is hungry and I realise we haven't kissed like this since before Kit left. His hands are on my ribs, and down to my waist, fingers kneading my hips. I kiss back, hard, and he is surprised. I can tell as he loses balance slightly, which annoys me. I need him to be firm. I need him to want me. I need to feel anything at all, anything apart from this. And I want him. I really want him.

So when he pulls me to him, whirls me round and lifts me onto the kitchen counter, I know that I am ready. That it's going to happen. Wrapping my legs around his waist, I almost feel relieved. That it will have happened. That it's over. All the want. The desire. The empty promises.

I close my eyes tight and remember the way his hands felt on my hair by the water. The way he murmured it had always been me. The harvest moon and the crack of the branches.

He whispers, 'Are you sure?' in my ear, but it's not what I want to hear.

Yanking off his top, he looks and feels so much different to Kit, I am momentarily caught off guard.

There are no hairs on his chest and his skin is taut. His arms are wiry, but there's definition, which excites me. I don't know where I belong on his body, though. I don't understand where I fit.

Frantic. That's what he used to call it. On the messages.

Sex for the first time between us would be frantic. Passionate. Animalistic.

He is moving fast and his hands are everywhere. Between my legs through my jeans, under my bra. The taste of his skin is becoming salty and his eyes are becoming foggy. The blue is turning to grey.

It doesn't feel like I thought it would. I close my eyes tighter and think about before. Think about the way it would feel to hear the gentle buzz of his phone and know it was him, before I even looked. The way he called me a goddess, and the way he saw me, the image of me I knew he was building up in his mind.

Quiet, strong Cass. The girl with the determined look in her eye and the fast walk. Cass, the girl who would scrape roadkill off the road to give the animal some last dignity. Cass, the girl who would lie about her school marks so as not to be labelled a swot. Cass, the girl who sat on the sidelines and watched the world so she didn't have to play. Cass, who wrote and wrote and wrote the songs that Joni sang. Cass, who reached out her fingers blindly to the edge of the dome and couldn't see the stars. Cass, watching the world turning too fast. Cass, who married the man who told her no one would love her the way he did. Cass, who looked out over the mills, the stacks, the burned-out steelworks and waited for the smoke to come for her.

'Do you believe in anything after death?' Kit once asked us all.

'God, I hope there isn't,' I had replied.

I feel Jamie inside me and the thickness of his breath dampens my neck. He drives into me and I move and gasp and the gnawing pain in my stomach goes away. The countertop scrapes the backs of my thighs and I see my jeans in a puddle on the floor and realise I don't remember when they even came off. I hear the words he is panting, but I don't understand what they mean. They feel like love, though, and I know this sex is not bad sex. It's not that kind of rough. It's not angry or possessive or controlling. It's collaborative.

I just wish I could feel it. Because all that is running through my head is Joni. Joni. Joni. Joni.

Afterwards, he makes me a cup of tea. I feel completely endeared by this, curl up on his lap, and lay my head on his shoulder.

'God, I love you,' Jamie tells me and I feel the smile on my lips and the warmth in my palms from the mug.

'I love you too,' I say. It does feel different now. I used to say it like a doll, with a cord in the back.

I don't anymore. His eyes are back blue again.

I cook for us later, after a slower, gentler second time in bed, and he cuddles me from behind, as the onions and garlic spit. He kisses in the crook of my neck and I remember, God, I remember how the first flush of love felt when you truly believed that it was sacred and just yours.

We distance ourselves a little when Millie comes home, but we all eat together. Jamie doesn't try to make jokes, or be her friend, and the mood is still sombre. We talk a bit about Netflix. Jamie's memories from the village. How much the high school has changed. Millie even asks a question about Jamie's job in marketing – it's snide, but he doesn't realise. Which makes it a little embarrassing for all when he answers it.

After Millie vanishes to her quarters, leaving her dirty plate on the table, I don't dare to argue and wonder if she's on the phone to Kit. Reporting in. Technically, Jamie's not meant to be here, but the rules have changed.

'So ... can I stay tonight?' Jamie reaches forward and tucks my hair behind my ear. For the briefest second, I want to slap it away and then I remember it is meant to be tender.

'Oh Jamie ...' I shake my head. 'I'm sorry, I just don't think it's a good idea. Kit—'

'Kit said I was banned from the house. And we've crossed that line.'

'Yeah. And I don't want to push it,' I say softly. 'I'm sorry ...'

'Feel a bit used here.' He is trying to joke, but it cuts. 'Why don't you come and stay at mine? Feels like you could use a night away from this village?'

'Have you ever seen that movie *Cabin in the Woods*?' I ask.

'No. I don't know. Not sure it sounds like my kind of thing.'

'It's a horror film. But, anyway, these teenagers are trapped in this kind of invisible electric dome, but they don't realise it. They think everything is real.'

'Like *The Truman Show*?'

'Yeah, I suppose ... Sometimes that's what this place feels like.'

'You could have got out, Cass. I don't get it. Out of everyone, I thought you'd be the first to leave.'

Jamie leans towards me. It's not the first time he has said this to me. I keep thinking he is looking for a different answer.

'Why would I want to leave?' I whisper. 'Just because I chose to stay in the place I was raised. With my family. My friends. Why should that go against me? Why does that make you better?'

'It doesn't make me better.' He reaches and grabs my hand. 'But you said it was a dome, that you couldn't reach the outside world. But you could. University was an option…'

'You know I couldn't leave my mum. And what would I have done at uni? An English degree? To do what? Be an English teacher? I could never stand up and speak to people at the front of a classroom. What would be the point? I'd still end up in a florist's.'

'You could be running your own chain of florists' by now.'

'What, if I had an English degree? Not sure how that would help me in any way at all. Can't you accept that I'm happy here? That I was happy here. I don't need rescuing, Jamie. I don't need you to take me away to your shiny towers in Leeds.' I pull my hand away. 'You say that all the time. That I deserved better than this. But what is so wrong with my life? And what do you mean by *deserved*? You act like this life is some kind of… punishment.'

'Cass. No.' Jamie shakes his head. 'This isn't what I meant. Not at all.'

For a second, we are back in the steelworks. The horrific taunts and then the sickening sound of bone splitting. The beads of blood on the back of my hand.

'Baby…' God. The sound of that word. Makes me feel sixteen again. The promises. 'I just want you to be happy. Just like I did back then.'

'Jesus, Jamie, my best friend is missing. What do you want from me?' I'm not angry and yet my words come out as if they are.'

'*You*, Cass. I want *you*. And you're not with me yet. I know, I know why. I know it's about Joni right now. And not us. But I need to know, this *is* what you want, isn't it? Am I still what you want?' He looks at me with such intensity. I nod and bring his hand to my lips.

Later, when we say goodbye at the door, I see Kit's van parked down the road. It's dark, so I can't see if he's in it. I don't mention it to Jamie, but I shrink back into the shadows after he kisses me goodbye on the cheek, then watch as he turns and walks towards his shiny dark blue Audi.

His headlights sweep the main gate and he does a three-point turn, and I catch the purplish outline of Kit, just for a second, like a ghost in the driver's seat.

I wait until Jamie has gone, still staring at the van. The interior light flicks on and he is there.

Watching me. Us. He wants me to see him. We both stay there, still, our eyes locked on each other for a minute, before I turn around and go back inside, locking the door behind me.

Men and their needs.

It isn't that late and I'm really not tired, so I open up the laptop again, relieved to be in my own head, my own space.

Back onto Facebook.

I let the cursor hover over 'Password'. Pause. Take a deep breath. And type 'applepip'.

And the screen springs to life.

12

Now

For a second, I feel dizzy with the anticipation of what I could be about to read. I can see notifications for unread messages and the first thing I do is click. The first ones are from Facebook Dating and I'm not going to lie – I didn't even know that was a thing. And I certainly didn't know Joni was on it.

There are loads of messages, telling her how gorgeous she is. No surprise there. She hasn't replied to most of them. I work out that your dating profile is different to your Facebook page, and it says they only match you up with people who aren't friends. Her dating profile picture is, of course, stunning. She's used one where her eyes are bright green and her freckles are prominent, laughing with a glass of wine in her hand, in a trademark kimono. I stare at it for a while. I took that picture in the pub. Not even that long ago. I wonder why she didn't tell me she was on Facebook Dating.

I do Facebook searches for every single man who has messaged her. It takes a while. But I list them one by one and put stars next to the ones who she's messaged back. I'm still doing this when Millie arrives home, with red-ringed eyes, I note, and not from crying. Chris is clearly a bad influence. But who am I to talk?

97

'What are you doing?' she asks, and she hooks her coat up behind the door. 'It's past midnight. You're not ... Wait.' She peers over my shoulder. 'You did it? You got in?'

'Don't be mad.' I look up. 'I guessed the password. I'll call Jenny first thing with it. But I couldn't help myself.'

'What was the password?' Millie sits down next to me, already engrossed. Morals and judgements out the window.

'FleetwoodMac,' I say.

'God, she needs lessons on password security. Even I could've guessed that. What have you found?'

I show her a brief but really sad exchange with a man whose wife is an alcoholic. It looks like she had been talking to him for a while. In true Joni style, she seemed to be more crisis line counsellor than sex chat. It seemed to be a theme. This isn't a woman looking for sex, I noted. Just ... connection? Attention? Validation? I don't know. Every time any of the men sent her an explicit photo, she told them off and sent links about informed consent. I couldn't see any hook-ups or dates being arranged, no matter how much they were trying.

'Millie, am I a bad parent, letting you see all this? You know this isn't—'

'Yes, yes,' she cuts me off. 'I know about porn sex and the dangers and I won't wax all my hair off or do deep throat on the first date because that's what he expects.'

They are so much more enlightened, this generation.

Millie is leaning forward, pen poised for any details at all that could help as we track through Joni's conversations with each potential suitor.

There's one that gives me pause. Matt18698. He doesn't have a profile picture of himself, though, it's a pic of the cover of *Rumours*. Interesting.

They've been talking for about six months. And it looks like they've definitely met up, from the tone of the conversations. I start to shiver.

The last message was the night before All Gallows' Eve. From him. She read it but didn't reply.

Tomorrow?

I go back to the messages and type in the box.

Who are you? Is Joni with you?

I don't even hesitate. I just press send.

'MUM!' Millie smacks my hand away from the machine. 'NO! Leave that to the police.'

'Shit, I shouldn't have done that, should I?'

I haven't entirely thought this bit through. I consider ringing Jenny, the nice DI, to confess, when a little ping comes from the screen. I move so fast back to it, I knock over my wine.

A message pops up.

ACCOUNT DEACTIVATED.

The wine is slowly spreading and staining the kitchen floor, seeping into the wood. I feel guilty letting it take hold, but I am staring so anxiously at the screen, I can't even begin to move.

Millie leaps up instead and snatches up a cloth.

'It's OK, I've got it.' I start scrubbing at the stain with hot water and soap. I'm so stupid. Too hasty. I didn't think it through. Now I've scared him off and we won't be able to track him. I've slopped so much water onto the floor, it starts to soak into the knees of my jeans and I don't even realise I am crying until I am curled up in a ball and there is soap on my cheek and Millie is over me, her arms around me. And it's not how it should be. I am the mother, not the child.

We lay on the floor together until my heart has returned to normal and my face is drying and my skin is too tight.

'She's going to be OK, Mum. She's going to be OK,' Millie keeps lying into my ears. Millie does not think Joni is OK. Millie is as scared and rattled as everyone else.

There have been so many times I have thought we should tell her. The truth. But I've never been able to find the words. They stick in my throat, like tiny metal fish hooks. Now, I'm so glad. She couldn't take that kind of pain. Or maybe it's me that can't.

I squeeze her back and we change into pyjamas. My mouth cascades apologies and reassurances. There is toast. We turn on some shit on Netflix about kids with unlimited clothes budgets and absent parents and I think about the dome.

I used to believe it was Mum who kept me here. She would always cry after one of her binges. The shame. The horrors of a child taking care of her mother; the shame I feel tonight too. The promises. The inability. Sheer inability to change. After a while, I believed it too – you could not do the impossible. It was unreasonable of me to ask her for it.

She loved me. She loved the village. But she didn't, couldn't, love anything as much as she loved the bottle. She told me she hated it. As much as she hated my dad. But just the same, she went back and back and back.

One night, when I was only about eight, I walked past the mills, up to the stacks. Joni was at the fire station with her dad and the village was empty. The streets were quiet, no kids out playing. Not that I would have joined in, but the noise would have been a comfort. The pub closed now on Sunday afternoons – not enough takings to pay the staff. No smells of beef fat or crinkling chicken skin from the terraces. Roasts too dear. Mum was asleep on the sofa. I'd moved her onto her side and put the washing-up bowl under her, a little bit of water and bleach like Joni had taught me.

The sky was bland. Not even any clouds for me to find comfort in. I climbed over the drystone wall into the field and over the stile. The hay had been baled. It took a couple of attempts to scramble up onto the top of one, my palms stung from the cutting of the cable ties I'd had to grasp for leverage.

I lay back and tried to look for omens in the skies. The signs I had become so accustomed to searching for. The two magpies. Waiting, eagerly, for a bird to shit on me. Funny, the things that keep you entertained as a kid.

I hadn't realised how tired I was. John-Paul Duggleby at school used to joke about how I always had bags under my eyes. But I didn't quite understand what he meant.

I turned on my side and saw a scarecrow at the edge of the field. Without the long sheaves and the tall whipping grass that shredded your knees, it was less impressive. Sacks and clothes hanging on a stick.

I'd always been afraid of the scarecrow bonfire. It seemed wrong. Like we were burning our protectors. They were made with such love. Kids would stuff old tights and holey jeans with straw and hope. We'd hang them on the gates and when you walked to school the next morning, it looked like the village has been massacred in a firing line. Heads and limbs drooping. But after school we'd run to see whose scarecrow had claimed the red rosette. I'd always loved them.

I think I'll miss you most of all, as Dorothy said to the scarecrow and the autumn golds tarnished to greys. The straw men burned before our eyes.

But this one. He was still here. I reached out my fingers and wriggled them slowly in a wave.

A magpie landed on his shoulder. Of course. Just one.

The sky was becoming dark but without the kiss of the sunset. Just darker grey. No shadows. As if someone had dimmed the lights. My legs felt heavy as I thought about the trudge home. The washing-up bowl to be cleaned. The homework to battle. Some kind of food to cook.

My eyes drooped and the scarecrow blurred. But I had to go home.

The moon would be here soon and little girls could not be in the fields after dark. Even in 1989, when the bogeymen weren't in the newspapers but only in the darkest corners of our minds and towns, and in the fields. The stacks. The mills.

'You'll look after me, won't you, scarecrow?' I whispered before I fell asleep.

I felt the arms lift me. I was being carried and the smell was strange. I tried to look up, but my face was buried in some old clothes. It was dark. Musty. But warm. I fell back to sleep, but when I woke, I was cold again, back on the ground. My short-sleeved rainbow T-shirt had not withstood the October skies. My jaw chattered and my hair was damp with mud. Underneath me, I patted, and it wasn't straw, or hay, but earth. I sat up, confused, into a bright light shining into my eyes and a strange creak, creak, creak noise disappearing into the distance.

Something stiff and rough scraped my back and I turned

to see I was under the Gallows Tree in the village. Rubbing my eyes, confused and bleary, I saw the dim outside lights of the pub and the cold street light glaring on top of me.

'Cass?' There was a voice from behind. Male. Dad-like. 'Cass, what are you doing here?'

It was him. Joni's dad. He squatted down next to me, a pint of milk in his hand. The shop was still open then. I looked at him and felt my bones grow even colder.

'Jesus, you're burning up.' His hand was clapped over my brow, but all I could feel was the wet mist of the start of the rain. 'What are you doing here?' he said again. 'Where's your mum?' He gathered me in his arms and his legs buckled as he tried to pull up both of us. I was tall then. Even for eight.

'The scarecrow brought me back,' I said.

And then I passed out.

13

Then – 1996

'Loads of people died in here, you know,' Kit said as we scrambled over the wall, through the torn-down wire, into the old factory.

'You mean the blast? In 1941?' I said and shuddered.

'That blast killed the Gallows Queen.' Pete wriggled his eyebrows.

'Oh, that's sad.' Joni wrapped her arms around herself.

'Yeah, but it was only the day after All Gallows' Eve. So, the village had voted to sacrifice her. And then it actually happened. I mean, that's proper creepy.'

'They weren't still sacrificing them in 1941,' Joni pointed out. 'You just got the best ribbon or something.'

'Weird that after she died, though, in the blast, the steelworks got rebuilt and it created loads of jobs. That's like the 1940s version of the crops growing,' Pete said.

'Come on then, are we going in?' Kit motioned to the door. There were holes in his sleeves that he'd been cultivating for some time. The cardigan had belonged to his grandad. There was no one in the world apart from Kurt Cobain and Kit who could pull off that look.

Tom and I exchanged glances.

'Didn't someone else die in there too?' Pete said. 'A few years ago. Or, like, in the eighties. Fell into the molten slag.'

'Molten slag? Sounds like a strip club,' Joni quipped.

'Come on.' Pete pulled a torch out of his pocket and Tom hurried to catch him up.

'Wait, I'm not going at the back again. Is there any light?' Tom said.

'If we can fix the generator,' Kit called back. His voice echoed from inside the entrance.

It was dusky and the clouds had rolled back. The eyes of the building were hollow. I felt as if a hundred jagged metal teeth could close around me at any time. But we trod into the deep throat of the steelworks.

'Woah...'

We followed Pete's voice and came out in the main cavern of the works. One giant room, the ceiling so high that when Pete ran his torch around the walls, there was a flutter and a screech and a pair of yellow eyes made Joni scream. We felt the wind of the owl swoop past before we saw it, and heard the pitter-patter of bat wings as we realised they were there.

'Bats? Fucking bats?' Tom started brushing himself down and cowering as if they could get their feet caught in his grade two.

'I love bats,' I said quietly and followed Pete's beam, hoping to catch a glimpse. There was a flutter and a scurry, and a fast shadow moved through the light. 'Oh my God.' I was entranced. I stood and stared, and Pete handed me the torch, which I took wordlessly, without looking. My eyes scraped all the corners. The windows, once boarded, were split now and rotten. The night thrust through the gaps in the woods and the roof seemed blue and broken with the weight of the sky.

All around us were horrible twisted shapes. Arachnid almost, or like some dystopian machine at the start of

Terminator 2. It looked as if creatures were crouching under metal shells.

I shivered and turned my gaze back to look for the bat roosts up high.

It was then I realised Kit was close to me. Closer than I think he had ever been before. He smelt of Kit. Chewing gum and fabric conditioner. No matter how grunge he tried to be, his mum, Sara, always made sure he was clean, albeit ragged.

I tried to keep my torch hand steady, but I could feel his eyes on me. Not moving. I dared to glance over and flashed a little smile.

'What?' I kept my voice low.

'I didn't know you liked bats.'

'Yeah. They're brilliant,' I whispered. 'Did you know they can fly up to sixty miles an hour and hunt in almost pitch blackness?'

'Did you know they are more closely related to humans than mice?' Kit whispered back.

'Yes!'

'Wow. Did you know you smile with your eyes?'

I blushed and looked down, then back up at the roof. I could feel some kind of prickle in the air between us, but I didn't dare believe it was real. I stared up at the ceiling and the gods were on my side, because there, in the beam, hung a tiny bat, scuttling along upside down by its feet.

'There ... there ... there ... there ... there ...' I pointed to Kit and he came in close next to me to follow my finger. We huddled together by the beam and watched as the bat swayed and then let go, making a break for the exposed timberworks.

'Cool.' He grinned and I turned to him, our cheeks so

close, I could almost feel the hairs on his skin brush against mine. I could hear the blood pounding in my ears.

'What you guys doing?' Pete pounced on us from behind, a hand on each shoulder, and Kit sniffed, shrugged and stepped away.

'You found the generator?'

'Nah, man, I think someone's nicked it. But this place is great. If we can work out how to get an electric hook-up, I think you're right – we could padlock the gear in there.' He nodded to the small office with the metal grate still intact. 'It's going to work, man.'

He slapped Kit on the back again and bounded off to rattle the office door.

'Don't you think this place has got bad karma or something?' Joni shuddered as she moved in closer to Tom. I couldn't tell if she was playing her damsel in distress card purposefully in order to make him feel more confident or whether she meant it. She did have a thing for karma, and her eyes were flitting around more anxiously than normal.

'Is it karma? Or a curse?' Pete turned and held the torch I handed back to him under his chin, wriggling his eyebrows.

It was getting much darker now and our outlines were becoming pencil drawings. We unconsciously started moving closer together.

'Do you believe in the Gallows Tree? Seriously?' Joni said. 'I mean, it must have come from somewhere. Myths are always based in fact.'

'Of course I believe in the Gallows Tree.' Pete shone his torch into her face and Joni squinted and held her arm over her eyes. 'I've seen it. I know it's real.'

'Don't be a prick. You know what I mean.'

'You mean the legend? That the village has to sacrifice someone to the scarecrows to make the crops grow?' I asked.

Kit was opposite me now. And for a second I could feel the weight of his eyes on me.

'Do you think it's just a song? Or did people actually do it?' Joni shivered and looked around.

'Or ... did the village *itself* kill the Gallows Queen? Like in here? Like that freak accident. Maybe it was a proper curse. Maybe people didn't really get hanged, but the village took them.'

'You've been watching *Children of the Corn* again.' Tom shook his head. 'No wonder people think this village is nuts.'

'No other Gallows Queens have died, though?' I pointed out. 'I mean, not that we know of, anyway.'

'Do you think this place is haunted?' Tom looked at Joni. 'I mean ... like you said, there's been so many accidents.'

'There's something a bit off about the energy,' Kit chipped in.

I looked at him oddly. It wasn't a very Kit thing to say at all. He caught my eye and for a second I thought he was going to laugh. His chin twitched.

I made a confused face and he turned away.

'Thought you believed in all this anyway, Cass,' Pete said. 'You not picking up any vibes?'

'Yeah, Little Miss You Don't Have to Believe In It, Just Believe I Believe In It,' Kit smirked.

'Hang on, you're the one going on about energy. You trying to impress her or something?' Joni laughed.

I could have killed her. Especially when Kit just shook his head and pulled his chin into his chest like it was the most ridiculous thing he had ever heard.

'Maybe it *is* haunted. Burnt victims of the explosion.

Maybe they are all crawling around the floor, just waiting to grab our ankles and drag us down to hell,' I whispered, feeling like I may as well play the part I had clearly been cast in.

'You know, my grandma used to say you could see the lights come on in here at night. Months after it closed down.' Tom's head darted around.

It was almost pitch-black now, the outside had bled in and infected every chink of light. We all heard the bat wings flutter above and Joni and Tom moved closer together. I was pretty sure her hand had laced through his. You could tell by the way their outlines had blended. Maybe even his arm around her. I looked on enviously.

'Yeah, I heard that too,' Pete nodded.

'And you didn't think to mention this before we all dragged our arses down here?' Kit said.

'Thought you didn't believe.' I raised my eyebrows.

Kit didn't reply. He just looked over my shoulder and furrowed his brow.

'What? What?' I froze.

'What's that?' he said. I couldn't turn round.

'What? What are you looking at?' Joni squealed and craned her neck. 'Where?'

'At the door,' Pete whispered. 'By the office.'

'Oh my God.' I ran towards Pete and Kit and threw myself in between them. 'I can't see. What is it? What is it?'

'Shine the torch.' Tom's voice was almost robotic.

'There's nothing there …' Joni's voice was small. 'What do you think you saw?'

'I don't know,' Kit whispered. 'But we're not alone.'

14

Now

I am woken by a hammering on the door and I automatically assume it's Kit, ready to yank Jamie out of our bed. I throw back the duvet, all full of protests and proof, and then I remember that, firstly, Kit saw him drive away, and secondly, we had medium-to-good sex on the kitchen counter, so my claims of innocence are moot. At least I think it was medium to good. I don't have much basis of comparison.

Blundering down the stairs, I double-check I have underwear on before I tug back the curtain over the kitchen window and am relieved to see it's DI Jenny, until I open the door and there's someone else with her. A tall man with a rumpled suit. No tie, though. Definitely not a reporter. There's no smell of despair and regret clinging to him.

I pull my grubby old shirt down to my knees, but it doesn't stretch that far; I open the door with apologies.

Jenny holds her hands up. 'Sorry, we didn't mean to wake you, but—'

'Has something happened? Have you found her? Is she …' I don't move to let them in and they stand awkwardly.

When Timothy Taylor was killed in a drink-driving collision, the police went to his mother's house. We'd all seen him leave the pub, stagger into his car and reverse it out the car park. We were just kids. We didn't know to stop him.

We didn't know we had that kind of authority. The papers said he was only eighteen. That his life had just begun. I remember thinking of eighteen as being so old. That his life was surely over.

We heard his mother's howls across the field.

I grab the door frame.

'It's not about Joni.'

I feel the adrenaline surge up through my thighs and into my gut.

'We needed to—' DI Jenny starts, but the man cuts her off.

'It's about the remains found at the church.'

I stare at the man blankly.

'I'm sorry. I'm Senior Investigating Officer Mark Easton.' He holds out his hand and I shake it without thinking, letting go of the bottom of my shirt. His nose is large, and his eyes are dark. He is not unattractive, but rather striking. His hands are strong and calloused. He doesn't feel like a cop. More like a landscape gardener with a minor drinking problem.

'I'll just fetch my dressing gown,' I say apologetically, forgetting I don't own one. When I get to my room, I pull on some jeans and an old Pixies T-shirt that once belonged to Kit but I shrank in the wash. It feels wrong somehow to wear it, but it's the first thing in the drawer and needs must.

Raking my fingers through my hair, I bob down to scribble concealer over last night's make-up and swirl my gob out with mouthwash. It's not a good look. Even I know that. But I feel less skanky with clean knickers. Downstairs, I hear muted voices. On the landing, I pause and try to listen, but they are too good. Everything goes silent as the treacherous floorboard creaks.

'Sorry about that. Late night,' I try to explain and then

wish I'd not said anything. Tell-tale red wine circles on the kitchen table. 'I mean, I'm not sleeping.'

I fill the kettle and Jenny and the Easton bloke sit down at the table. He accepts my offer of coffee. Jenny does not.

'So, the results have come back on the remains.' Jenny looks at her boss, questioningly. As if she has to ask permission to speak. Her voice is more tentative than normal and it reminds me of the time someone came in to observe our Year 9 English teacher. Her lesson was less fun. More guarded. Proper phrases.

I am still completely unclear why they are telling me this.

'So the tests date the bones at about twenty-five years old.' Jenny looks at me carefully.

'Right.' I look at her and then Easton. 'And do they know how they got there?'

'Well, it does appear they were buried. *He* was buried. And from the soil samples in the ground, it looks as if he was buried very close to where he died. There will be an inquest. But the coroner's office puts him at one or two days old.'

'He?' I say quietly.

'Cass, at this point do you think that there could be any connection between Joni and this baby?' Jenny looks at Easton and I bristle.

'What do you mean?'

'Well, we originally thought these remains were older. But now it transpires that when this child died, Joni would have been about sixteen.'

'And?'

The kettle is bubbling viciously and we all hear the click, but I ignore it.

'Cass, could this baby be Joni's? Could this be why she … ran?'

I stare open-mouthed at both officers until it becomes uncomfortable. It's only when they start shifting in their seats that I realise they are expecting me to say something.

'Sorry, I don't quite get what you mean. Are you saying she ... dug ... Sorry, I don't understand.'

'Did Joni have a pregnancy when you were teenagers?' Easton sits forward in his chair and, like two dance partners, I immediately lean back.

'No!'

'Do you think there is a possibility that Joni could have had a baby in secret?'

'I said *no*. Why would you make this connection anyway?'

'One theory could be that Joni may have had an episode, or perhaps some kind of repressed ... breakdown. She could have exhumed the bones. Or perhaps, someone else did. To frighten her perhaps? And she ran. Scared of getting in trouble.'

'It's just one theory. We just need to rule it out.' Jenny reaches over the table and grabs my hand. I don't squeeze back and let it flop limply in hers.

'Can't you do some kind of DNA test?'

'We haven't been able to collect a sample of Joni's DNA from the house.'

'Jesus. How could you even ... I'm telling you – if Joni had a baby, I would have known about it.'

'OK. Thanks, Cass. We know this is difficult. There will be media today, we should think. The information has gone out as a press release.' Easton sits back in his chair, his arm hooked over the back, which I think is wildly inappropriate.

'That Joni had a baby?' I ask in alarm.

'No. That the bones date back to 1997. There's an appeal for anyone to come forward with information,' Easton says.

'Well, it's macabre and horrible. So, great for the papers,' I point out.

'They'll get bored of it soon,' Jenny says.

'And bored of Joni?'

'Cass. There's something else.' Jenny looks at Easton just as my phone starts to buzz on the table. We all look down at the screen and see it's Kit calling.

'I'll let it ring,' I say and the two make eyes at each other.

It stops for a second, but then starts again. Not like him. I frown and reach for it.

'Sorry, I'd better get it. He must need—'

'Just wait a second.' Jenny puts her hand out, but I've already grabbed the phone and am swiping the sticky screen.

'Kit? Any news?' I don't even say hello.

'Are the police with you?' He doesn't bother with pleasantries either.

'Yes ...'

'Thank God. But you're OK? You're OK, right?' His breath comes out as a whistle.

'Why wouldn't I be OK?'

There's a brief silence. 'They haven't told you?'

'About the baby?'

'What baby?'

'Kit! What are you talking about?'

'Cass.' He pauses again and I look up at the officers quizzically. They must be able to hear Kit's tinny tones through the handset. 'There was another noose on the Gallows Tree this morning.'

'What do you mean?' I say slowly.

'A new one.'

'Oh my God ... Is it ... Did it have anything of Joni's on it?'

'No, Cass. It had ... it had a doll on it.'

'I don't get it.'

'A doll, Cass. *Your* doll. The one from ... that night. The one you lost. It was burned. I didn't say it was yours. Don't say anything.'

'Kit ...' I let the phone drop down to the table with a clatter and stare at the officers. They look a little shifty now.

'Another noose appeared on the Gallows Tree this morning,' Easton says. 'I assume that's what that call was about? Did they tell you what was found on it?'

'A doll?'

'Yes.'

'Why would someone hang a doll on the tree?' I say carefully.

'Well, we were wondering if you could tell us? We've bagged it for evidence, but, yes, we would like you to see it. That's the main reason we are here.' Jenny raises her brow softly. I wonder if they train them to make that expression in police school.

'When? Now?'

Jenny nods and reaches down into a black leather bag that looks a bit like a medical one. I listen to her unzip it and brace myself. When she holds it up, I can only really see the remains of one glassy blue eye and a tuft of blonde hair. Half the face is melted and grotesque, and the body is black and shrivelled. I clamp my hand over my mouth.

'Do you recognise this doll?' Jenny asks with a softness she must reserve for children mainly.

It's her. It's Annie. Of course it is. I look at her deformed, ghoulish features and shudder. Burned alive. My hands begin to shake and I sit down on them so they don't notice.

'No,' I say. 'I've never seen it before in my life.'

The police officers exchange looks.

'You're sure? It didn't belong to Joni?' Jenny asks.

'I'm sure. I mean, I don't remember ever seeing it.'

'And you're positive you don't think this doll ever belonged to you?' Easton says.

'I mean, I didn't really have any dolls. I was more the kind of girl who wanted to climb trees and build dens. And Mum didn't have a lot, so ... Why do you think it's mine?'

'Just thought we'd check. It seemed like it could be some kind of threat perhaps. A message? Or maybe it's just a prank. One of the local kids.'

My phone buzzes again and both officers glance at it.

'A threat? To me? But why?'

'Because it had your name pinned to it,' Easton says. He is quiet and calm and yet the words feel like they've come out of a megaphone.

'What?' I stammer.

'Do you have any idea who might want to upset you?' He doesn't raise his eyebrows. His face is still very steady.

I shake my head. 'No. Not ... not like this. I don't understand. When ... Why did ... Who reported it?'

'I believe it was someone from the pub. They saw it early this morning when they went to let the cleaner in.'

'And has everyone seen it?'

'I don't think so. We took it down as soon as we could.'

'You think it's a joke?' I press. Easton stays silent and Jenny starts talking, but I jump in. I can see I'm being rude. It's almost like I have some kind of out-of-body experience, but I stare straight at the man. 'Sorry, I don't know how I'm meant to address you.'

'Mark is fine.'

'OK, so if you're the senior ... What is it?'

'Investigating officer.'

'Right, *you* tell me please. Is this a joke? Do *you* think this is a joke?'

'No, Cass, I don't.'

'And you're taking it seriously?'

'Of course we are. We think it would be a good idea if you went to stay with someone for a few days.'

'I'm not leaving Millie.'

'And your daughter too.'

'You think she's in danger?'

'It's just a precaution,' Jenny says, but I look at Easton. I suddenly get a funny feeling she isn't as kind and on my side as I had thought.

'Where are you suggesting I should stay?'

'Well, at this point, perhaps away from the village.' Easton shifts his weight and leans forward in his chair.

'I don't have any friends outside the village.'

'No family?'

'No, I'm an only child. I never really knew my dad and my mum ... my mum died about fifteen years ago.'

'I'm sorry to hear that,' he says.

'I don't want to leave. Besides, half-term is over and Millie has school.'

There's a knock at the door and I jump, knocking my knee on the table and spilling my coffee over the back of my hand.

'Shit.'

Jumping up, I wipe my hand on the back of my jeans and open the door, half expecting another reporter. But it's Kit.

He looks grey. All black and white, his skin like news-paper. Scrunched and delicate. The grey at his temples is more pronounced. His forehead looks more domed, and the shadows under his eyes look sore.

He seem shorter somehow, as I go towards him. Our eyes are almost level. It feels strange not to be looking up. He opens his arms and I don't think twice. I feel them wrap around me, the smell of paint on his overalls, the loose skin on the creases of his forehead where his head leans against mine. Kit. Kit. Kit.

'So, what's happening?' he says, his eyes over the top of me, locking on the SIO. Mark.

'Who are you?' he asks and Kit looks taken aback.

'This is ... my husband,' I say. 'We've recently separated.'

I can feel Kit stiffen. His arms drop and I step back. He looks at me, and for a minute I think he is looking at my breasts, but then I realise it's his Pixies T-shirt that I'm wearing. He has clocked it and I can tell he doesn't know what to make of it.

'And do you live here too?' Easton asks.

I see Jenny shake her head subtly.

'It's my house.' Kit's jaw clenches.

'He's staying with a friend,' I explain.

'We were just saying that perhaps Cass and Millie should stay with someone else for a few days. While this dies down.'

Kit makes a strange noise, somewhere between a cough and a strangled, bitter laugh.

I know what he is thinking.

'We won't go there,' I say quietly.

Jenny is interested and coughs. 'If there is somewhere you could go outside the village, I do think it would be in your best interests.'

'My daughter is not staying with *him*,' Kit spits.

'Maybe I should leave ...' I place my hand on Kit's arm

to keep him steady. 'And Millie could stay here. With you and Tom?' I look at him questioningly. 'I don't want her in a strange place either. Or being disrupted. She needs to keep going to school. This has been horrifying enough. For everyone.'

Kit bobs his head up and down but won't meet my eyes.

'Just for a day or two?' I look questioningly at the police officers, who remain poker-faced.

Things move fast after that. I call Jamie, who tells me he is going to leave work now to come and get me. I try to argue that I can get a lift to the station and come on the train, but he is insistent.

The police officers hang around a little longer. Ask more questions about anyone who might want to hurt me; who could be connected to Joni. I mention Facebook Dating again and Matt18698. They nod and say they are on it, but clearly aren't, otherwise they would see a message has been sent from her account since she's been missing.

But I don't mention it. Best not at this point.

By the time I get a bag packed, and leave strict instructions about picking Millie up from school, and no one breathing a word about the other noose, or the doll, the police have gone.

I'm just zipping up my bag and keeping an ear out for Jamie's car when Kit turns to me and motions for me to sit down.

'I don't want to sit down,' I say. I know I'm being churlish, but I feel like a caged tiger. I don't understand what's happening. I want to stay. I want to stay so, so much. Just the thought of leaving the village is giving me palpitations. Joni used to joke I get some kind of weird agoraphobia, that

I would implode if I set one foot over the road where the steelworks ended and the stacks began.

I hate the thought of even being in Sheffield, with the trams and cars and dying high street, the boarded-up department stores. The sad, lonely kids' fairground aeroplane ride that no child ever goes on, and the soullessness of the Peace Gardens. The trendy young professional square, all glass and chrome and vacant eyes.

Leeds will be worse. I've never been to Jamie's flat. When he first told me he lived in a flat, I thought it'd be like the ones in Middlewood – stacked, probably dodgy cladding, dogs called Mitchell. Then he showed it to me on FaceTime and it looked just like the Peace Gardens. Chrome. Transparent walls. Bright city lights below. Navy blues and shiny floors. It didn't look like a flat to me.

I can't imagine lying in his bed, listening to the rush-hour traffic, like the sea. The fumes, the chatter and footsteps, the mania. Beeps. Horns. Takeaway latte cups. Ironed shirts. It's another life. A life I don't understand. One I only see on Netflix. And I'm going to it. Even just a few days, it feels all wrong. I feel all wrong.

'Cass.'

'What?' I look at Kit, almost surprised he is still here.

'I thought you lost that doll. That night.'

'I did.'

My tongue is stuck to the roof of my mouth. Kit looks at me and I realise what that awful, thick, brewing expression in his eyes has been, since the morning Joni vanished. It's fear.

My words are barely a croak, a scrape from the throat.

'Someone knows.'

15

Then – 1996

It was as if the blackness of the steelworks was recoiling, shadows scurrying back into the girders, and Pete's torchlight shakily cutting through the huge, gaping factory floor.

And there it was. A tall figure. In black. Wearing some kind of dress, maybe even a robe. A hood.

I screamed first before Kit grabbed me and slapped his hand over my mouth. The bats broke from the roof and shrieked.

'Don't show you're scared,' he muttered. 'Probably just some homeless guy.'

We froze. The figure didn't move. Not even to raise his hand over his eyes as Pete flashed the torch onto his face. There was nothing but a black shroud there.

'The fuck...?' Joni burrowed into Pete's side.

'There's five of us, it's all right,' Pete whispered. Then jutted out his chin in the way I'd seen him do before at the rusty gate of the Miles's shack. 'You all right, mate?' Pete called. But the figure remained silent. It stood. Tall. Hunched, though. Arms hanging loosely at its side. Almost primate.

'Why is he just standing there?' Joni's voice was barely audible.

'Can we help you with something?' Pete shouted again. I had no idea how he could possibly sound so calm.

Still no word. No movement. Tom took a step back.

'Listen, just move along, yeah? We don't want any trouble.' Kit's voice was loud and clear, but I could see his hands were shaking.

The figure looked up. Then slowly crouched down to the ground.

'What's he doing?' I whispered. 'Jesus, he looks like an animal.'

'He's picking something up. There's something in his hand,' Pete said and pulled Joni tighter. 'Don't worry, I've got you.'

I felt the emptiness of the air around me and a cold rush of adrenaline pump through me. My knees bent slightly. Ready to sprint. Or spring.

We watched as it stood up, Pete following it with the torch. Its hand raised slowly and for a second I thought it was a snake writhing in his hand. Something thick and looped.

'Jesus Christ, it's a fucking noose!' Kit pointed at the figure and reached out blindly, holding his hand up as if to try to warn it back.

'RUN!' Tom shouted and yanked Joni in the direction of the entrance where we'd come in. We turned to follow, but where there had been an open doorway, there was now just blackness.

'What the fuck? Where's the door?' Pete shone the torch over the wall to get the grates lit up, while Joni and I screamed to keep the light on the figure. He whirled back round. But the figure was gone.

'Shit. Shit.' Joni and I clung to each other, while Kit and Pete turned in slow circles. 'Where's he gone?'

'I'm here.' There was a low guttural voice close to my ear.

Clamping my hands to my ears, I screamed and screamed and screwed my eyes shut tight, like when we were little and playing hide-and-seek. If I can't see you, you can't see me. But it could see me. I could feel its hot breath on my neck and its fingers reach out and grab the back of my T-shirt, and a strange noise. A noise that didn't sound right. Animalistic almost.

It was only when Joni put her arms around me, I realised it was laughter.

'You fucking bastards!' she shouted. 'Look how scared she is.'

'I'm really, really sorry.' A voice I didn't recognise.

I opened my eyes slowly and felt a rush of pain through my head. Pete and Tom were doubled over laughing.

Kit was smiling, but somewhat shamefully. And there was the stranger, in black jeans and a hoodie, now pulled down, holding some kind of blanket.

'Payback, bitches,' Pete spluttered.

'That was so cruel, you guys.' Joni tried to look mad, but her mouth twitched until she started laughing too. 'Oh my God, it's not funny. This is hysterical laughter, I'll have you know.'

I looked at the stranger, into his salty blue eyes.

'I am so sorry,' he smiled. 'It was just a joke. I got talking to these guys this morning, you know. I've just moved here. They said it would be a laugh.'

'Who the fuck *are* you?' My words trembled so much, I sounded like a thirteen-year-old boy with a breaking voice.

'This is Jamie,' Kit grinned. 'Meet the new frontman of the band.'

★

It wasn't long before Jamie became a permanent fixture. To start with, he was Kit's shiny new toy. He liked the right albums, always bought the cans and the cigs. Yeah, he was a little bit clean-cut, but he did the bankrolling.

I was waiting for the inevitable Joni pounce. I struggled to find much to say to him really. Without shared village history, I wasn't sure what people talked about. Besides, I assumed he was much more interested in getting to know Joni. In the biblical sense. Of course, it only took three weeks, maybe four at the most, before he came up in conversation.

'What does sex feel like?' I asked. Joni's hair was flowing off the end of the hay bale and it made it look like it was being licked by flames.

'What do you mean – the pain?' She rolled over onto her stomach and looked down at me, sat cross-legged on the crops.

'No. Well, yes, I guess I do. I just mean, the feeling. Like, what's good about it?' I leaned my head back against the bale and looked at her upside down. The sky was a peculiar shade of blue.

'Hon, you've not, you know ... touched yourself?'

I shrugged and screwed up my nose. 'I tried. I don't think I'm doing it right.'

'There is no right. It's what feels good for you.'

'Well, it feels OK. But, you know, just like a neck rub does.'

'Yeah, you're definitely not doing it right,' Joni laughed and I reached up and swatted her arm, which was dangling down and pulling little bits of hay out of the bind and sprinkling them in my hair. 'You just need someone that gives you the fanny gallops. Then you'd know what to do.'

'Jesus, Joni.' I looked back down and my neck cracked.

'What?!' She laughed again. 'Don't take it all so seriously, Cass. It's just a vagina.'

'I just have no idea what I'm doing.'

'You need a night alone in the steelworks with Kit.'

'That just sounds threatening.'

'Fair. But I'm not sure a night in your bed under your care bear duvet would set the right tone.'

I didn't reply, but we both knew what she meant.

'Cass?' Joni asked after a minute or two of us listening to the caw of the crows.

'Yeah?'

'Jamie. Yes or no?'

'Yeah. He's nice, isn't he?' My eyes searched the borders for scarecrows.

'Nice? That's a bit knicker-drying.'

'Oh, you meant like that?'

'Yeah. I mean, I had a go at fantasising about him last night and it was surprisingly easy,' Joni said casually.

'I thought you weren't having anything to do with boys our age?' I reminded her.

'I'm not. Too easy. I want someone I can feel proud of myself for conquering. I don't mean that to sound arrogant. I just mean, I want someone to look up to. You know, to admire. Not feel like I'm throwing them a bone.'

'There's not a boy or man in this village who wouldn't lie down at your feet.'

'You say the sweetest things.'

'It's true.'

'It's only because I'm obvious.'

'Yeah. Obvious beauty. What a bitch.'

'And everyone knows I'm a slag. I'm easy. It's like a lamb bone at the butchers.'

'Don't, I hate that word.' I turned round. 'I hate it when you do that.'

'But it's true.' Joni smiled and shrugged. 'I'm not ashamed of it. It's OK to be a teenage girl and want sex.'

'Doesn't make you a slag.'

'Well, what is a slag? Someone who likes sex? So yeah, I'm OK with that.'

'Good job you're so gorgeous then, so you'll never have to go on the game for it. Feels like the best shot I've got at losing my virginity.'

'Cass, you're so beautiful. You have no idea. Your eyes, your hair, that smile. You're so funny. Like wickedly funny. And know all the words. You're the most loyal.'

'Thanks, I mean, that's all very nice, Joni, but it's not helping Kit notice me, is it?'

'You know, I think you should maybe think twice about Kit. Maybe he's a bit up himself?'

I didn't say anything, but rested my chin on my knees and felt my skin swell through the rip in my jeans. I knew what she was doing.

'I mean, the more I think about it, I'm just not sure what a great match you are. I mean, he's so moody.'

'You said that was sexy before. Brooding.'

'Yeah, I know, but I was wrong. He just looks like a toddler who's been told he can't have a biscuit. You don't want to be giving up your virginity for someone who's going to then go home and light his nag champa and write a mawkish song about how hollow and empty the soul of a woman is.'

'Oh my God, Joni, that's exactly what I want! Don't you know me at all?'

We both laughed and I heard her stomach rumble. It was definitely past lunchtime and all I had in my pocket was a half-empty packet of fruit Polos that had clumped together into one purplish, sticky lump.

'I'd settle for a proper kiss. I don't even want sex. I wouldn't have a clue what to do.'

'Didn't you get off with Tom once?' Joni propped her face in the cup of her palm.

'Yeah, but we were kids and it was a shit dare at form time. It really wasn't good. Our teeth kept clashing together and he opened and closed his mouth too fast. I think it might have been his first one too.'

'Didn't fancy going for round two then?'

'Nooo. Anyway, he's only got eyes for you.'

'Hmm, I wouldn't be too sure about that, chick.'

'What do you mean?'

'Nothing. Anyway, I just think maybe Kit would end up treating you like shit. He's got that look. I know that look.'

'I wouldn't even know what I was doing anyway. It's embarrassing.'

'Practise on Jamie.'

'Jamie doesn't fancy me either. No one fancies me.'

'They do. You just don't know it. And you probably don't fancy them back, that's the problem.'

I stared at the way the treetops scraped the sky and lay back in the grasses. The clouds were thick and spreading, moving fast. I tried to imagine it was the field that was moving, spinning, and the sky still, until I felt sick.

'Joni?' I said after a while. There was no reply. I squinted and held my arm over my eyes and looked at her. She was fast asleep.

I looked and looked for the scarecrow, but I couldn't see it. I felt lost and safe both at the same time. The birds landed gently and pecked and nibbled around me. Turning on my side, I tried to catch the eye of a blackbird about three feet away. But it wouldn't look back.

Sometimes I tried to do that with Kit. Will him, will him, will him to glance in my direction. I thought about the way it would be. Maybe he would come and hold a boom box over his head, playing Radiohead instead of some eighties shit, just like John Cusack in *Say Anything*. Outside my window. Throwing stones. And I'd pretend I had been sleeping, even though I had full make-up on and smooth, shiny brushed hair.

I'd only been to his house once and when I saw his bedroom, it made me ache. Actually ache. Articles from *Kerrang!* and *NME* all over the wall. Dark, acerbic paintings. I think it was probably stuff he'd done himself in GCSE Art. Well, I knew really, because it was mounted on sugar paper and had been on display in reception for a while until a parent complained it wasn't appropriate and it got taken down.

I wanted so much to lie on those unmade sheets and bury my head into his pillow and smell him. Smell the salt and sugar of him. His cheap deodorant. His earrings on the bedside table. I wanted him to kiss me until I bruised. Make me feel desired. Loved. Needed. I dreamed of spending the night. My mum might not even notice. The thrill of the idea of a used condom on the floor. Not that I would have any idea of how it worked or what to do with it. Tom and Pete turning up unannounced and seeing the tips of my toes pull in from underneath the grey covers, and realising that I was as much of a woman as Joni.

Joni. Joni who went to a gig in Bradford last night at Rio Rocks. Bradford. I'd never been to a pub outside this village, let alone a club in another city. A band in a van came and picked her up. She'd met the bassist in Sheffield. Did some work for her dad apparently. Good lad, her dad said. So he let her go. She tried to get me to come, but I was too scared – I knew what would happen. She'd do my eye make-up and scrawl my lips with Black Cherry lipstick. I'd wear my mum's black Lycra body and tie-dyed tassel skirt and Joni would wear some incredible concoction, her creamy breasts bursting out of it, her legs Amazonian. I would loom like a tall, spindly insect. No boobs. No hips. I'd hide behind my hair and not be able to offer any witty comments, or even *any* comments. At all. I'd be boring. Everyone would wonder why she had brought me. Joni would try, of course, to cajole me. To tell funny stories to make me look cool. But it would all fall flat. I'd get paranoid from the weed and not drunk enough off the Blastaways.

Then Joni would disappear into the dark somewhere. The club would be loud and smoky and the guitars would ignite my soul, and I'd see all the men, surrounded by beautiful, sexually experienced, bombshell-type women, and I'd press myself up against the wall among the Newcastle Brown and the Castaways and think, for the millionth time, it's more lonely to be in a packed room than on my own, curled in a ball, on top of a haystack before the rain.

Last night, Joni said she'd given a blow job to a guitarist who signed her arm afterwards. It made me feel utterly sick. The thought of some guy holding her head like that, not caring about her, not curling up with her after. And it wasn't even so much that. It was the fact that she didn't want that either. She didn't care. I couldn't understand it.

That was when the first crack appeared.

16

Now

'Someone knows. This is a sign. A warning.'

Jamie stands with arms crossed against the back door. Tom has his head in his hands and Pete is leaning against the fridge. I have to ask him to move so I can get the milk.

'Cass, why are you making tea?' Kit continues. 'That fucking kettle is on all the fucking time.'

'Kit.' Pete looks at him and gives just a sharp little shake of his head.

'And you never found that doll again? After that night?' Tom raises his head. He looks absolutely awful. And for a minute, I see that stocky teddy bear of a boy again. He is as scared now as when he first walked through that railway tunnel.

'No. I mean, I assumed it got ... destroyed with everything else.'

'It went missing, though. Do you remember? Before we left ... you couldn't find it earlier that night,' Kit says.

I am surprised he remembers.

No one speaks. I pour the tea that nobody drinks apart from me. And that's only to prove a point.

'Look, lads,' Tom says. I assume I am counted as one of the lads. Like always. 'If this is one of you playing silly buggers, please say. Please. Because I'm really struggling here.'

'Not me.' Pete shakes his head. 'I'm on the verge of being arrested as it is. Think I'd be involved in this?'

'It's got to be ... I don't know.' Kit looks at me. 'Cass, I know you're going to go mental, but are you *sure* you don't know where Joni is? Is she in some kind of trouble? And you're covering—'

He ducks before the milk carton can hit him and it explodes all over the wall.

'You think, you *actually* think, I could put Millie through this? Put us all through this? You IDIOT!' I screech.

'Don't you fucking dare call me that, you little—'

'Hey!' Jamie hits Kit on the back of his shoulder. 'I don't know what you were about to call her, but I suggest you SHUT. YOUR. MOUTH.'

Pete and Tom are up, chairs flying back, before the first punch is even gestured, throwing themselves between them.

'Stop it,' I cry. Then I grab a tea towel and start mopping up the milk, my chest heaving and my sobs the only sound in the kitchen, save for the deep, rasping breaths of the boys. My boys. I collapse back into a sitting position and Pete comes down to give my shoulders a squeeze.

'Cass, no one thinks you're covering for her. You're just worried. Right, Kit?'

I don't look up, but I feel Pete's glare as much as I sense Kit's nod.

'Is she dead?' I ask. My voice is emotionless and flat.

'You can't think like that,' Tom says. 'There's nothing to suggest—'

'OK, I think we need to tell someone. About what happened that night.' Jamie stands up straight. 'This has gone on long enough.'

'No. No way.' Kit starts shaking his head. 'We have a *kid*,

Jamie,' Kit says. It's so full of nuances, but I decide not to bother getting riled up.

'But ...' I look at the boys. 'If there is any reason, any suspicion, that what happened to Joni was connected to what happened that night, surely the police need to know.'

'Do you want to end up in jail, Cass? Because we could. You do realise that, don't you?'

I think I'm going to pass out.

'But what we did ...' The tears start to burn my cheeks.

'We didn't do anything.' Kit's fist slams against the wall. 'We ran. It was an accident. That's what all kids would do. We didn't even know.'

'We did.' Pete turns away. 'Fuck. OK, fine. Fuck it – that's what me and Joni were arguing about. The night she ... disappeared.'

'What?' I don't understand.

'We were getting ... wound up. Upset.'

'Why were you even talking about it?' Tom says. 'We don't ... We said we wouldn't. You said. We promised.'

'Because sometimes I find it hard to look in the fucking mirror.' Pete's voice has changed. There is something lower. Something rotten.

I get up off the floor.

'What about Joni?' I ask. 'What was she saying?'

Pete sighs. 'She was babbling something about us all being punished. I don't know. Saying she was lonely, that it was all because of what we did. I tried to tell her I've been thinking about it recently. About maybe even confessing. She kind of got mad and pushed me. I didn't hurt her, I swear. But I did grab hold of her. Honestly, just to calm her down. Then she started to scream. And I just got scared. I just ... ran away.' He slumps down next to Tom. 'I left her alone. I knew she was drunk. And I left her ...' His voice cracks and his head bows. 'I'm a piece of shit ...'

'Mate. We all know what she was like when she got like that, when she'd had a few.' Tom puts his hand on Pete's shoulder and I bristle.

'Don't start that. This isn't Joni's fault,' I say.

'It's not Pete's either.' Tom's eyes harden. 'We should have done what I said in the first place. It wasn't on purpose and we were kids. The guilt has just eaten us all up. For years. Why else haven't we been able to move away from this place? Or even make anything of our lives. It's because we don't feel we deserve it.'

'We should never have left.'

Jamie just shakes his head and that annoys even me. For a second, I can see him through Kit's eyes.

'You don't really think that's got anything to do with Joni going missing?' I ask. 'I mean, God, why? Why would that happen now? After all this time, I mean. Even the noose and the crown. It could all be coincidence, right? Maybe Joni really has run off. Gone to some yoga retreat or something. Especially if she was feeling ... depressed.'

'And your doll?' Kit says. 'How do we explain that?'

Pete looks back up. 'Unless ... someone knew. And maybe they were using that Facebook Dating to get to her. I mean, there are some real weirdos on there.'

'How do you know?' I ask.

'What, Joni's the only one who gets lonely?' he says.

'You're on it?' I ask.

'No. Not that one. Sometimes, you know, I use other apps. For hook-ups.'

'Oh.'

'Don't be judgey, Cass. We all have needs,' Pete says.

133

'Why couldn't you just shag each other if you're that desperate?'

'Nice, Cass.' Kit shakes his head.

'Sorry ... I just ...' I look down. 'I get it. But it seems so anonymous. Just, not Joni. At all. She's so ... you know, ethereal and spiritual. It's just not the kind of thing I thought she'd be into.'

'What have the police said? Anything?' Tom asks.

'About this Matt guy? Nothing. Closed his account. Nothing to trace him with. And as they keep telling me, no real reason to suspect him of anything criminal.' I shrug. 'It still seems so creepy to me. *Tomorrow*? The night before she goes missing. Just ...' I shudder.

'I think it's just better that we sort it out ourselves.' Kit looks up. 'There's only one person who knew we were there that night.'

'Who? Andy?' Tom asks.

'No way.' I shake my head. 'Just ... why? Why would Andy even think about it? Make the connection?'

'Well, I think it's worth a visit.' Kit looks at Pete and he nods quickly. 'Hopefully this is all just some kind of twisted game. We can put an end to it.'

'Look, I just want to get Cass out of here. And Millie ...' Jamie says, but Kit's jaw clenches and his voices drops.

'Millie stays here,' Kit says and Jamie just nods. 'All right. Cass, get your stuff,' Kit directs.

I don't remind him I'm already packed and was ready to go. I don't need his permission.

Jamie rolls his eyes slightly but reaches down and lifts my bag up off the floor. I'm going with him. I'm leaving the village. Something inside me feels sick, but I follow him out and sit in his heated leather car seat, and wonder how I ended up here. I can see Kit, Tom and Pete all sat round the kitchen table through the window and I hate it. I want my home. I feel invaded. Passed about. Like no one thinks I can take care of myself. Or Millie.

Then I think about my doll. Her face deformed and melted. The noose. I know what I feel is fear. But it's a strange fear. There's something coming for me. I feel the way I did when the grey sky rolled and I woke under the Gallows Tree.

But the scarecrow isn't there to protect me anymore.

Because we killed him.

Jamie's fridge frightens me. There're gadgets and buttons and I don't understand any of it.

There's a bit for water. But why not just get it from the tap? I ask Jamie this and he laughs.

'It's filtered.'

'So?'

'It tastes better.'

'It's water, you knob.'

He comes to me and puts his arms around my waist, his chin resting on the top of my head.

'I know it's bad of me to say this, but I am so happy you're here. I know, I know. It's so fucking awful of me. But I can't help it. You don't know how long I've dreamed of it.' He kisses my crown, then my neck. And although every muscle in my neck has solidified into hard, gnarled lumps, it makes me sigh, and I feel tingles, prickles, a sign of something, somewhere, relaxing.

'That night...' I can't help it. It's burrowing into my brain like a parasite.

'Best and worst night of my life,' he says. 'I still don't regret it. Any of it. Because it meant having you in my arms.' He turns me around to face him and gently presses me against the Bosch gunmetal-grey American-style fridge. I think of my under-the-counter white one that makes a funny noise at 1 a.m. and always slightly smells of fish. 'The way you felt. Beautiful, Cass. Your eyes. Your hips. The touch of you.'

He kisses me hard and, God, it's amazing. He squeezes his fingers into my waist and I don't even care about the extra couple of inches since Millie. I want him. I love him.

You can lie to your friends. You can lie to yourself. You can lie to him. But don't lie to me.

I hadn't seen Jamie in more than twenty years when I clicked on 'Add friend'. Even as I was doing it, I felt sick to my stomach. I'd looked for him over the years. He who shall not be named. I didn't even dare tell Joni in case she accidentally slipped some information to Tom and Pete, which would have undoubtedly made its way back to Kit.

His profile picture was gorgeous, of course. Someone's wedding. Stubbly. Not the clean-cut, fresh-faced boy I used to know. It was black and white, but the eyes still sparkled. An open top button. That killer dimple.

Worked in marketing. Of course.

Relationship status – not filled in.

A man like Jamie wouldn't be single. And it wouldn't matter because I wasn't anyway.

That night had been a bad one.

I'd tried. It had been busy in the florist's. My fingers were pimpled and prickled from the holly and I had a rash on the creamy, tender flesh on the underside of my forearms. When I came in, there was no smell of cooking, not that it was usual, but the kitchen light wasn't even on and it seemed colder inside than out. We were always stringent with the heating, but it was December. The week before, I had come home to find Millie trying to do her homework in fingerless gloves.

'Millie, it's freezing. Put the heating on!' I had said, as she pulled her duvet around her shoulders.

'It seemed a waste when it was just me home,' she'd replied.

That wasn't the exact moment the resentment started, but it was when I started to defy him. Money was tight. We didn't know any different. We were the generation of free school dinners. Findus Crispy Pancakes. Extra jumpers, not radiators. Sharing bath water. It was all normal for us. But when I first heard that heartbeat, I swore it would be different for Millie.

I never wanted her to cringe in Home Economics because we couldn't afford the ingredients. Or to have to wash her period-stained knickers in the sink because the washing machine had broken and we couldn't afford repairs.

One night it all came to a head. Millie was out. Over at a friend's from school. Probably eating dinner from a table with serving bowls in the centre and white wine for the mum.

Kit was upstairs. I could hear him finger-picking as I walked into the living room, up the open stairs. It was never a good sign. Strumming could go either way. Blues riffs. Doom.

'Kit?' I shouted up the stairs. The house was so small, I knew he would be able to hear me. But there was no reply. I closed my eyes for a second, trying to shuffle through the day, that morning, even last night. Wondering what I'd done or said. If it was even me. Had Tom made a glib comment that pissed him off? Not referred a job his way? Did Pete owe us money again? Had Millie rolled her skirt up too short for school?

I could feel the oppression as I started up the stairs. I often remembered how Joni and I had watched *The Amityville Horror*, and talked about the house in that story, the fact you can almost feel the weight of the negativity. The utter despair. Hopelessness. The dread.

I always tried to mask it when Millie was home. Music on. Oven blasting. Offers of Netflix and wood on the fire. Kit would either engage or he wouldn't. He sulked upstairs, or at the pub; we ignored it. It was better that way. Never begged him to come down or join in. It would make it worse. Having him there with his face on. Staring into space. Feeling his disdain at the domesticity.

And yet never liking me out of his sight. He'd been texting me that day. Asking why I wasn't replying straight away, even though I told him I was in the shop on my own. The suspicion began long before there was anything to be suspicious of.

'Kit?' I pushed open the bedroom door. He didn't look up and just carried on plucking the strings. 'Kit? I'm home.'

Nothing.

I turned to go and start cooking something. I was starving, even if he was going to be a moody prick all night.

'You used to love watching me play,' he said suddenly.

I looked back, but he was still sat on the edge of our bed, his back to me.

'I still do. When have I ever missed a gig?' I replied. I knew I shouldn't start asking questions. He would start on at me for grilling him, not accepting how he feels.

'I mean, just us. Remember, you used to sit behind me, me between your legs, your arms around my waist.'

He stopped playing. But his eyes were still down on his frets.

I didn't say anything. There was plenty I remembered. And plenty he didn't.

'Maybe ... maybe that's why ... I don't know. It's not been working down here.'

'You mean the other night?' I ventured tentatively. 'Because that was a one-off.'

'It wasn't though, was it? We've not been having sex. Like, at all.'

'Well, yeah. But ...'

'But maybe that's why. Why I don't even bother trying anymore. Why, you know, the other night it didn't happen. You're so cold now, Cass. I just don't feel wanted. You know?'

You don't feel wanted? I wanted to scream. *You* don't feel wanted? Is that another thing on my list of daily jobs? Do the washing, clean the house, go to work, come home, fight with Millie, feed everyone, clean up, battle with Millie, sort Joni out, feed Pete. I don't even have time to change my tampon. Now I have to add 'make Kit feel wanted' onto the list?

'I do want you, Kit,' I said quietly. 'I've always wanted you. Since well before you decided you wanted me. How can you say that?'

'You never show it.'

The room was cold. There was a crack in the plaster in the roof that made me shudder. He knew how much I hated it when the house was in any kind of need. I'd asked him time and time again. It was a five-minute job, he kept saying. But five minutes never came.

'It's like you resent me or something.'

'Kit, it's you who resents me.'

'Don't start, Cass.'

'I can't help it. I *know*. I know what you gave up I know you could have gone with the band. But, Kit, you did it for Millie remember? Not me. You did it to be a dad.'

'They only wanted Joni anyway.' Kit rubbed the bridge of his nose. 'They only offered me the gig because they thought it would make her come too.'

'You hate that indie jingly jangly music anyway,' I pointed out.

'I wouldn't have hated the money, Cass. That song got to number two.'

'Kit, you made the right choice for the right reasons,' I said. 'Or are you saying you should have made a different choice?'

'Don't you mean you? *You* should have made a different choice?'

'Where is this all coming from?' I shut the bedroom door and perched on the other end of the bed. 'What's happened?'

'I went on the laptop to do an invoice. Your Facebook was open.'

'And?'

'I saw you'd looked him up.'

I went cold.

'Kit. I just... God, Joni and I were just talking about old times, wondered what happened to him. I looked him up to see, that's all.'

'Are you sleeping with him?' Kit's voice was so brittle. So matter-of-fact. Like it was a done deal. That's how little he thought of me. Of us.

'Kit, I haven't seen him. Not since... well, you know. I've not spoken to him. I know nothing about him apart from his Facebook profile picture.'

'Bit weird, isn't it? You stalking him like that. He'll know you've been looking for him. How do you think that makes me look?' He turned his head then, to the side. The sharpness of his cheekbone was starting to fade. Like the Celtic tattoo band around his arm that was bleeding into a grey, shapeless ring.

'He won't know,' I said. 'Facebook doesn't work like that.'

'Yeah, well, you'd know. You spend more time on it than with me. With us.' He put his guitar down and leaned forward, so now I couldn't see his face at all.

'That's not true.'

There was a painful silence. And then he said, 'You don't have to stay with me, you know. I've never forced you into this marriage. You could have gone to uni or whatever. You didn't have to stay here for me.'

'I never said you did.' I furrowed my brow.

'I feel it. It's like you think that you're meant for more than this.'

'Don't, Kit. Don't project how you feel onto me.'

I cringed then. I knew I shouldn't have said that. I could almost see the hackles on his neck rise, like a stray dog. The snarl was coming.

'So I'm a failure, right? You do think that? I could have gone, Cass. I could be famous by now. I could be … they fucking headlined the Leeds Festival three years ago.'

As if I hadn't seen. Or felt his pain that entire weekend.

'Kit.' A year ago, maybe two, or maybe, if I was honest, even five, I would have reached forward, wrapped my arms around him. Convinced him of his talent, his amazingness, how he still rocked my world. But those words just seemed to have been recycled and recycled until there was nothing left of them, like one of his work T-shirts that eventually would just fall apart in the wash. Disintegrate in front of my eyes.

'Cass,' he replied. He didn't know what to say any more than I did. That beautiful, brooding boy had grown into a man, but he had not grown apart from the dark moods. And now, the brooding, the disgust for society, the angst, the blame, the fuck you attitude. It just didn't suit a man of his age.

He was right about one thing.

He did tell me to go.

I couldn't leave, though. I could never leave.

The day we buried my mother in the village churchyard, I watched them lower her into the ground and, for a minute, I wished I was with her. Curled up in the coffin next to her, her hand on my head. We would both melt into the earth, feed the roots of the trees. Become the oxygen in the air. And I wouldn't be here. Alone. Even with Kit on one side and Joni on the other.

Her death wasn't a surprise. Doctors had warned her. I was an orphan at thirty-three.

No one prepares you for how that feels. Pathetic really. A grown woman. But now I'd never have it. I'd never be someone's child again. I'd never feel as if I belonged to someone. I'd never feel her hand on my hair.

Only Joni's.

Had I stayed here for something that didn't exist? Could I have got in the car that day? With Jamie. Watched the villages disappear in the rear-view mirror? Gone with him to uni. Shared some dodgy damp flat, worked shifts stacking supermarket shelves. Held him back. Neither choice was ever about me. Where was I? What was I meant to be? What was I for?

We didn't bother with a wake. It felt too awkward to raise

a glass to a woman who, by all intents and purposes, had drunk herself to death.

Instead I walked across the cornfield, looking for him. Always, always, looking for him.

And, as usual, he wasn't there.

Back in our bedroom, I tried to open my mouth. To soothe Kit with balmy words of comfort, medicinal coos of love, of promises. But instead we just let the silence hang over us. The village around us felt it too. It was crumbling before our eyes. Just like us.

He went to the pub that night with Tom. Spent our last tenner on shit beer and false smiles.

And I opened Facebook, and clicked on 'Add friend' on Jamie's profile.

It was time. Just like he always said it would be.

Now, Jamie makes love to me in front of the huge window that reaches out over the cityscape. The stars here are the lights of the towering buildings that fill the skies. The meadows are the people below us, wavering like blades of grass. The sex is so different with him. It's not like it was with Kit, where I felt I had to get there too, otherwise he took it as a personal failure. I can relax now and not feel so much intense pressure to make sure it ends the way it is supposed to.

His hands are softer, but his mouth is harder. The way he moves is unfamiliar and thrilling. I don't know what's going to happen next, and he doesn't know me inside out; he doesn't know where the curves of my body dip and contract.

'Tell me what you like,' he whispers and I realise I have absolutely no idea. I know what I like with Kit. I don't know what I like with this man. He tells me not to be shy, but I can't explain to him it's not shyness keeping me from telling him what to do. So I just kiss him back harder and ask for him to surprise me.

He keeps murmuring in my ear, telling me how much he loves me, how long he has waited for me. The rug is soft and thick underneath my back and the lamps are expensively soft. He moves inside me and I close my eyes and allow myself to feel it for what it is. No results required. My breathing is quicker and his is deeper and that makes me move with him until his hands begin to grab my skin that little bit harder, so it almost burns.

His shoulders are high and his knees and feet firmly planted into the floor, as if he is about to begin the hundred-metre sprint. In the reflection of the glass, he looks like a panther, or some creature about to attack. It thrills me and I close my eyes and allow myself to feel wanted, to feel loved, as he tells me he adores me. That it's always been me.

I think about the night I saw such pain in his eyes when I closed door on him. On us. And I feel relief. Relief I have taken away some of that pain.

He moves faster and deeper and I moan to let him know that it's OK. My back arches and I widen my hips to let him in further, and his eyes bulge and his hand creeps up. And then it happens. His hand is round my throat.

My immediate reaction is to pull away. Something flashes in my head. Some memory, but then I remember that this is what people do now. This is a thing. It's OK. Sex has moved on from tying up with scarves. It's progressive.

My mind flashes to the websites, but I shake my head to knock the thoughts of Joni out. I can feel my body start to tense as I think of her and I try to get myself back into where I was, and find I can. I love the feel of his strong body over mine. I feel safe. I feel protected. I even feel controlled, but in a good way. I open my eyes to smile at him and his face is so near mine, his forehead touches mine and our eyes are close, I feel so connected.

His breath is heavy and his eyes close, so I close mine too and just let myself feel everything. His hand tightens on my throat. At first, I think it is because he is just moving position and wait for his grip to release. But it doesn't. My eyes open and I put my hand up to his hand to let him know I can't breathe.

But his eyes stay shut and when my palm touches the back of his hand, his fingers clench tighter.

I try and shout, but it comes out like a croak and that's when the panic starts. It rushes up through my thighs and my heart races, and I start to thrash.

Suddenly, there's a rush of relief and air floods down my throat. I gasp and Jamie, still moving, still undeterred, asks me if I'm OK, was it too much?

'I'm fine. I just couldn't breathe,' I say and let him apologise and stroke my hair. I let my heartbeat settle, but I can't seem to get back into the rhythm and my hips move awkwardly and bang against his. He doesn't seem to notice. When he comes, his fist clenches in my hair and he collapses onto me, his face buried in my neck. And I stare out the window and my hand strokes the back of his head automatically, like I am soothing a child.

There are sweet words tumbling out of his lips that I try to catch and keep, but they disintegrate through my fingers.

The sky is ink.

I remember saying I did not want to believe in anything after death. Now I'm not so sure.

Where are you, where are you, where are you?

17

Then – 1991

The mouse twitched its little nose and scrabbled tiny claws against the side of the mug.

'It's so cute,' I beamed at Pete. 'Thank you.'

'I don't think it's hurt. You just need a shoebox or something to put it in. Or, like, some kind of cage. I can ask Billy. Bet he's got something lying about.'

I poked my finger into the mug and patted the tiny brown creature on the head. It shook, so I blew little kissing noises at it. It didn't seem to make much difference, but I liked it.

'What will I feed it?' I asked.

'Dunno. Leaves and shit? Carrots? I'll ask Billy. He'll know.'

According to Pete, Billy knew everything. Since the day he handed him a Mr Freeze, Pete had started spending actual time at the shack. Tinkering with all the weird and strange items. Helping fix things. Maybe it was because he didn't have a dad about, or brothers, but he was oddly excited when Billy taught him how to wire a plug. Then, one day, Billy produced a knackered bike frame he'd found in a skip. Him and Pete set about rebuilding it from scraps and bits found in the garden, in skips, in the bins behind garages. It was going to be wicked, Pete said.

'But what do you talk about?' Kit had asked. 'I mean, why are you hanging out with the village weirdo?'

146

'Maybe *I'm* the village weirdo,' Pete had pointed out. 'Why is he hanging out with me?'

'Well. Yeah. That's what we're asking. Does he ask you to come inside to see his puppies?' Tom had teased.

'Dickhead.'

'He's like the doc in *Back to the Future*,' Joni had said. 'Just a bit creepier.'

'And not building you a time machine,' I'd added.

'How do you know?' Pete had wriggled his eyebrows. We had laughed and let him get on with it.

In fact, there was an element of me that was jealous. We played Bad Eggs and Block 123 in the street. Kicked a ball about. In the evenings, we played in the fields and watched the hay and the crops turn honey-coloured as the sun trickled down. Then everyone would go home, leaving me and Pete, dragging our feet. Pete's mum worked nights in the nursing home, so he was often home alone in the evenings. My mum would normally be passed out on the sofa or crying. We took the long route back.

But now Pete would be rushing home to sort out some tyres. Or go skip cruising after nightfall.

I think, looking back, perhaps that's why he caught me the mouse. Prised from the jaws of death, he said. Big'un, the huge black panther-esque cat who lived in the alley behind the pub, had jumped up onto the wheelie bin with it in his mouth while Pete was rummaging for steel wire.

We called him Mickey.

Joni had squealed 'get that thing away from me' when we proudly showed him off at the rec, but that didn't deter me. I happily followed Pete up to the shack, where Billy made good on Pete's expectations and fashioned me a home for my new pet, created from some chicken wire and a plastic tub. We got sawdust from the mill and I put a little egg cup in there with water, and an old smoked glass ashtray with bits of bread, grass or anything that looked tasty for him.

Every morning, I'd wake up and clamber out of bed to see him. He started coming to me, sniffing my finger. I'd lie awake at night and listen to his scratching and rustling. It was so soothing, so peaceful. I'd talk to him about my day as I drifted off to sleep. I imagined getting another mouse, and having mouse babies, and my dreams were full of mouse palaces and cardboard toilet-roll tunnels.

It was the happiest I'd ever been.

'That vermin has got to go,' my mum said one night, after she staggered into my room. 'It's not a pet, Cass. It's disease-ridden. I'll buy you a bloody hamster if you're that bothered.'

We both knew this was a lie. I let it wash over me.

Mum's hours had been cut at the pub. Not enough customers to warrant a cleaner every morning. Not enough glasses to wash. Things were tighter than usual. We'd had porridge for tea the last two nights. She wasn't drinking because she couldn't. Instead, her eyes were cold. She was tired but couldn't sleep. Snappy. Pacing. Banging.

Then, one night, I had a nightmare. I dreamed she cooked Mickey in the oven and made me eat him. After that, I couldn't leave him in the house. I was terrified she would do something to him, get rid of him. I started taking him with me when I went out in an old teabag box.

The others noticed, of course. But they didn't say anything. Not really.

Then, one day, it happened.

We were playing in the fields, Block 123. I'd left Mickey in his box on top of a hay bale where he'd be safe. The

THE VILLAGE

scarecrow was watching over him, after all. It was an epic game, one that would have gone down in history if it hadn't been for what happened next. Tom was seeking, Joni and I hid in the hollows of the oak at the edge of the field. Pete had headed into the stream, and under the bridge. And Kit had managed to scale one of the ashes so high, he was almost touching the magpie nests.

By the time we all beat Tom back to base, I'd almost forgotten about Mickey.

Just one more game.

One more.

I left him in there too long. I didn't understand about air holes.

The gang helped me bury him. Under the scarecrow so he would always be protected. My tears dripped over his little body and Joni sang 'When a Knight Won his Spurs'. Pete suggested we give him a Viking funeral downstream and send him to Valhalla. But when Kit pointed out we'd have to torch his little body, I became inconsolable.

Pete and Joni sat with me until the sun went down.

I'd never known loss like it.

Perhaps I'd never really known love before.

I walked home and emptied the makeshift cage of sawdust and leaves. Washed out the ashtray and egg cup and put the plastic box in the back of my cupboard so I didn't have to see it. I fell asleep aching for his velvety head and his little pink claws and begged, begged, begged to something, anything, for forgiveness.

The next week, Andy's mum took a nasty spill down the stairs and ended up on crutches. Mum got some shifts behind the bar. Cash in hand, of course. We had pork chops for tea that night. Then, on the Saturday, we went to the jumble sale in the next village so Mum could look for some jazzy tops for her Saturday night shifts. There, on one of the stands, was a plastic-bottomed hamster cage, a greenish cloudy water bottle still wired to the side. The door was off the hinge. It would have been perfect for Mickey and I felt a lump in my throat and I walked away to look at the one-armed Barbies.

On the bus home, Mum kept her black bin bag of loot close to her. And the next morning, I woke up to the orange hamster cage, the greening water bottle full of water, and a little white mouse we named Martha.

Sometimes good things can happen in the darkest of places. If you're willing to make a sacrifice for it.

18

Now

After Jamie has gone to work, I sip at my coffee before realising it has gone cold. I wonder how long I have been sat at the kitchen counter for. Or is it a breakfast bar? It's all so shiny and marbly and chrome here. I can see my reflection everywhere, in every surface, like some kind of crazy hall of mirrors.

He didn't want to leave me alone, but I insisted. I see Millie has been online again, posting like a demon. She seems to be loving the drama. Kit said her phone had been buzzing non-stop. And Chris had been round again. Kit wouldn't let him in the house, though. It was really embarrassing. According to Millie.

I wonder if the boys have been round to see Andy yet. God knows what they'd say. We don't know what he knows. If he ever put two and two together. Maybe it will do more damage to bring it up? God, my head is spinning. I'm about to call Kit to tell them to call it off, but my phone buzzes before I get chance to dial.

'Kit? Did you see Andy? Did he seem shifty? Did you go round? What did he say?'

'His dad's in hospital.'

'What?'

'He's been with his dad in hospital. For the past couple

of days. It can't have been him.' Kit's voice is flat. 'He didn't hang that doll. He's not been here.'

'God,' I whisper.

'There's another one, Cass,' Kit says.

'What? What are you talking about?' I pause with my mug raised halfway to my mouth.

'Another noose.'

'You're kidding me? Was there anything tied to it? Another doll?'

'Pete's goggles. You know. The ones he always used to wear. Those dumb glasses.'

'The ones he was wearing? That night?'

'Yeah. All melted. Like, they'd been burned.'

'Are you sure they are the same ones?' I ask.

'As sure as you are that that was your doll.'

'Shit. Have the police seen?'

'No. I just took it down. Before anyone saw. Not even Pete. I was up early. Thank God.'

'Have you told Pete? Have you told the police?' I ask.

'I don't know. I don't know what to do. Are you OK? I mean, are you safe?'

'Yes, it's like Fort Knox here. Honestly. There's a doorman and about fifty locks. It's well posh.'

'There's a surprise,' he scoffs.

'Please don't.'

'Millie's asking some questions, Cass.'

'Like what?' I sip my coffee again, forgetting, and then take it to the microwave.

'About gigs me and Joni did. With the other band. She wants venues. You know. Dates. So she can share on that Faceache site.'

'Well, give her them.' I slam the microwave door and heat up the coffee.

'Do you think that's wise?'

'Kit, I just want to find her. If Millie thinks that's going to help, then fine.'

'Don't you think Millie has been through enough?' Kit shoots back and I bite down so hard, I feel a molar grind and chip. 'Why, Cass? Just ... how could you do this to me?'

There's a terrible, horrible sound. A howl almost.

'Oh God, Kit. Please don't cry.'

I haven't heard that noise for years. Not since we were sixteen.

'Was it him? All along? Was it him? Always him?'

'Nooo.' I start to cry too. 'I swear.'

'Did you fuck him? In our house? While I was at work? Pulling double jobs.'

'No. Kit. NO. It wasn't like that, I swear. We've been over this again and again. Nothing happened. Nothing happened until after ...'

'How can I believe that?' Oh God, that noise.

'Kit, you left me. *You* left *me*. Remember?'

There is a strangled silence, and then I hear him choke. I put my hand gently to my throat.

'But I left because you weren't there. You were a ghost. I didn't mean it. I thought you'd do something. Say anything. To make me stay. But you didn't. You just watched me go.'

'Because it didn't feel real.'

'Come back to me, Cass. Please ...' He is begging and my guts slither so violently, I think I am about to be sick. 'We can start again. It's us, Cass. It's me and you.'

I close my eyes and I can sense his forehead on mine.

The pain is so deep, I can almost feel the cuts in my skin. I wonder how long I can bleed for.

'I can't, Kit. I can't. Not now.' The words blister my lips.

'Cass ...' He is crying fully now and I want the world to stop turning.

But, most of all, I want Joni.

After the tears dry and shallow goodbyes are forced, I move over to the sofa. It's upright and uncomfortable. Not the kind you throw yourself into and bury yourself in the cushions. I log into Joni's Facebook again. There are a few new messages. I wonder if there are sickos who know she is missing or just don't watch the news. I ignore them all. Even though Matt18698's account has gone, I reread the messages, but it makes me feel ill, so I just sit back on the sofa and stare out over the sky.

Leeds looks different in the daylight. The bricks look cleaner, but the air seems dirtier. It's all shades of grey and the people outside look like insects. Parasites. Crawling over the carcass of something rotten.

I want to go home.

But I can't.

The flat begins to feel like it's closing in on me, so I grab my coat and bag. I want to go somewhere else, somewhere I can feel her again. Cities aren't me. Or her.

Jamie doesn't live far from the station, but still I walk furtively, as if I'm doing something wrong. That I shouldn't be outside. Avoiding eye contact, I pick up my pace. The streets aren't that busy. It's morning, a weekday, and the pavements smell of coffee and good intentions. The station itself is huge. Hardly like the two platforms in Thistleswaite. Starbucks and Subway, mini supermarkets, bars. It's like being on holiday. I expect.

I buy my ticket from the machine. I can't cope with looking anyone in the eye today, even though I'm not exactly
sure what counts as off-peak and peak, and head through
the barriers. I have to watch someone else scan their ticket
as I really have no idea.

There isn't a direct line to Haworth. I have to go to
Bingley and then I try and fail to work out the buses and
end up in a taxi instead. I instantly feel my shoulders drop
as the driver pulls up at the pub at the bottom. The hill up
through Haworth winds high and crooked and I stand and
gaze at the cobbles and the squat little shops. It smells still
of lavender bath powder and liquorice.

The first time we came here, Joni's dad drove us. We were
twelve. He had some job to quote for nearby and thought
we might like the quirky old bookshops and apothecaries,
plus we were reading *Jane Eyre* at school and he thought
we might want to go to the Brontë Parsonage. We didn't
want to.

Spooks, with the little black outline of a ghost on the
signage, was the first shop we saw. Joni had dragged me in
squealing and cooing over the tarot cards, the crystals. She
bought some nag champa incense and begged her dad for a
tenner for a card reading. He flatly refused.

I bought the old-fashioned hard liquorice sticks from the
penny sweet shop and we climbed to the top of the hill until
we were out of breath. We tried to buy half a shandy in the
Black Swan, but they laughed at us, so we sat on the wall and
waited until Joni's dad was finished. Watching the people go
by. Brontë die-hard fans. Grannies. Locals. The sun stroked
the chimney pots lovingly and I told myself if I was ever to
leave Thistleswaite, this is where I would live.

After that, whenever Joni's dad was out this way on a

weekend, we'd hitch a lift. Even though we never had any money to buy anything, we'd wander around, even the crazy bric-a-brac shops selling headless Labrador china figurines and caliper boots as plant pots.

When we were fifteen, Joni managed to save up enough babysitting cash to get her cards done. Jobs were few and far between; no one had the money to go out and pay for a sitter. Just took their kids to the pubs instead. But Joni struck lucky with a single mum who worked night shifts and had no family to help her.

'God, aren't you scared?' I said as she handed over her bag of pound coins to the man with the leather waistcoat behind the counter.

'No. Why? Do you think it's going to be bad?' Joni's eyes widened theatrically.

'No, just ... I don't know. Bit scary? Are you going to ask any questions? Do you want me to come in with you?'

The leather waistcoat guy was locking up the shop and flipped the door sign over to 'back in half an hour'. I guessed it was a one-man show.

'Ummm, no. I'll be OK.' She squeezed my hand. 'Thanks though.'

I wasn't being kind. I just wanted to hear what he was going to tell her. Joni was the kind of girl who believed anything you told her if you had enough of a convincing argument. I didn't want her worried.

'You OK here?' the man said and gestured to the stool where he had been sitting.

'Erm. Yeah, sure.' I came behind the counter and perched on it, wondering if he had CCTV, or just his psychic powers to rely on the fact I wouldn't rob anything.

Joni gave me a faux-anxious grin and then followed him down the stairs into the basement.

A door clicked below and I gazed around the shop. Some of the stuff was a bit intimidating. Symbols, talismans, spell books even. A book of shadows. Other stuff was gentler. Essential oils. Unicorn pendants. I let my fingers brush across the boxes of tarot. Rider Waite. The Old Path. The Tarot of the Fairies. The velvet bags of runes.

I felt nothing.

After listening to the ticking of the clock for longer than was comfortable, I hopped off the stool and round to the bookshelves, looking for something to read while I waited. Ghost stories, folklore. I plucked one off the shelf and settled back on the stool.

Occasionally, I heard the unmistakable tinkle of Joni's laugh. But they began to get fewer and fewer, until eventually, I thought I heard a strange kind of mew. Cocking my head to the side, I listened sharply. It was snuffly, but definitely not a laugh of any kind. A sigh. Another mew, then rapid intakes of breath. I got off the stool and went to the top of the stairs, staring down the cold hard cement flight. Should I go down?

Then it stopped. There was silence and then the hum of a soothing voice. I couldn't make out the words, just the calm, rich tones.

A sharp peal made me jump.

For a second, I had no idea what the noise was, and then I heard angry rapping at the window and a middle-aged woman in a kaftan pointing at the 'back in half an hour' sign. I shrugged and mouthed 'I don't work here,' but she just furrowed her brow and carried on gesticulating. In the end, I gave up and went back to return my book to the shelf.

But before I could replace it onto the shelf, I heard the door open downstairs.

'Joni?' I positioned myself at the top of the stairs. 'You OK?'

'I'm fine ...' She smiled up at me, but she was pale and looked almost distracted. The leather waistcoat man had his hand on her shoulder.

'I think you've got some customers,' I said apologetically.

'Ah, that will be Fat Babs,' he said with a shake of his head but offered no further information.

I took a closer look at Joni. 'Joni, are you OK?'

'Yes,' she nodded with thin lips. 'Sorry, must have been so boring for you, having to wait.'

'No, it's fine.'

I followed her to the door and we stood back as, who I could only presume to be Fat Babs, came rushing in, babbling about sage bundles.

Leather waistcoat man held the door and I felt the heavy weight of his stare. I looked up at him and his blue eyes locked onto mine. He had wrinkles in the corners and stubble with flecks of white, but he was otherwise ageless.

'Take care of her,' he said to me quietly. I just nodded.

It was only in the van on the way home I realised I was still holding the book in my hand.

My phone rings as I stare at the door sign now. 'Back in half an hour'. Just like before. Tarot readings have gone up to thirty quid now.

I fish about in my pocket and answer without even looking to see who it is.

'Hey. Where are you?' It's Jamie's voice.

'Haworth,' I say, almost robotically, and get closer to the

shop window. I see my haggard-looking reflection and realise I have become Fat Babs.

'What the hell are you doing in Haworth?' Jamie sounds shocked.

'How did you know I wasn't at your flat?'

There is a pause. 'I didn't. I just, well, I called you and you sound like you're outside.'

'Really?'

'No. I came home on my lunch break. I just wanted to check and see if you were OK. I had a heart attack when the flat was empty. Christ, I wish you'd told me. I thought something had happened. What are you doing in Haworth?'

'I like it here,' I say simply. 'It reminds me of Joni. I just wanted to feel close to her. Just for a while.'

He arranges to pick me up at 6 p.m. despite my protests that I can get the train.

It's definitely edgier here now. Gift shops more expensive. The weird old bric-a-brac joints have jacked up their prices and become all hipster.

As I hike up past the comforting old cafes that still have their green and white checked tablecloths and red writing in the window, I see a gallery tucked away on the left. It's not the gallery as such that grabs my attention; it's small and unassuming, all windows and white and clean lines. There's a sign above it that says 'Abrahams'.

It's the picture in the window that makes me almost gasp for breath. Steelworks in the background, against a fiery sky. With a group of children, all boys, tiny in perspective, playing football, dwarfed by the industrial backdrop, comforted by the sunset.

My eyes skim for the name. *Star of the Future*. I am captivated by it.

I see us all there, even though the figures are all boys in the painting. Jubilant. Arms raised high. Stripes. Messy hair. I can hear the shouts and the catcalls in the painting. I can smell the rain on the air and hear the sizzle and spits from the kitchens and the barks of the dogs.

I have never felt so at home and yet so far away.

I see Tom and Pete. Kit. Joni. Me.

Before Jamie. Before that night.

Would we have scattered? Left the village? Would we have believed we were, and could be, stars of the future? Did we stay because, deep down, we didn't deserve a fresh start? That we were in fact, and in some strange way, co-dependent on our guilt? That had become so big a part of us that we couldn't exist without it.

I hold up my phone, take a picture of the painting, and head back down the hill to Spooks. As I push open the door, the same bell rings and the shop looks almost exactly as I remember it. A smile almost flickers on my lips.

He is greyer, gaunter. His stubble is no longer stubble but a whiskery tangle of a sparse beard. His eyebrow hairs are long and straggly. But he is still wearing a leather waistcoat. And his eyes are still the same blue.

'Can I help you?' he says, peering over the wire-rimmed spectacles.

'Yes.' I clear my throat. 'I was hoping you'd be able to do me a reading.'

'Oh, I'm sorry, I think we're almost fully booked today. I can check with Saskia though, but she's just with someone.' He opens a book and shakes his head. 'She might be able to squeeze you in a bit later ... say—'

'Actually, it's you. You I wanted a reading with,' I say. 'I'm sorry. I'm sure your colleague is great, but—'

'I don't do commercial readings, I'm afraid,' he says with a smile and those crow's feet crease in exactly the same way. Just a little deeper.

'You used to,' I say softly. 'You read for my friend. When we were teenagers. She's missing now.' My voice catches and I look for a flash of recognition. 'Joni Blackwood. You must have seen her in the papers.'

His eyes change, shift a little. 'I have. I have seen it. I'm very sorry.'

'You read for her. When we were fifteen.'

'Did I?' He doesn't look uncomfortable. Just empathetic. 'I'm sorry, I don't think I'm able to help if that's what you're after. I don't remember readings. There's too many, there's—'

'No, I know. But will you read for me? Everything you said to Joni. It all came true.'

He looks at me without blinking.

'I've retired now, my girl. I am truly sorry. But I am sure we can fit you in with Saskia. I'll—'

'Please.' My voice is high and I am aware I sound as if I am begging. But my dignity is at the door. 'She ... said it was as if you could look into her heart.'

'People are often seeking answers when they come for readings. They can feel that way sometimes. Perhaps she was looking for affirmation. Something she already knew. Deep down.'

'She didn't know.'

A strange look clouds his eyes, and it's clear to me, for a second, he remembers. If not Joni exactly, something darker. A memory. A feeling.

'And you told her what was going to happen to the baby.'

19

Then – 1996

'I might not come tonight,' I said. I was lying, of course. I mean, what else was I going to do? But I knew what the night would entail. Band practice. Joni and Jamie singing. The boys playing. Badly. But holding it together. Me sat on some old girder, as if I had a function or anything useful to contribute. I needed to feel needed, though. I wanted them to want me there, even though I couldn't imagine why they would.

'Of course you're coming. Don't be daft,' Joni said. 'But maybe we should do something different. I hear what you're saying. It is getting boring. God, I can't wait until one of us can drive.'

'Dream on.'

We laughed, but it was hollow. Kids in school got driving lessons for their seventeenth birthdays. No chance of that for us. A Chinese takeaway if we were lucky.

'You know what we could do?' Joni slit the stalk of a daisy with her thumbnail and started to make a chain. 'We could go shrooming. Pete says the field behind Billy's is full of them.'

'I'm not taking mushrooms,' I said. 'Besides, knowing Pete, we'd get the wrong ones and poison ourselves.'

'No, we won't. The worst we will do is get a bit of gut rot. Come on. It'll be brilliant.'

'I'm not going home tripping my tits off. Our parents will spot it a mile off. Well, your lot will.'

'Well, we could camp out there tonight? It's warm enough. Take sleeping bags. Build a fire. It could be good. I mean, they are going to start this regeneration work on it soon. We won't be able to hang around there as soon as construction starts. Be a good way to end the summer.'

'Mum won't let me camp in the steelworks,' I pointed out.

'Your mum won't know.' If anyone else had said this, it would have made me wince. 'Anyway, say you're sleeping at mine. I'll tell Dad I'm at yours.'

'What if they ring each other?'

'When have they ever rung each other?'

'True.' I watched as Joni's fingers worked deftly. My chains were always rubbish. The flowers too far apart and the stalks too thin. I was running out of excuses, but I didn't want to spend the night in the creepy steelworks; the fear of a scary bad trip was even worse.

'Give you a great chance with Jamie. Snuggle up next to him in the sleeping bags. Oh, we should take teddies and pyjamas, we'd look well cute.'

'I don't fancy Jamie,' I protested. 'He fancies you.'

'Oh my God. We could pull the *mother* of all pranks.' Joni stopped her floral workings, her eyes huge. I noticed she ignored my last comment completely.

'Joni...'

'Oh come on. There must be something we can do.'

'It's too expected now.'

'Hmm. Never say die. I'm going to have a think.'

'I'm just a bit nervous about it, Joni. I mean, surely some

grotty steelworks isn't the best place to take mushrooms for the first time? Shouldn't we be in a field somewhere?'

'Oh you sweet summer child,' Joni laughed. 'Come on, let's ask the lads what they think.'

'Why bother? When did they ever not do something you wanted to?'

'You'd be surprised.' Joni climbed down off the hay bale.

'Are you going to get off with any of them?' I asked after a beat.

'Depends how bored I get,' Joni replied and my bones chilled. 'Come on then. Let's go knock for them.'

As usual, everyone loved Joni's idea and the rest of the afternoon was found sourcing steel bins for a fire, blow-up beds (no one had any), sleeping bags (only two of us had one) and trying to score some resin from Scabby Dave – fifteen quid for an eighth. Four quid each, a packet of Marlboro Lights because Marlboro Red made your lungs bleed apparently and a packet of king-size Rizlas. Always a giveaway at the shop, so Tom went on his bike two villages over where no one would be suss. I hoped Joni had forgotten, or at least had had second thoughts, about the mushrooms.

So my heart plummeted into my stomach when Pete pulled out an old scratty carrier bag from his backpack.

'OK, me and Jamie have pretty much cleared the field. Going back to mine now to make them into tea.'

'That sounds rank.' Tom stuffed his hands in his pockets and his eyes were on the floor. I got the feeling he didn't want to do it any more than I did.

'You sure they're the right ones?' I chewed on my bottom lip.

'Yeah. Everyone used to go shrooming back at my old school,' Jamie said. 'These are the ones for sure.'

'You done it before then?' Kit jutted his chin up.

Jamie paused. 'I've had a little bit. Not enough to fully trip, though.'

That seemed to satisfy Kit.

I had a terrible feeling as I boiled up some pasta for Mum's tea and scribbled out a note to say I was sleeping at Joni's. I kissed her goodbye and she stirred. Part of me wanted to climb into bed with her, like when I was little. She said I was the only thing that would make the headaches go away, that I was magic. I believed it for a while. I would touch her brow when she was sleeping and try to see if the magic dust was coming out of my fingertips to heal her head. Sometimes I thought I saw it. Little golden sparkles. When I got older, I realised it was dust particles in the light.

Joni and me drank the last of Mum's wine that I found on the living-room floor and Joni dressed me up in her dad's Pearl Jam T-shirt that she cut the neck off, and a skirt. The T-shirt pretty much covered the skirt. But she said I had legs up to my armpits so I should stop pretending they were made of denim. Mini plaits in my hair and black eyeliner. Not quite Black Cherry – I wasn't that brave. Rum Raisin lips.

'You look *just* like Milla Jovovich,' Joni sighed. I had no idea who she was talking about. Whoever she was, she sounded cool, but I didn't feel it. Not even sat on a metal girder, waiting for them all to finish band practice. Despite Jamie muttering about Kit being the fun police, the music came first. I was getting chilly and was eyeing Joni's pink fluffy duvet that she'd made me help her carry through the village. Hardly the queens of stealth.

Jamie and Joni were trying to get the melodies right on a

Pixies number and Kit was getting more and more frustrated. I could always tell. He started to hunch like a vulture and his eyes would become fixed. Almost blank. Tom was happy now he had mastered the drum intro, and, as usual, Pete didn't really give a fuck about anything. He was perched with his bass next to Tom, his weird glasses still on his forehead, his beige mac looking filthier by the day. I wasn't contributing anything apart from the arrangement of the cushions. Joni's old teddy bear, Dogly, was on top of her duvet, an old blanket on the ground underneath. We'd found the driest spot we could and put plastic sheeting down, which basically made us look like we were planning some kind of murder.

Annie, my one-eyed bald doll that Mum had bought me from a charity shop in Stocksbridge, was on my pile. Unlike Joni's endearing Little Princess bedding, I had an old orange sleeping bag I had found in the attic that I assumed had once belonged to my mythical dad or the last inhabitants of our house. Either way, it wasn't clean and didn't smell good. But it was the best I had.

'Guys, let's just nail down these chords while you two sort those harmonies out elsewhere?' Kit piped up. 'Otherwise we're going to be here all night.'

'We *are* going to be here all night,' Jamie said. 'I thought that was the point?'

'Don't be a dick,' Kit said and there was the knife's edge of a silence.

I leapt up. 'Maybe we should take a break and go for a walk or something? Or have a smoke. Then try again? You've been at it a while?'

Joni nodded. 'Good plan.' She came over and sat next to me, rummaged in her bag. 'I'll roll.'

Kit sighed, and for a second I thought I'd pissed him off,

but he came over too. And, to my shock, slumped down next to me. 'How's it sounding? Is it shit?'

'No, it's not shit at all. Just needs a bit of tightening up.' I had no idea what this meant but had heard them talking about it before and Kit nodded, so I'd obviously got it right.

'Hard. You know? There's, like, different visions.' He looked over at Jamie, who was joking about something with Pete. The two of them, almost identical heights, couldn't look more different. Jamie in loose jeans, red lumberjack shirt and work boots that were far too clean. Pete in skinny black jeans that were widely unfashionable for the nineties and a Sisters of Mercy T-shirt. And the mac. Always the mac. He smiled widely, though, at Jamie. I could only catch some of the conversation. Something about the maths teacher, the formidable Mrs Cook. That's how they'd met. He sat next to him. Both in top set.

Jamie's voice was rich and dark brown. Deeper than the rest of them. Pete was almost high-pitched next to him. I guessed that was why they thought he'd make such a great frontman. The touch of the Lou Reed about his vocal tones. And there was no doubt he could sing. The first time he came to rehearsal a couple of weeks ago, we all were taken aback. His voice, with Joni's supporting, could really make them do something different, Kit said. Not grunge by numbers, like Courtney and Kurt. If Jamie could, you know, grub up a bit more. Jamie had laughed at that and said he didn't own a single cardigan, let alone one he could create holes in, although he did have an old The Wonder Stuff T-shirt with a fag burn in it if that helped.

'Bloody Wonder Stuff. Jingly jangly violin shite,' Kit had said.

'What? You like the Levellers?' Joni had pointed out.

167

'They're political. They've got a message,' Kit had shot back.

'Oh here we go…' Joni had swatted him on the arm. 'You know it's OK to like music just because it's fun. You don't have to feel tortured by it to make it acceptable to listen to.'

'Listening to the Wonder Stuff is torture. Pete, back me up.'

'I like *The Eight Legged Groove Machine*.' Pete had held his palms up.

'Yeah, but you buy "Best of" albums. You musical tourist.'

He said 'buy'. He meant shoplift.

'You're such a pretentious muso, you sad bastard,' Pete had jibed. There was a brief uncomfortable silence. And then Kit had laughed. Rare occurrence. I didn't know he had teeth.

'Hah. Yeah, you're right.'

Only Pete could get away with that.

Now, I cleared my throat. Fear was bubbling up, but I had to do something.

'I don't think it's different visions,' I said carefully. 'I don't think you've decided on your vision yet, that's all. So it's going to go off on tangents until you agree on what it is you want to be. I mean, you've got Joni who is all Janis Joplin or Stevie Nicks. Then Pete is kind of Talking Heads, Tom is more like, you know, late-eighties rock. You're punk slash grunge. And Jamie—'

'Should be in a boy band…'

'Hey. You wanted him in this band. It was your idea.'

'He's bland though.'

'So add some flavour. You've got music through the ages with the others. Make that the thing. Maybe it's good Jamie doesn't fit into a musical box. That way, he's like the stone in the middle of the water and you're all the ripples. Beautiful. But you all need each other.'

'Jesus. You're right.' Kit looked at me. His eyes were wide and he smiled, that vampiric smile with his pointed incisors that made my stomach flip. There was a moment. An actual moment. Fuck. His eyes had got brighter and he wasn't looking away.

'Can I borrow this one?' Joni's face appeared between us. 'Need her for a second.' She hauled up me and I wanted to kill her.

Tugging me, I stumbled a bit but followed her out the main entrance and watched as she lit up two cigarettes for us. This was my favourite time of the day to smoke. I loved the way the red fiery ends bobbed and lit up in the dark. I liked the smell more than the taste. It warmed me and made my throat relax and my shoulders drop. Could never face it in the daylight, but as soon as dusk fell it was like being a toddler with a sparkler.

'Jamie. Likes. You.' Joni's grin was so wide, I thought her face was about to split in two.

'What? How do you know?' I tried to turn my head to see if Kit was still sitting in the same spot, waiting for me, but Joni dragged my jaw back.

'Because I asked him.'

'*What?*' Oh, the horror, the horror. I could have curled up and died there and then.

'Relax, he's into you. I asked him what his girlfriend situation was back at his old school, and he said he's broken up with someone and wasn't in a rush to get his heart trampled on again. So I said, that's such a shame because I know someone who likes you ...'

'You fucking didn't?'

'I fucking did. And he was so cute and started looking at his feet and being all shy.'

'Jesus, Joni. He probably thought you meant *you*.'

'No. No way. Like, no chemistry there. Anyway, then he said … get this: "Please tell me it's Cass." '

'He didn't?' My heart was in my Dr. Martens.

'He did. So I said yes, it's Cass. And he smiled. Like properly smiled.' Joni threw her arms around me and squeezed. I wondered if Kit was looking and what he thought was going on.

'And then what?' I mumbled into her shoulder.

'Well, nothing. I came and got you. We need to sort out your game plan.' Joni let go and held me by the shoulders. I thought she was about to shake me.

'What game plan?'

'How you're going to get off with him. Go and ask him to go for a walk.'

'Cringe. No. Obvious,' I hissed. 'Did Kit hear? Did he hear Jamie say he liked me?'

'He's looking. Oh God, he's coming over.' Joni raised her eyebrows and I widened my eyes. Then, suddenly, Jamie was there.

'Hey. Cass, can I talk to you a second?'

Before I replied, Joni had bolted, giving us both the kind of knowing smile that your aunt does at Christmas at the working men's club when a boy that is even remotely your own age walks through the door. If I had an aunt. I've heard that's what happens.

Then it was just us two. Jamie smiled at me and dug his hands deep into his pockets. His skin was smooth and his hair all chestnut and shiny. It suddenly occurred to me that Joni had never thought to ask me if I did actually like Jamie.

And it never occurred to me to think about it. He liked me. He liked Me. A boy liked me. And that was enough to make me like him. A boy in a band. A boy who was taller than me. A boy with bright eyes and a clear smile. The one he was giving me now.

'So, Cass. I, erm ... well. Joni's been meddling.'

'I know.' I felt the heat rise to my cheeks and looked down, dropping my cigarette and stamping it out probably a little bit too aggressively, but at least I was doing something.

Then I felt it. The finger under my chin. The boy throwing stones at my window. John Cusack with a stereo over his head. His finger lifted my face up towards his. And then it was happening. I was kissing Jamie. He was kissing me. And with only minimal teeth clash. His hands were round my waist and squeezing and he was breathing deeply. I let my arms go around his neck and he pulled me towards him, my body locked into his. My spine curved to fit in his arms. I felt a gnawing in my stomach and the thud of the blood in my ears. His tongue was in my mouth and his hand working his way over my shoulder and down my chest.

My entire body tensed, knowing all he was about to feel was Gossard Wonderbra's finest attempts to give me a womanly figure. But he didn't seem to care. His eyes were closed and his hands were strong. And I felt it. For the first time, in this way. I felt needed. I kissed back, hard.

And at that point, I couldn't have cared less where Kit was, if he was watching. If he could see that I was wanted and desired. That's what I kept telling myself.

It was two hours until midnight.

Two hours until our world burned to the ground.

20

Now

By the time we get back to Jamie's, it's getting dark and the city looks friendlier from the top of the block. Lights are flickering across the skyline and it no longer feels so mechanical and rigid. Reflective almost. All the buildings with their mirror-like windows. As if anyone wants to look at themselves.

Jamie pours me a glass of wine and we sit down on the sofa. He kisses my neck, strokes my head. And I lean into him and let him pet me like a cat. It feels safe and warm and I close my eyes now, to not let anything else in, like Joni's mindfulness tricks she was always trying to get me into.

My eyes feel heavy and I think about the last time I slept. Really slept. Without feeling the absence of Kit. Without feeling the presence of Jamie. Without my fingers reaching out for something that was never tangibly there.

Jamie whispers to me how much he loves me. I think back to the messages. The promises he said he was aching to make me. The words he couldn't say. He's saying them all now. This should be perfect. This should be my happily ever after.

Rain begins to fall against the window and I let my eyes open and watch the drops get heavier, smearing the view until the lights become blurred and smoggy.

'Do you want to watch some TV or something?' Jamie kisses the top of my head. 'What do you need? Anything at all? Hungry?'

'Can we just watch the rain for a bit?' I ask.

'Of course, baby.' I can feel his stubble on my cheek, which is unusual for him. He's normally so clean-shaven. I did notice in the car the shadows under his eyes and blamed myself for keeping him awake last night with my tossing and turning, and, in general, having a stranger in his bed. I haven't really thought, haven't stopped to think about how all of this would be affecting him too. A wave of selfishness washes over me and I let my hand snake across his stomach and pull myself tighter into him. His body stiffens, but in a good way, and I hear him exhale.

'Jamie, I'm so sorry,' I say and feel the tears start to build up behind the backs of my sore, dry eyes. They feel welcome.

'What for?' he says gently.

'All this. Everything. You didn't ask for this. This isn't the way this was supposed to happen.'

'You're in my arms, Cass. I've got everything I ever wanted.'

A tear slides down my cheek. I am the worst person in the world.

'If I hadn't messaged you, you wouldn't be caught up in this nightmare.'

'Baby, it's going to be OK. We've got each other. We'll find her. We *will* find her, I promise. I was thinking, maybe we could look into private investigators? What do you think? I'll pay for it. Whatever it takes.'

I raise my head and look into his eyes. They are so clear. So perfect. His words are like a waterfall. When he looks at me, it's me he sees. Plain and simple.

I climb on top of him and kiss him deeply. 'I love you so much,' I say between kisses. 'I'm sorry. I'm so sorry for what I did before. For choosing him. Not you. I'm so—'

He silences me by kissing me back, slowly. Firmly. His hands tighten on my waist and for a second I think back to last night and then knock it out of my head. I'm too naive. Too vanilla. I don't understand how sex works now. That's already been made clear. I'm an old married woman.

Or I was.

And now I'm free.

Of Kit. Of secrets. It could all come tumbling out now and I wouldn't care. It's as if my ribs have burst open and I feel lightness in my chest.

Jamie stands up, with me wrapped around him still, and presses me against the window. The rain is hammering by my head and drowning the howls inside me.

We fumble and remove clothes, propped on the window-sill. We are too high up to be noticed from the ground and part of me doesn't care if we're seen anyway. It feels different. Everything feels different.

The man from the tarot shop infiltrates my brain for a second, but I squeeze my eyes tighter and don't let those thoughts in. Bad thoughts. I am free, I can make my own choices.

I feel Jamie's fingers hook my knickers and start to slide them down and I ever so slightly thrust my pelvis to make it easier for him. I need to feel him inside me and, when I do, it feels better than every other time.

Now, I kiss him and let my entire body move with his. My back begins to feel damp with condensation on the window and there are beads of sweat in my hairline. I have never wanted anyone so much. His face. His eyes. His stubble. His smell. He loves me. He loves me. He loves me.

After, when he is in the shower and I am curled back on the sofa wearing his work shirt and waiting for the red rash on my chest to go down, I see that the rain has stopped and the lights are no longer ghosts and the sky is beginning to clear again. I could do this. I could be with him. I could be happy.

Maybe even without her.

No.

I can't even let a sliver of peace into my heart. Sadly, I stand and walk over to the kitchen.

After my mum died, I would spend hours walking in the fields. By the works. The stacks. The mill. I think I was looking for her everywhere. She couldn't just have gone. How could a person just disappear? They couldn't. How can someone stop existing? It couldn't work.

The place where lost things go. Things we never find again. Dolls. Jewellery. The odd sock. The best handbag. I used to imagine a huge room, filled with trinkets and treasures. A scrawled phone number on a piece of paper. Tenners left unguarded. Keys. They must be *somewhere*.

Things can't just vanish.

Where are you, where are you, where are you?

Jamie's laptop is on the kitchen counter. I eye it up for a while as I pour another glass of wine. It's open already from when he ordered the pizza before getting in the shower. I can't help myself. I want to see if Joni has any new messages, so I go to log into Facebook, but just as I am about to type, I see there's already a username there. Ready filled in.

Matt18698.

21

Then – 1996

'That's weird.' I pulled back the vile orange sleeping bag. 'My doll has gone.'

Joni pulled herself up onto her elbow, all snuggled in her pink clouds, hugging Dogly to her chest.

'Annie?'

'Yeah. She was here.' I looked under the pillow and all around the circle of blankets and duvets.

'Do you mean that terrifying-looking toy that could come alive and stab us to death at any time? Chucky's girlfriend?' Tom laughed and pulled his hood up. 'God, I'm cold.'

'Yes, have you seen her?'

'No and I'm glad. This better not be another fucking prank. I'm not going to wake up with it hanging from a noose over my head, am I?'

'You will if you've touched her.' I could feel the anxiety start to rise. It was so hard to explain why a doll that cost fifty pence from a charity shop meant so much to me.

'OK.' Joni threw her covers back. 'Operation Annie. Everyone hunt. She's got to be here.'

'Come on, guys, it's not cool if someone's hiding her,' Jamie said. I wanted to hug him.

'Why would we nick a horror-show doll?' Tom said. 'It's not here, Cass, sorry.' He shone his torch over all his bedding.

'Well, where's it gone?' I chewed my fingernail. 'She's got to be here somewhere.'

'Let's look in the morning. It will be easier by daylight,' Pete said. 'She'll be here, Cass. It's too dark. And it's time for…' He pulled out two Thermos flasks that had seen better days. I felt sick and swore under my breath.

Joni leapt up and started pouring into mugs like she was serving us afternoon tea.

'One for you,' she said, handing a battered camping mug to Kit. 'And one for you.' She passed one over to Tom. He took it but wrinkled his nose.

'It stinks. What does it taste like?'

'It's not great,' Jamie admitted. 'But just knock it back. It's a means to an end.'

I didn't like the sound of that.

'I'm cold.' Tom placed his cup on the floor. 'Shall we get the fire going?'

'Is a fire a good idea?' Pete asked. 'We don't want anyone knowing we're here.'

'Well, who's going to come down this way at this time?' Joni pointed out.

Kit stood up and pulled his cardigan round him. I looked at the shaved side of his head and I still wanted to stroke it. 'I'll try to get one going. Before this kicks in.' He upturned his mug. He'd finished the lot.

'Woah, that was fast!' Joni grinned and handed me and Jamie a cup each.

I looked down into the fluid, a yellowish murky colour with skinny-looking toadstools bobbing in it. Pete couldn't even open a tin of soup. God knows what it was going to do to me.

A pair of hands appeared around my waist and Jamie pulled me back into him.

'You OK?' he whispered and an electric shock went all the way through me, from the tips of my toes to my head. 'Nervous?'

'Yeah, a bit,' I admitted and let him draw me in, wrapping his arms around me and spooning me in his expensive red and black sleeping bag.

'Get a room.' Tom rolled his eyes. There was a clatter from the steel bin as Kit started to lob in the wood we had collected earlier.

'Want to get in here with me?' Jamie whispered into my ear. I suddenly didn't feel that cold anymore.

Joni flashed her torch over at me and I could see her grinning.

'Stop that.' I buried my head into the damp cushion under my head.

'OK, everyone, come on, it's really not that hot,' Pete said apologetically. 'Just swallow it down.'

I watched Joni wince as she gulped her mug down alongside Pete. Behind me, I could hear Jamie taking long sips. Tom and I locked eyes. As if we were both daring each other to say no. And longing for the other to do so.

'I'll get the fire going.' Kit pulled out a can of lighter fluid and a box of matches.

'Go easy,' Jamie said. We all tensed, but Kit just clenched his jaw and I saw a muscle twitch.

Tom and I looked back at each other. I widened my eyes and lifted my shoulders, as if to say *what can we do?* He just shook his head, his eyes equally as big.

'That's going to taste gross if you let it get any colder,' Jamie said. 'Come on.'

'If she doesn't want to do it, she doesn't have to,' Kit said without even looking up. 'I knew she wouldn't be into it.'

Without thinking, I tipped the entire contents down my throat. Down in one.

'YES, CASS!' Joni squealed, and jumped up and down, clapping like a little girl. I couldn't meet Tom's eyes. I felt like I'd betrayed him.

'Jesus, that's foul,' he said, and I heard the clink of his mug on the concrete.

'Five for five,' Pete grinned. 'How long does it take to kick in?'

'About half an hour,' Jamie said as he scooped his arm around my waist and drew me back into him. It was the first time I had been so close to a boy. I could smell his Lynx and it gave me a little shiver.

Kit had a face like thunder. A tiny fizzle of regret shot through me. It wasn't really a moment between us earlier, was it? I was reading too much into it. Just because I was so used to wanting it so much. I'd been hanging out with Kit for more than a year, maybe even two. Most nights, every weekend. And he barely even acknowledged my existence. Until now. And even then, it was so fleeting, you couldn't even catch it in your hands.

No. A fit boy with a killer smile and a voice that would make the entire female population of the lower-sixth melt into their stripy purple tights. And he wanted me. Me. For tonight anyway. And I wasn't going to let that go.

The fire whooshed and Kit stood back quickly. The shadows on the wall leapt as well and the bats broke free. Joni screamed, but I sat up fast, fumbling for the torch. 'Don't scare them!' I scolded her. The fire settled and the orange on the walls felt apocalyptic somehow. 'Have they gone?'

'Here.' Kit shone his torch into the far corner where

we had been watching them for the past couple of weeks.
'There's still one in the roost.'

I wriggled out of the sleeping bag and felt Jamie's arm
move back. It was freezing in the night air as I stepped over
Tom, trying not to stand on Pete.

'Ow!' Joni howled. 'That was my leg.'

'Sorry, sorry, I can't see ...'

Kit held his arm out to me and I reached over and
grabbed his hand to steady myself. It was the first time I had
ever touched him. Wobbling, I hopped over and followed
Kit's torch light.

'Oh, he's so cute,' I whispered. 'Look at the way his little
claws move like a monkey across the bars.'

'I think we should call him Ian,' Kit smiled and I laughed.
He let go of my hand slowly. But his index finger traced my
palm. I felt it everywhere. He must have heard my breath
shake. Because he came in closer. I kept my eyes fixed on
the roost.

Jamie must have been able to see every single move we
were making. As well as the others. Even in the dark, the
silhouettes cast by the fire were unforgiving.

'Let's try to get closer?' Kit said. And I nodded, keeping
my eyes firmly on Ian the bat. It wasn't like we hadn't tried
to do this before. We edged as close as we could, even attempted to climb onto the rickety roof of the old office
door, but we dislodged something and the ruckus spooked it.

'I'm not climbing onto that roof in the dark,' I said.

'No, it's OK, you don't need to,' Kit said.

'What you doing?' Pete called.

'Just trying to get near this bat. Going to turn the light off
so he isn't scared,' Kit said over his shoulder, and switched
off the beam.

'This fire's going out,' Jamie said. 'Have we got any more wood? It's caught too quickly.'

'Yeah, it's here,' I heard Tom say and presumably Jamie started collecting it.

I was stood there, next to Kit. In the dark. Only the sparks of the dying fire in our eyes. I felt his fingers thread through mine again, and he guided me into the corner, underneath the roost. I listened for the scuffles. But my blood was pounding in my ears.

'Cass.' His face was close to mine. Would he kiss me? What would I do? Could Jamie see? I needed Joni. I was so far out of my depth.

'Yes?' I murmured back. *Please kiss me. Oh God no. Please don't. Please do.*

Kit reached towards me and tucked my hair behind my ear. His scalp almost glowed in the moonlight coming through the cracks. For a split second, he looked almost skeletal. Demonic. But beautiful.

'Not him, Cass. Not him…'

And then, he turned and walked back towards the fire, leaving me alone in the dark.

Anger rose up in my chest and I started to shake. I had no idea what had just happened. What Kit was trying to prove, what he was trying to make me feel? All of a sudden, I felt like he'd done that, coaxed me away from Jamie, taken me into the dark, just to prove he could. And I hated him for it.

I began the walk back over the debris and the puddles, barely able to see, when suddenly there was a sharp pain in the ball of my foot and I let out a shriek. The pain was so intense I thought I was going to be sick. It was like standing on a plug, or Lego, but worse. Because whatever I had trod on was still in there. I could feel it.

'Cass?' I could hear a murmur of voices. 'You OK?'

'Ahh fuck. FUCK!' I tried to move my foot, but it was stuck. 'Oh fuck, what have I done?' I yelped and squealed again, the pain was in my entire foot now and I felt woozy. A pair of arms were suddenly there, hoisting me up, and a torch light was shining down on my foot.

'I can't see, just don't move,' Jamie said and motioned to Tom to keep hold of me while he bobbed down to the ground. 'Shine that down,' he said to Joni, who was already on the floor, trying to see.

'What is it? What is it?' I gabbled.

Kit stood on the sidelines. I met his eyes and narrowed mine.

'You shouldn't be walking around here without shoes on,' he said. 'There's dodgy shit everywhere.'

'Yeah, well maybe you should have waited for her since you had the torch. Prick,' Jamie spat.

'Fuck off, you fucking southerner. Who the hell do you think you are?'

'I'm from Leicester!'

'That's fucking south to me.'

'Stop it, you idiots,' Joni said. 'Cass, it's a nail. It's gone right through.'

'Oh my God, oh my God…' The adrenaline started to kick in and I felt a strange rush of something begin to travel up through my legs. I went hot, then cold.

'OK, let's see.' Jamie crouched next to Joni. 'Tom, hold her tightly.'

Pete came over and got on the other side of me. 'Got you, Cass. Don't worry. It's going to be all right.'

'Yeah, it's OK, Cass. You've got this.'

'OK, so the nail's attached to this bit of wood. So we either need to carry her with the plank attached—'

'I think I'm going to be sick...' I said. Even Kit was looking worried now.

'Or we need you to pull your foot off the nail yourself, Cass.'

'I can't, I can't...'

'Babe. You can. You absolutely can.' Joni stood up and grabbed my hand. 'I'm right here. Just grab my hand and squeeze as much as it hurts. Remember? Like when we were kids? As soon as it hurts, just squeeze my hand and the pain will transfer to me.'

'That was such bollocks,' I gasped.

'I know. But do it anyway.'

I grabbed Joni's hand, and Kit came over.

'What can I do?'

'Here, we need to ease her foot up. Can you hold the torch?' Jamie looked up.

'Yeah. Course.' Kit got down beside him.

'Right, Cass. Do *not* look down. Look straight ahead,' Jamie said.

'Or look at me,' Joni added. 'Just look at me. Squeeze my hand. The boys have got you.'

I tried to look at her, but felt my eyes fill with tears so turned my head and took a deep breath, focusing my vision on the gap between the old office and the wall, where Kit and I had just been. I raised my eyes and looked for the bat, but I couldn't see it.

'On the count of three...' Jamie lied. 'One...' and on the two, a searing pain, so much worse than the initial one, went through my skin. I could feel metal against raw flesh and my eyes bulged and then screwed shut. I squeezed Joni's hand as I felt the delicate bones scrape.

'Nearly there,' someone said. Possibly Kit.

There was a pause and I opened my eyes.

Everything seemed to be swimming, but there was a figure there in the background. Someone stood in the gap. Something. Tall. Stopped. It had a face.

'There's someone there,' I tried to say, but the pain started again and instead I screamed. It was short and intense and my foot felt on fire, and suddenly very wet. I looked at the gap and it was still there.

'You goddess, Cass,' Joni was crooning.

'You are fucking hard as NAILS!' Tom shouted.

'There. Is. Somebody. There.' I tried to point at the gap, but Joni still had my hand and Pete had hold of my other arm and shoulder.

'Babe, it's the mushrooms, they are kicking in.' Joni glanced over. 'Just shadows.'

'I swear. There was someone ...' I looked down and saw the amount of blood that had soaked into my sock. 'Oh Jesus.'

My legs disappeared from under me and Jamie carried me back to the sleeping bags. If I hadn't been in so much pain, it would have felt like the most romantic moment of my life. Instead he peeled the sodden sock off and Joni was rummaging around in her bag.

'Does she need to go to hospital?' Tom asked, worried. I knew why. Not for the stitches. But that we'd get caught for camping out. And Tom's gran would not be impressed.

'Erm. Dunno. It actually doesn't look too bad. It went through the skin between your big toe. It might not be that bad. Fucking lucky, mind,' Jamie said.

Pete crouched next to him.

'But, like what about tetanus?'

'We can't go to the hospital,' Pete pointed out. 'We're all coming up ...'

Joni looked at me, trying to read what I was thinking. I didn't want to go to hospital any more than Tom wanted me to. But not because I'd be in trouble. But because they would have no one to call to pick me up. Mum wouldn't answer the phone. And when she did, she'd be a mess. And we couldn't drive, so we'd have to get a taxi that we couldn't afford.

'It'll be fine. Can we sterilise it or something?' Joni said.

'Yeah, have we got any spirits?' Jamie asked.

'No, rich boy,' Kit scoffed. 'We've got some Mad Dog 20/20 or Newcastle Brown.'

Everyone looked at each other and started to laugh. Even me. It all seemed so funny suddenly. Especially when Joni decided to gaffer-tape up my foot.

'You're so pretty,' I said, stroking her face, and she tore strips off with her teeth. 'You're soooooo pretty. Like, everything about you is perfect.'

She shimmered in the darkness. The fire embers had come to life and fairies danced on the ground by my feet. I tried to pick one up, but it bit me. I giggled.

Joni leaned in and kissed me on the lips and I licked her. She shrieked, then leaned over and licked Pete. It connected us. We were one. I tried to explain this to Tom while Pete chased him round, with his tongue out. He needed to be licked. The shadows were merging and slobbering on each other. The sounds of everyone's laughter was ricocheting off the walls.

My eyes kept straying to the dark and hollow office building, though. I could see things there. *Demonic things*, something whispered. At first, it was as if the bats had grown legs, walking and scuttling on their stumped wings. One by one, they crawled from the roost and began to line the walls, like some kind of macabre tapestry.

'Look,' I pointed. No one looked. But I was transfixed. I could hear Kit strumming on his guitar, but it was like it was underwater. Joni's laugh became shrill and horrifying, like a ghoulish clown in a funhouse. The floor was shimmering, like it was covered in petrol. Purple and greens.

There were eyes all around. I could see their orange irises from the corner of my eye, but when I whipped my head around, there was nothing there. I could hear them, though.

You're all going to die tonight.

'Joni,' I said, but it didn't sound right. Like my tongue was too fat for my mouth. It was long and slow.

I desperately tried to make eye contact with her, but she was dancing around the fire and her hair was now completely engulfed in flames. Why wasn't she screaming? Why wasn't she in pain?

'Joooonniii!' I tried again and began to crawl to her on my hands and knees. The eyes were back. The walls were now completely lined with the bats. Wing to wing. Their heads were moving, following me. We were in the dome of their leathery wings.

'Cass is a dog,' I heard Pete laughing. 'Come here, doggy. Come here.' He was patting his knees.

Was I a dog? My breathing became laboured and I started to pant. I was turning into a dog. I let out an involuntarily whine. Joni continued to burn alive next to me.

'Cass.' I felt something touch my hair and I screamed and scuttled backwards into a nest. It was the bat nest. I was sure of it. A prehistoric bat nest. They were going to feed me to the bats.

'Shit, she's having a bad trip.' I heard a voice. Maybe Jamie's? Maybe the devil.

I curled into a foetal position. And then I saw it. The

shadow in the gap. But it wasn't a shadow at all. It was a scarecrow. And it was walking towards us. I screamed to warn Tom, who was still sitting on the girder, and he looked behind him and jumped up in fear.

'Fuck!' he shouted and backed over towards me, knocking the fire bin over, stumbling over his feet, and he tripped and fell.

I saw the bats crawl towards him, like miniature dragons, walking on their wings.

'They're going to eat him,' I screamed again. I had to save Tom. I leapt up and grabbed a burning stick from the fire.

'Cass!' Kit tried to grab the fire from my hand.

'The bats!' I screamed.

Tom was being yanked up by Pete, who was looking at the scarecrow in horror. It was black and bony and beckoning.

'Don't go with it, Pete, don't go!' I yowled as Pete took a step towards it. 'It's a demon.'

My eyes started to sting. Everything seemed grey and I couldn't make out Joni. For a second, I didn't understand why. It was as if a cloud or fog had descended on us, a hot, angry cyclone. I tried to inhale to shout, but my lungs were filling with smoke and the back of my throat closed.

'Jesus CHRIST!' I heard Pete yell. 'Don't leave me.'

That's when I saw the flames. Crawling, slithering, prowling towards us, faster and faster, in straight lines. One caught the end of Kit's combats and I smelt the horrific stench of burning hair.

'JESUS,' Kit shouted, slapping at his leg with Tom.

'Pete!' I tried to yell. 'Don't go with it.'

But he couldn't hear me. The fire had already started to spread. Like some kind of domino fall, lines were appearing from nowhere, joining together, emulating something living and breathing. Something monstrous. Rising.

'We've got to get out of here.' Kit's face was contorted with pain as he limped over to me and Tom. Joni appeared next, but Pete was trapped, with a wall of fire between him and us.

'What was that?' Joni shouted and clung to me so hard, I could feel her fingers pressing into my bone. 'Pete, COME ON!'

'It's the demon. It started the fire. It wants to kill us!' I tried to shout, but Jamie grabbed my arm.

'Cass, come on. It's the mushrooms. They've turned on you.'

I wouldn't leave Pete. I couldn't. The fire was climbing the walls; I couldn't see the demon anymore, but I knew it was there. It was here to claim Pete's soul. With an almighty shove, I pushed Jamie off me and blundered into the smoke. Grey, withered hands clawed at me, and twisted misshapen faces lunged as I staggered to where I could see the outlines of Pete and the creature. It was dragging at him, yanking his shoulder.

I plunged at it, and raised the stick, bringing it down heavily on its head. It didn't even make a noise, just slithered down to the ground. I couldn't look, I just grabbed Pete, who was crying and pulling at his hair.

'What have we done? What have we done?'

My eyes felt like they were melting, the skin on me crackling and oozing from the heat. Pete dropped to his knees and was feeling around as if he had dropped something.

I could hear the voices of the others as if we were at the bottom of the sea. Dropping down to the ground, I crawled towards where I thought Pete was. Each breath was like a knife in my lungs. My throat was raw and I could see my skin blistering, fat yellow pus-filled boils exploding and popping all over me.

'PETE!' I called. 'Where are you?'

All I could hear were muffled screams and animal-like howls. I lay down. Let the bats take me.

Then there was a weird sensation in my stomach and I was being lifted, my head swinging, the floor underneath me. Was it the scarecrow? The demon? I tried to fight and struggle, but I was being moved away from the black smoke, the heat was simmering. And then there were stars and cool, wet grass. My skin was normal again. I took a huge shuddering gulp of night air.

Above me, there was a crackle as glass windows shattered in the heat.

'Pete,' I coughed.

'He's here.' Jamie's face was hovering over me. Too close. The pores on his skin were making puckering, smackering noises. I screwed up my eyes. 'Kit got him. He's OK. Everyone is out.'

You're all going to die.

'Everyone OK?' Jamie looked round us all.

Tom was puffing on his inhaler but gave a thumbs up. Kit was wincing but nodded; Pete was curled up in a ball. For a minute then, I saw him as a five-year-old. Knees hugged to his chest, jumper stretched over them. A little cocoon.

'We've got to get out of here. Someone's going to call the fire lads soon,' Kit said and Jamie nodded.

'Shit! My dad!' Joni squeaked.

'No, we have to warn the firemen about the demon!' I looked back over my shoulder. 'It's inside!'

'You didn't see anyone. It was just a shadow. You're having a bad trip,' Kit said.

'Should we go back and check?' I tried to get to my feet, but my legs were like jelly.

'Fuck no,' Jamie said. 'We've got to get out of here. We're in so much fucking trouble. We're going to be done for arson. It's suicide going back in.'

'We. Need. To. Go,' Tom said. 'I'm going. Now.'

'All our stuff is in there,' Joni said, her voice high and frightened. 'They're going to know it was us in there.' She turned and looked back into the steelworks, almost frozen.

'It's all burned. They'll think it was homeless people,' Kit said. 'Pete. You OK, man?' He squatted down next to Pete.

'There was someone there. Someone grabbed me.' Pete's words were mumbled. But I heard each one so clearly.

'Christ, not you too. That was me, mate. I grabbed you. I dragged you out.' Kit pulled him to his feet, as Jamie hoisted me up and wrapped my arm around his neck. 'Come on. We've got to go through the back woods. No one can see us.'

'Did you really see a demon, Cass?' Joni's voice cracked and Kit roared.

'She. Is. Having. A. Bad. Trip.'

'Do you believe in God?' Joni grabbed me. 'You don't, do you?'

'Stop it.' Jamie gently peeled her fingers from my shoulders. 'It's OK. Everything's going to be OK. We can talk about this later. We need to go.'

The moon shone through the trees and the crack and spittle and rattle of the fire lit our way. We knew these woods like the backs of our hands. We carried on, up the banking, the mud between our toes and, above my head, the bats danced.

22

Now

My fingers shake.

Autofilled password. I click on login.

Do you want to reactivate your account?

I feel faint.

I have no idea whether the water is still running in the bathroom. Or on the window. All I hear is the thud of the blood pounding in my ears.

'Cass?'

He's there. At the bathroom door. Towel wrapped round his waist. He glistens with beads of water and his eyes sparkle.

'What are you doing?'

'Nothing.' I slam the MacBook shut. 'Just checking the news. Seeing if there's any update. Sorry, I borrowed your laptop. My phone was dead.'

And that second it starts to vibrate. Both our eyes fly to it.

'Almost dead,' I say weakly and grab it. It's Kit. His name is flashing on the home screen and I try to answer, but Jamie is quick. I've barely slid the green button and his hand is round my wrist. I cry out and try to wrench it away, but I fall sideways off the bar stool and there is a shooting pain up my arm and into my shoulder joint. My legs are scurrying, flailing, trying to get a grip, my feet trying to plant on the floor.

LISA ROOKES

'Cass, wait. Don't—'

'Cass? Cass?' There's a tinny voice from the phone and I scream Kit's name.

Then there's a smash and I see my phone fly across the room and bounce off the fridge. There's a sickening crunch and in that moment I have no idea if it's my phone or a bone. Then I'm on my feet. Jamie is holding me, my arms pinned up against my chest. His towel is on the floor and this huge, imposing man is gripping me and whispering to me, like some dark lullaby.

'It was just sex, Cass, just sex.' That's all I can hear.

I try to find his eyes with mine. I search for them, the way I did just an hour before. When my back was pressed up against the window and my legs around his waist. I can't believe it's true. But it is. It is. I can't bear it.

'What did you do to her?' I croak.

'Nothing, Cass. Jesus. NOTHING.' My wrists feel as if they are about to snap. 'Believe me, baby, please. Please. It was just sex. I was lonely. I was haunted by you. You. Kit. What we might have been. I had no idea you were going to come back to me. I just wanted to be near you. Close to you. It was the only way. I just came across her. I always use that fake account on dating sites, you know, until I get to know someone and can trust them. It's embarrassing otherwise. She just popped up. And I couldn't help it. I swiped.'

His lips are so close to my ear, his words feel wet, rubbery. Intrusive.

'You lied. You lied to me.' My eyes are screwed so tightly shut, I feel as if my skin will rip and tear across my forehead.

'I didn't lie. I swear I didn't lie …'

'Where is she, Jamie? Where IS SHE?' I scream the last words and bring my knee up high.

Stood naked in front of me, exposed and vulnerable, Jamie lets out a yell and doubles over, letting go of one of my wrists to cup himself. I pull and yank and use all my strength to loosen his grip, but he won't let go.

'Let go of me, Jamie. Let me go!' I kick out at his shins, but it doesn't seem to be making much difference. 'You're hurting me.'

'Cass.' He winces. 'You *have* to listen to me.'

'I don't have to do anything. Not now. Let me go, Jamie. I fucking MEAN IT.' I bring my foot up and stamp down hard on his, again and again, with my heel until his grip weakens.

'It was sex, Cass. I swear. That's all. And we stopped. The minute you left him.'

'Oh my God.' I pull my arm away and hold it with my thumb and forefinger. 'You were sleeping with her? When you were messaging me? When? That time? At the reservoir?'

My head spins and I can see us there. The way he held my cheek in his face and the way the curve of his shoulder slotted into mine. It was as if all the trees stopped swaying and the shadows apologised and tiptoed away. The lake stopped rippling and the foxes froze. All yellow eyes on us. We were the only people in the world.

It had been weeks of messages. Nothing wrong. Nothing cruel. Pictures of his cat. Memes. My heart began to leap when I saw the little flag on the corner of my phone. The gentle buzz on the sofa arm. Kit was even next to me. I couldn't tell him, of course. His hatred of Jamie ran deep, even after all these years. But it didn't feel wrong. It was like speaking to an old friend, or, even better, making a new friend. The kind you make that feels like you've known them a lifetime. Or so I am told.

I was someone new with him. I could be someone else. Someone vibrant. Someone funny. Quick with the jokes. The pictures of my baking. I could be anyone. I could shake off the shackles of Kit and Cass. Selfies of me and Millie. Socked feet in front of the fire. Floral arrangement pics on Facebook. Look what I can do. See me. See me. See me.

See me. I can be her. I can be Joni. I can light up your eyes.

'Cass,' he says. 'Don't do this. Please.'

'I have no choice,' I say. I bend over and pick up my shattered phone. 'Come near me and I'm calling the police.'

I only stop to grab my crumpled jeans off the floor, and I leave. I have no shoes. No underwear. Just my jeans, Jamie's shirt and my phone. I go for the door and look at the screen on my phone. It's an utter mess. I don't even know if it will work. Who will I call? How will I get help? But I run for the door anyway. I can hear Jamie calling, but he does not appear to be chasing after me. Instead, I can hear bangs, shatters and crashes.

I wrench open the door and he's there. It's him. It's Kit. I have no idea how. Or why. But he is there. His face is haggard, but his eyes are strong.

'Cass.' He looks up and down at me in horror and the pain is real. 'Are you OK? You forgot your laptop ... I—'

'No,' I say. 'I'm not.'

When the police arrive, I am still clasped to him, in an age-old embrace that feels, at that second, like it is where I have always belonged.

23

Now

'Fucking knew it.'

We're sitting in Tom's kitchen. It's the house he grew up in. His grandma left it to him when she died. He became a homeowner at twenty-two. He was so proud of himself. Invited us round. Beers in the kitchen. Barbeques in the backyard. Told us of his grand plans to knock through. Open-plan living and kitchen. Wet room upstairs. Like a proper one, not a grandma one.

The wall is still up between the kitchen and the living room. With the serving hatch. The green and white tiles that have been there so long now they could be classed as fashionable. Blue kitchen cupboards. He did do the bathroom, though. Given he's a plumber.

'It …' I just trail off. There's no point.

Pete, Tom and Kit are all standing above me and I'm sitting on a stool, being given endless sugary cups of tea. For the shock. I'm still in his shirt. No underwear. Barefoot. Kit made a big show of carrying me from the van.

'He took you in. Took us all in. Again.' Pete shakes his head and he and Kit exchange a knowing look.

'So, have they charged him?' Tom is chewing on his knuckles. 'I mean … what do they think?'

I shake my head. 'He's just been taken in for questioning.'

'Well, they took *me* in for questioning,' Pete says, obviously bitter. 'That doesn't mean anything, does it?'

'Well, I guess he didn't lie. Just didn't tell anyone.' It feels like there is a bowling ball in my throat.

'What ... didn't tell the police that he was on those sites, didn't mention that he's been fucking the missing person.'

It's like a sledgehammer in the stomach. But there's nothing I can do. No emotion I can show.

'It looks well bad for him,' Tom says. 'Fuck. If he's done something to her ...'

'Stop it, stop it, stop it.' I screw my eyes up. 'I can't bear it.'

Kit bobs down so his hands are on his knees, and his face is in front of me. 'Cass, it's OK. You don't have to be embarrassed. That's what these people are like. They prey on you. On your insecurities. He will have known just what to say. Just how to behave. To reel you in. I knew this wasn't you, I knew it.'

He reaches out and I feel his hand cup my head, my face.

'It's OK. I'm here. You're home.'

There is a darkness in my heart so great I feel eclipsed.

The mood becomes, not exactly celebratory, but there is relief. Mutterings. A sense of finality.

'I mean, it all makes sense. I bet he's had your doll all this time. Like some creepy maniac.' Tom sniffs at one point. 'He's just been hoarding it since that night.'

'Maybe he didn't do anything to Joni,' I say, forcing down a mouthful of toast that Tom has wordlessly put in front of me. Toast and a sugary cup of tea. For the shock. The apocalypse could come to Thistleswaite, and everyone would simply pop down the toaster and get the Utterly Butterly out. 'Maybe he was just messing with our heads with the nooses. I mean ... maybe that's why he came back into our lives. Maybe he just had a grudge or something. I mean, that night he left the village was awful. Maybe Joni really is OK? Maybe he knows where she is?' My voice cracks.

Pete bobs down in front of me. 'It's been three weeks now. Three weeks, and two days. It's not looking good, Cass.'

I stare back down at my plate. Everything is swimming.

'You need some sleep,' Kit says. 'Come on. I'll take you home.'

'What about Millie? Where is she?' I ask.

'At Chris's,' Kit replies with a grimace. 'Yeah, I know. I don't like it, but it's probably the best place for her. Away from all of this. She's been calling up all the pubs, you know. I gave her a list. She's trying to get them to put posters up, in case anyone remembers her.'

'I hate to say it, but maybe he's just confessed where she is,' Tom says quietly.

No one says much after that. I tell them I'm popping outside to give Millie a ring. The black air is crisp. The stars are pocketed and nestled and there is no breeze.

I walk and feel my lungs fill with the pure air until it's time to go back.

I let myself back in and the atmosphere is still thick and unyielding.

'I'm exhausted,' I say. 'I think I really just want to go to bed.'

'Yeah,' Kit nods. 'I'll stay at the house. On the sofa.'

I don't protest.

Pete and Tom follow me and Kit out the front door and light up.

'Look, call in the morning, yeah? We probably owe Andy an apology as well,' Pete says awkwardly. 'We sent some pretty intense texts, especially with his dad dying.'

'I feel really bad about that now,' Tom says. 'It's not going to make us look good, is it?'

They start walking with us back up the slope and into the village centre. Kit's had a couple of beers and has never ever driven drunk, even after half a shandy. Said he would never forgive himself. Which is ironic really, given the things he has managed to forgive himself for.

We don't say anything for a while. The way we walk up in a line brings back memories. Apart from the gap on my left-hand side – Joni always in the middle. I was always on the end.

'You really don't think ... that these nooses, these ... things ... are connected to that night, do you?' I say, pulling the jacket around me, before something catches the corner of my eye as we approach the pub. The lights are off and it makes me realise how late it must be. 'Oh Christ, Kit, I thought you said you took it down.' I turn away from the Gallows Tree.

'What do you mean?' Kit looks at me and then back at the tree.

'The noose ... the ...' I look at the others. 'You said it had all gone.'

'It did. It had.' Kit puts his hand on my shoulder.

'What are you on about?' Tom says.

'Didn't you tell them?' I snap.

'Tell us *what*?' Tom's eyes are darting between us.

I look at Pete, but he just looks down.

'I only told Pete,' Kit sighs. 'I didn't want to freak Tom out.'

'ABOUT WHAT?' Tom shouts and Pete reaches out and puts his hand on his bicep to steady him.

'Kit found my goggles. The ones, you know, I used to wear,' Pete explains.

'I don't think that's them.' Kit squints at the tree.

'No, you're right,' Pete says and starts walking quickly towards it. Tom swears under his breath and jogs to keep up.

'Stay here,' Kit commands and turns to follow.

'No, I'm not staying here on my own.' I stride behind him.

'I mean it, Cass.' Kit walks faster, but he forgets my legs are just as long as his.

'SHIT.' I see Pete and Tom ahead. Pete is grappling with the noose and Tom is just stood frozen to the spot, clutching something that looks like a stick.

We both start to jog, as well as I can in Tom's too-big wellies.

'What is it?' I call over and Pete shushes me.

'It's new,' he says.

'What do you mean?' Kit starts to help him untie it.

I glance at Tom. His eyes are wide and his chest is rising and falling too fast.

We all look at it. The blackened, charred end of one of Tom's drumsticks.

'Do you think anyone has seen?' Tom asks. His voice is too high. He sounds like the little boy who ran from Billy Miles's house with me. His palms chubby and damp. I want to cradle his head to me.

'No, they'd have taken it down. Or called the police. I don't know.' Pete drops the noose on the floor. 'Shit, maybe they wanted to fingerprint it?'

'We're not telling the police.' Tom shakes his head and takes a step back. 'We can't explain this. I can't ... *Fuck*. Someone knows. Who is it?'

'Why now though? Why would someone do all this now? It's Jamie, I know it is,' Kit says and kicks the noose as if he is testing it, seeing if it is going to come alive, like some kind of snake.

'That's impossible. He's in Leeds. At the station. I want to go home.' I turn and start to walk. I hear footsteps behind me. I know they are Kit's so I don't turn round.

Above the steeple, the sun is beginning to rise.

★

Neither of us sleep. Kit covers me in a blanket on the sofa and builds me a fire. I let him. I let him take care of me. I have to. I call and call the police station, but no one can tell me anything. I can't feel her anymore. Every time I try to close my eyes, all I see is Jamie's face. And hers. I try to pull Sausage onto my lap, but she's having none of it and stomps away. I just want to smell her. Joni. Her perfume on her fur. Anything, any little piece of her that's left.

After a while, I have a shower and get dressed. My jeans are hanging off my hip bones. All those diets and look at me now. If I had the energy, I could smile ironically. But I've nothing left.

I tell Kit that I'm going to check on Carlos. The neighbours are feeding him and seeing to the pigs. I wonder how much longer for? Will they have to be rehomed? The thought of dismantling Joni's little smallholding ... The house. What will happen to her house? Will the bank take it? I walk faster. The thought of people rummaging around in there. Breaking it up into little pieces. I can't handle it. I need to protect it.

I start to run. My legs are trembling and my heart is pounding as I sprint up the hill – the hill I get breathless even walking up. I see Stella in her garden, but I don't stop. I can't bear the small talk, or, even worse, the talk about Joni. All I see now is sympathy; it hangs around everyone like some kind of aura. It comes off them in waves. Poor Cass. She can't survive without her. What will she do now? I am like Peter Pan's shadow. I have come undone, unstuck.

I climb over the fence and draw Carlos to me, burying my face in his neck, the wet grass and earth seeping into the knees of my jeans. He doesn't smell of her either.

I am nothing without her. I am defined by her. Or I was,

Until Millie came along. Then my heart doubled, rather than halved.

When Millie was little, it was me and her against the world. I saved every conker she peeled. I used to put the leaves in her hands so she could feel the changing seasons. We would walk for hours in the fields.

One day, we saw the scarecrow. I stopped still. I hadn't seen him in years. I held Millie's hand tighter.

'What's the matter, Mummy?' She looked up at me, her hair the same colour as the pumpkin we had just carved. The wheat was low and the trees were bare.

He stood in the field across, over the drystone wall, his red shirt still the same. The crows around his feet. Millie followed my eyes.

'Are you looking at that man?'

'Yes, sweetheart,' I whispered.

'Don't you like him?' she asked.

'Have you seen him before?' I said.

'Sometimes,' she replied.

I smiled at her. Then at him.

'He looks after us,' I said. And we carried on walking into the trodden corn.

I used to look in her eyes and feel like I'd been given the world. Now I watch her pulling away, and yes, it's all so normal. It's healthy. It's what they are supposed to do. She is finding herself. Finding her freedom. But the more she pulls, the thinner, the more fragile I feel that cord is. I am scared that one day it will break entirely. I can see her eyes changing. He has found her. I am sure of it. She's pulling more and more towards Joni. Like some kind of invisible umbilical cord. Nothing will ever be mine.

24

Then – 1996

When I woke, Joni's hair was matted on the pillow next to mine. We'd slept, like we always did, nose to nose, curled up together like otters in my single bed. The sheets felt damp and the sun was bleeding through the gap in the curtain.

I turned onto my opposite side slowly and carefully so as not to wake her. My radio alarm clock said it was just before 10 a.m. I didn't want to go downstairs. I couldn't face the carnage we'd created. My room was tidy. Everything was completely in place. That made it worse somehow.

It wasn't big. The bed was pushed up against the radiator under the window. I had a cheap chest of drawers and a knackered built-in wardrobe with sliding doors that kept coming off the runners. Incense sticks and a rag rug on the floor. An old mirrored throw on the bed that I'd got for Christmas the year before. The wallpaper was raised and weird and didn't match the room. Cream. Textured. Lumpy. Like curdled milk. I reached up and started pulling the lumps off, in whatever act of defiance I could stomach.

The pain in my foot was still there. In fact, it felt hot and I started worrying about infection. I thought about Kit's leg and the worry really began to churn. It was a nasty burn. He would scar. He couldn't see a doctor. He wouldn't be able to come up with an excuse. Major fire at the old steelworks,

THE VILLAGE

third-degree burn to this leg. I could say I'd trod on that nail anywhere really. Kit was going to have to suffer.

My mind flicked through the events of the night, shuffling them like a deck of cards.

The kiss. Kit. The flames. The kiss. Jamie. Kit. Joni.

The bats. The fire. The figure. That dark figure. It wasn't the pain. I wasn't hallucinating. I was sure of it.

The way that Andy waved at us from his bedroom window and we just pretended we were drunk and had been getting stoned in the woods. We waved at him merrily back, and pretended we didn't see the fire burning up the sunrise, or me limping. Or Kit hobbling.

He'd thrown open his window.

'What's going on up there?' he'd called down.

Joni had frozen and Jamie had pulled me towards him, arm around me.

'Dunno, mate. Looks like some kind of fire. Maybe one of the farmer's. We've just been in the woods.'

'Yeah, Andy, don't tell anyone you saw us. We kind of lied to our parents,' Pete had said and given him a goofy grin that made me so nervous that it had just naturally slid onto his face.

'Secret's safe with me, pal.' Andy had looked at the way I was nestled into Jamie and raised his eyebrows. 'Think I should call the fire lads? That smoke isn't looking good.'

We all had looked behind us.

I think now of the painting I had seen. The steelworks filling the sky with shadows, with blackness.

Then we'd heard the sirens.

'Someone's beaten you to it.' Kit had grimaced, pretending he wasn't in agony.

'That doesn't look like a field fire,' Andy had said slowly.

'Nah, you could be right,' Jamie had said. 'We better skedaddle before it wakes everyone up and we're not in our beds.'

'Yeah, later, mate.' Andy had stared out at the skyline. 'I think it's coming from the steelworks.'

Once we got to the top of the hill, the boys had decided to sleep at Kit's and Joni at mine. Jamie didn't seem happy about unwrapping his arms from around me and asked me a million times if I was OK.

I wasn't.

'Sleep tight,' he'd whispered in my ear. 'I don't want to let you go.'

'What time is it?' Joni's words sounded thick and stringy now. I could tell without turning over that although her mouth was moving, her eyes wouldn't be open.

She never was a morning person. Found it impossible to get out of bed. She used to deliberately drink water before going to sleep on a school night so the need for a wee would force her up when the alarm went off.

I fished about on the end of my bed for my dressing gown. I couldn't keep one hung on the back of the door anymore after Tom had told me his grandmother's dressing gown once waved at him when he was a kid from where it was hung. That and *Bedknobs and Broomsticks* had developed enough of a fear of clothes moving about without people inside them that I had to remove it every night.

'Just gone ten.' I swung my legs over the bed and tried to stand up, but the pain was shooting up my sole and into my leg. It hurt so much, I yelped out loud.

'Whasrong?' Joni's lips smacked together. 'Noreadyet.'

'I'm going to see what's going on,' I said back and shrugged my dressing gown on.

Wincing, I hobbled to the top of the stairs. Mum's bedroom door was still closed, so I managed to do a mixture of a hop and a limp down the stairs without arousing too much suspicion.

I couldn't see much from the living-room window. Just the street. Nothing unusual going on there. From the kitchen, though, I could just about make out the tops of the works. There was smoke in the sky and between the trees were flashes of colour. People, it looked like. I wasn't sure, though.

After a couple of hours' sleep and the mushrooms wearing off, the night before didn't seem real. The fire. Had that really even happened? The demon. I almost laughed at the absurdity. The embarrassment. Maybe it had just been a little bin fire. Maybe we all just overreacted. Maybe it was all OK.

Flicking on the kettle, I leaned against the counter and by the time I'd brewed us both a cuppa, I had convinced myself that there was no need for worry. That we would just let it play out.

I chewed on my nail and for a brief moment I let my brain block everything out other than *I have a boyfriend. Someone wants me. To smell my hair. To be close. To feel part of me.* I could feel a rise of panic in my chest. Or maybe he didn't. Maybe that monstrous thing might have made him think I was a lunatic.

Smoothing out my hair in the reflection of the kitchen window, I let myself think about last night and his hand on my hip as I lay on my side, stroking down into my waist. No one had ever touched me like that before. I'd felt as if my body was moulding under his hands, my skin pliable and smooth, stretching into his touch.

Kit's dark eyes.

I gulped, and thought of the blisters on his calf. The nail in my foot. What if it got infected? What if someone put two and two together? How much trouble would we be in? The smoke was still caressing the sky. I wondered how much damage there would actually be. The building was wet, damp. Perhaps this would all just blow over. It was abandoned anyway. No one was hurt. Surely that was the most important thing? It was just a shell. It had no heart left. No soul.

Shuddering, I picked up the teas and headed back upstairs. It was harder to hobble with the scalding water sloshing over the rim of the chipped mugs and turning the white flesh on the side of my hand red.

I placed both mugs on the bedside table, then perched on the end of my bed and brought my foot up to my knee. It didn't look good. The puncture wound was weeping and slightly yellowing around the edges. The skin around it was grey and puffy and swollen, like some kind of bloated fish. I screwed my face up. I had no idea what kind of first aid we even had in the house. My mum was never the sort to sit me on the kitchen counter to apply TCP or Germolene. Joni's dad gave me it once when I fell off my bike. I spent all afternoon inhaling the scent from my hands.

'How is it?' A wild-haired Joni struggled up in bed, the duvet almost fully shrouding her still.

'My foot? Dodge. There's tea there.' I nodded at the table.

'Angel girl.' She reached over and took a sip, not even noticing the heat. Asbestos mouth. 'What time is it?'

'I don't know. Gone ten.'

'What's happening? Do we know anything?'

I shook my head. 'No ... God, did it really happen? No

206

one's come knocking. Should we maybe get dressed and wander down? I can't tell what was real and what was just the mushrooms.'

'Yeah.' Joni nodded and rubbed her mascara even further down her face. 'Here, let me see that.' Joni clambered out of the duvet and crawled along to the edge of the bed. Her legs, her thighs, so white and full. Nothing like my spindly bird legs. She always used to moan about her shape. But the nineties heroin chic look would soon give way to the bootylicious trend. One of us was always falling foul of fashionable body types.

I put my foot on its side so the sole was facing her. I'm sure I detected a slightly weird smell coming off it. Metallic. Maybe just dried blood.

'It needs cleaning up,' Joni grimaced. 'Have you got any Dettol?'

'Don't de daft. If you need alcohol, we could probably manage it, though. Try under the kitchen sink.' As Joni left the room, I squeezed my foot to see if any pus would come out. It didn't, but it killed me. I took a sharp intake of breath.

'No medicine,' Joni said apologetically when she returned. 'But I boiled some water and added salt. And there's some banana liquor? What do you reckon? I brought it up just in case.'

'That shit has been in the cupboard since Mum's friend from work went to Benidorm,' I pointed out.

'Rich bitch.' Joni rolled her eyes. 'Who can afford to go abroad?'

'It was five years ago.'

'I still think it might be OK. We'll try it. Here.' Joni put the washing-up bowl at my feet. 'Stick your foot in here.'

I winced as the salt water seeped into the wound, but the

warmth felt nice. Joni crossed her legs and used a flannel that had seen better days to clean off the crust.

'Do you have dressings?'

'A dressing?' I baulked. 'Do you think this is an episode of *Casualty*? We don't even have Savlon.'

'A plaster and a clean pair of tights to wrap round?'

'Might be able to do a plaster ... or I've definitely got some gaffer tape in the shed.'

'That'll work!' Joni exclaimed. 'We could rule the world!'

I actually laughed and my heart felt just that little bit lighter as she foraged for resources and set about her project.

'Joni?' I asked as she cocooned my foot in a pair of hideous nude tights that we'd fished from my mum's drawer. 'What did you mean last night when you said, "*Do you believe in God?*"'

Joni took a deep breath. 'I dunno. I was probably just tripping.'

'Well, do *you* believe?' I asked.

'I never used to ...'

It was my turn to stay a little bit quiet.

'Yeah. I guess I do. I don't know if it's God exactly, though,' she said as she tied a knot on the top of my foot.

'Like ... good and evil?' I suggested.

'Do you believe in the devil, Cass?'

Something about that word made me run cold.

'No,' I said, perhaps too quickly. 'Do you?'

'Well, if there was no evil, then you're not making the choice to be good. You'd just be good. But without its opposite, it's not a choice. So therefore you need the dark for the light to make a difference,' Joni said.

We got dressed in silence.

I was ready before Joni. As usual. But I couldn't complain

since she'd done my eye make-up and made my bland boring hair look a bit more grunge. We tied up our boots, Grolsch bottle tops plucked out of the pub bins and now dangling from the laces.

But just as I went to open the door, Joni lay her hand on top of mine, on the handle. 'Wait.'

I turned around.

'Cass, I need to tell you something.'

Her eyes had paled.

'What's wrong?' I let go of the door handle. A billion thoughts flashed through my mind. She'd done something with Jamie or Kit? God, not Kit. Tom? Had she slept with Tom?

'Cass ... something really bad has happened.'

'Joni, when? Just now? What's going on?'

She just shook her head. 'You can't tell anyone.'

'I won't.' I grabbed her hands. 'You know I won't.'

'You love me, don't you?' Joni seemed smaller somehow. Not exactly waif-like. There was something different – I couldn't put my finger on it. She looked like Pete's cocker spaniel on Bonfire Night. She was afraid.

'I'll always love you, Joni. No matter what,' I said.

'Really?' It came out a strangled choke.

'Joni, there's nothing I wouldn't do for you.'

She opened her mouth and I steadied myself.

Then the phone rang.

25

Then – 1996

'He can't be dead. Billy can't be dead.' Pete's eyes were so swollen, he looked deformed.

'They found him … his body. Fuck. Fuck.' Kit's hands were wedged in his hair.

'How was he even there? I mean … how? *Why*?' Jamie asked.

We were all crammed into Joni's bedroom. Her Pearl Jam poster was already hanging from one drawing pin from the sheer number of bodies leaning up against the wall.

Tom hadn't said anything since we got there. He just sat, motionless, staring straight ahead.

'I told you I saw someone.' I released my puffy face from my hands. Make-up all down my cheeks. Black eyes.

'Shit, do you think that was him?' Jamie asked. He came to me on the end of the bed and got down on his knees. 'No, Cass. Honestly. You were banging on about a demon. It was just a bad trip.'

'But I hit something. Someone. Someone was holding Pete. I thought it was trying to drag him into the fire … Maybe it was trying to drag him away.'

'I'm so sorry, Cass. We should have believed you.' Jamie looked as if he was in agony and got up and moved away. He banged his head against the wall and the poster gave up and fell to the floor with a whoosh.

'No. We would have all seen him. Whatever you saw, Cass, it was just the mushrooms.' Kit shook his head. 'I bet Billy just saw the fire and cycled down. Got trapped somehow.'

'No, I felt something too. I saw something, I think Cass is right. It must have been him. Doing his rounds. Heard us there and came to check on us,' Pete said, then sank to the floor. 'Oh God, oh God, oh God, oh God, oh God, oh God...' He rocked back and forth.

'Pete.' I jumped up and wrapped my arms around him from behind. 'Oh God, I know. I know. I killed him. I killed him.'

His hands grabbed my forearms and he stayed there, locked to me, rocking back and forth like a mother and child. Except I wasn't sure who was who.

'Guys.' Kit bobbed down in front of us. 'Even if he was there, even if you did hit him, Cass, you didn't know it was him. No offence, but a blow from a tripping girl with a stick wouldn't have killed him.'

'We left him there to die!' I shouted.

'We didn't know!' Jamie said, making eye contact with Kit. 'It was just an accident. A terrible accident.'

'Thing is...' Joni said from her old battered armchair in the corner. 'No one knows exactly what happened. It could have been a hallucination. I mean, no one else saw anything, right? Pete, not even you.'

'I did. I saw... something. I think. I don't know.' Pete wiped the back of his hand over his face, leaving a trail of snot.

'And no one knows we were there,' Kit said. 'And that's the way it needs to stay.'

'You've got a fucking massive burn on your leg,' Pete

pointed out. 'No one is going to believe we weren't there when it broke out.'

'Well, can't we just say we were there ... and a fire started somehow and we legged it?' I asked everyone, my eyes wide. 'I mean, that's the truth. Maybe it was just a vision? I mean, I'd know right? I would have recognised Billy. I would, wouldn't I?' I rambled, trying to convince everyone, but mainly myself.

'Cass, either way, a man is dead,' Kit said. 'We made a fire. Our fingerprints will be all over the bin. We're fucked if anyone even places us there. It's manslaughter.'

'FUCK OFF!' Pete pushed Kit so hard, he toppled over. 'He was my *friend*!'

I fell back and Pete turned to me.

'Cass, I think we should go to the police. You'll come with me, won't you?'

'Of course I will.' My head went to his shoulder. 'Pete, of course.'

Jamie pushed himself away from the wall. 'Cass, I don't think that's a good idea. Guys, if we go to the police, we're pretty much hanging Cass out to dry.'

Kit turned round. 'Look, I'm not being a twat here. We're not from the same place. We don't have parents who can afford lawyers. They're relying on us. They're relying on us to start working for them when we finish school. Or get a proper job and help out. I can't do it to my mum, man. I just...' He looked down.

'Kit...' Tom reached out his hand and placed it on his shoulder. 'What's the matter?'

'It's back,' he said quietly.

We all knew what he meant. All but Jamie. No one

explained it to him. But Kit's mum had been in remission from stage 3 breast cancer for months.

'FUCK!' Pete lashed out and punched the wall by his side. I tumbled back and Jamie came towards me, hand out, ready to help me up.

I shook my head and clambered up myself. It didn't feel right, for some reason. Like we were ... flouting something.

'He was my friend.' Pete rocked back onto his heels. 'He was my friend. We killed my friend.'

'We didn't kill anybody.' Joni's voice was almost robotic.

'It was an accident. We don't even know if he was there when we were.' Kit put his hands on Pete's shoulders. 'God, he could have started the fire himself. Remember ...' He looked at me and his voice grew in excitement. 'Remember, Cass said she saw someone earlier. It was probably him. He was spying on us. He probably started the fire himself.'

'KIT!' I shouted for the second time.

'He wouldn't do that. He wouldn't.' Pete was shaking his head, his hands over his ears like he was trying to block out a deafening thunder.

'Whatever happens now, we're in this too deep,' Jamie said as he ran his hands through his hair. 'We've either got to go and confess. Today. Like now. Or we're going to have to pretend last night never happened. It's the only way to protect Cass.'

'No. If that was Billy I hit, I need to hand myself in. I can't live with the guilt. I can't.'

'But, Cass,' Joni pleaded, 'we will never know. We were all tripping. None of us knew what was real. You could be confessing to something you didn't do.'

'And you were trying to help me,' Pete said quietly. 'You were trying to protect me. I can't let you get in trouble.'

'There was nothing there.' Tom cleared his throat and we all looked at him. 'Cass, you were just hallucinating. Everyone was. Apart from me.'

'What do you mean, apart from you?' Joni said.

'I didn't take the mushrooms. I poured them down the grate.' Tom looked at the floor. 'There wasn't anything there. You guys were just hallucinating something. So there's no need to go to the police.'

The relief hit me in my stomach first, then all the way through my body.

'Tom, are you sure?' I asked.

'I'm sure.' Tom didn't look up.

'What about our stuff? Our sleeping bags? Cass's doll? I mean, that's all going to get found, isn't it? They're going to know someone was there. They'll be able to trace it somehow,' Kit said.

'Won't it all have burned?' Joni said. 'It'll just be ashes now.'

'No, that material, it melts, it doesn't burn. Fuck.' Kit stood up. 'We need to go down. See what they already know. See, Cass, it's OK. No one has to go to the police. We just need to keep our noses clean, and this never happened. Agreed?'

'Yeah. How's your leg?' Jamie nodded at Kit's calf, covered up by his loose combats.

'Fuckin' kills.' Kit stared at him aggressively. 'Why? Is that some kind of veiled threat?'

'What you on about?' Jamie screwed his face up. 'Is what some kind of threat?'

'You going to pin this all on me, aren't you? I've got the evidence burned into my flesh. Yeah?' Kit stood and squared up to him, despite being a good few inches shorter than Jamie.

'What you on?' Jamie shook his head. 'I only asked how it was. How paranoid are you?'

'I'm not paranoid, mate. I just don't fucking like you,' Kit spat. 'Why are you even here?'

'You asked me to be part of this band, remember?' Jamie half laughed. 'You just couldn't handle it when I turned out to be decent. Did you want to look good? Is that it? Is that why you wanted me to sing? So I would turn out to be shit and you could save the day? Be the big man?'

'Decent? You're not even half decent. You're not even half shit. You're just shit.' Kit went to turn away when Jamie pulled back his arm and punched him straight in his jaw.

Saliva flew, Joni screamed, Pete jumped up and Tom went to grab Jamie and pull him back before he went for him again. Kit just stood there dazed, as if he couldn't believe what had happened.

'You prick. You total *prick*.' He felt his jaw. 'You broke my jaw.'

'Don't be such a pussy, of course I didn't break your jaw. No one ever hit you before? Because, fucking hell, you've been asking for it.'

I backed off towards Joni in her armchair. She opened her arms up and we snuggled up together. You could almost see the testosterone dripping from the walls, like ectoplasm.

'Guys, now is *not* the time,' Joni barked. 'You think this is helping?'

'You think he is?' Kit pointed at Jamie. 'Everything just started getting fucked up since you landed. Why don't you just back the fuck off? Leave us alone.'

'You mean leave her alone, don't you?' Jamie shook off Tom's arm. 'Let's not pretend this isn't about her.'

'Holy shit,' Joni whispered. 'They're going to fight over you.'

'Who? Cass?' Kit scoffed and I felt a dagger gut me from

my heart to my belly button. 'You're welcome to her. If she's daft enough to fall for it.'

'Hey.' Tom put his palm out towards Kit and grabbed Jamie's shirt in a fist at his chest. 'Easy, Kit.' He stood between them and looked to Pete for help, but he was a crumpled wreck. He simply laid his hand on Kit's shoulder. 'Come on, man. Please.'

There was something in Tom's voice that made Kit soften. And Jamie.

They stared at each other for a moment and then Jamie just shook his head.

'You're right. This isn't the time. We just need to figure out what's going on.'

'I vote we go down the works,' Joni said. 'Half the village is there. We'll be conspicuous by our absence.'

'And what if someone asks if that's our stuff?' Kit said.

'Say we brought it down earlier, but it got too cold and we came home?' I suggested.

'Why didn't we bring it home with us?' Pete asked.

'It was too dark, too cold? We decided to go to the pub instead? Couldn't be arsed to carry it?' Joni suggested.

'What about Andy?' I looked up. 'He saw us. He saw us coming back. He knows we weren't downstairs in the pub.'

'Fuck, you're right.' Kit looked nervous.

'Andy won't say anything,' Jamie said.

'What makes you think that?' Joni asked.

'I'll make sure of it,' Jamie replied.

'What kind of cryptic shit is that? Who do you think you are?' Kit shook his head, then started to laugh, and pace, hands grabbing tufts of his hair. 'My fucking leg is fucking killing me.'

'Let me look.' Joni struggled out of the armchair and motioned for him to prop it on the bed.

Kit rolled his trouser leg up and if I thought there was a strange smell coming from my foot, that was nothing.

It had already blistered a sickening yellowy orange bubble, wrinkling at the edges.

'Oh. That needs popping.' Tom's nostrils flared as his eyes widened.

'No. God, *no*. That'll get it infected. It needs washing and wrapping,' Joni said.

'What, gaffer tape again?' I asked.

She rolled her eyes. 'It needs cling film. Just wait here.' She crawled over the bed and out of the room, presumably to the kitchen.

Pete rolled his neck around his shoulders and we all cringed at the two loud cracks.

'So, are we going down there then?' I asked.

'I think it would be a good idea,' Jamie nodded and Kit rolled his eyes, but he didn't disagree.

'Yeah. I mean, I don't know but ...' Tom trailed off and looked at me for support. He was scared. We both were. We were kindred spirits like that. 'Still.'

I nodded. 'We need to. I think we will just look more guilty if we don't.'

'And if they ask us? If that's our stuff?' Kit wouldn't even make eye contact with me.

'Then ... we tell the truth. That we were down earlier but it got cold. We left and came home.'

'It's pretty much the truth,' Jamie added.

We all pretended to agree.

Joni came back and started cleaning Kit up. I watched him breathe deeper, his dark hair falling into his eyes. My heart fluttered. I looked up and saw Jamie watching me. I gave him a weak smile and he winked back slowly. His shoulders all broad. My thighs shivered. I had never felt so confused.

And why was I even confused? When Kit had never shown any interest in me until now. Was it even interest? Was it just utter hatred for Jamie? Why did I even care right now?

I am a terrible person, I thought.

Once Kit was ready, we set off through the village. The birds weren't in the skies. The clouds were painted a strange, thick grey and seemed almost curdled; the air smelled off. Not just of smoke or embers. But of intrusion.

None of us really said much as we walked down. I looked up at the window of the pub to see if Andy was still there, watching. But the window was dark as if the curtains were closed. We ventured on down the hill. Some of the old dears were out in their front yards, peering over their fences, chatting with each other, making those same soft crooning noises that they always did, whether it was good or bad gossip they were passing between them, like a ball of wool.

My foot was sore but I tried not to limp, although it was especially painful on the cobbles. Jamie held my hand, and I squeezed it. He squeezed back and I felt it go all the way up my arm. Joni looked at me from the corner of her eye and smiled.

Tom walked behind. I wanted to turn around. To ask him if he was sure, ask if he was positive it wasn't Billy's skull I'd split.

To ask him over and over and over and over until I believed his sweet little lie.

But I didn't.

I never asked him again.

26

Now

That day, the one after the fire, we walked down to the steelworks, chewing on lips, eyes darting like startled rabbits, ready
to bolt. Of course, they wouldn't let us near. The fire lads and
Joni's dad sent us away. They were still damping down, and
the whole site just seemed to sizzle, like someone throwing
water over an instant barbeque. But there was nothing inside,
they said. No clues as to how it had happened. No half-
charred sleeping bags or melted dolls. Nothing. Not even
the bin we used to make the fire. It had all just vanished.

Tom wanted to believe it had all burned away. Kit suggested maybe Billy had been trying to move it, rescue our
stuff for us, and became overcome by the smoke. Pete got
upset at that and then Tom pointed out that it wouldn't
explain where it was.

Kit's calf healed by itself. He still has the scar. I find it
hard to look at. Always have. My foot became infected, and
I had to spout a pack of lies to the doctor for the antibiotics.

Each day I'd wake up with nervous dread in my stomach.
Waiting for the knock on the door. I couldn't eat. When
school started again, I couldn't focus. My homework went
undone. Mum started getting calls, but at least she could
never really muster up the energy to do anything about them.

I spent a lot of time at Joni's. She too was becoming

withdrawn. She stopped wanting to hang out with the boys so much. She even stopped encouraging me to see Jamie.

Sometimes she would disappear. Not be in when I went to call for her. Her dad said she was on one of her walks. But I knew that wasn't the truth. Late at night, sometimes even in the dead zone when it seemed the entire world was asleep, she would throw handfuls of gravel at my window. I used to wake, thinking it was rain to start with. But there she would be, huddled up in a floor-length sheepskin coat that used to be her mum's.

She never told me why she would just turn up. And when I asked if she was OK, she wouldn't answer. We used to walk around the village, into the churchyard, even though I was scared of the gravestones in the darkness of the night. There was one, a weeping angel. Tall and majestic, once white, I assumed, now grey and marbled, cracked. She only had one arm now, and the top of the left wing was chipped. She stood watch over a child's grave.

Benjamin Grayson, died aged eleven. In the daytime, I used to love looking at her, thinking of the family from the late 1800s who must have lived here. Were they rich land-owners? They must have been to afford such a gravestone. Or did they scrabble together everything they owned just to give their little boy the best resting place? The safest. I would think about his bones under the ground. Little bones. Little skull. Asleep in the ground. Tucked up safely in the earth. Sometimes I was jealous.

In the witching hour, though, the angel seemed cruel. Her face all angles, her wing sharp. Despite defying age, she was crumbling away, disintegrating like the little boy underneath her. Jealous of our youth. Our heartbeats. I used to turn away from her on the bench.

Joni liked coming here but wouldn't explain why. I tried to ask her more about that night, about her sudden flirtation with religion, but her jaw would stiffen and her eyes would darken.

Sometimes there were tears too.

I couldn't help but wonder if they were for Billy. Or something more.

I never did find out what she wanted to tell me that day.

The band splintered. Sometimes we would sit outside the pub. Copper up for a drink. Or just bring one from home. And sometimes I would catch myself laughing at some daft thing Pete had said, or a silly joke. And then I remembered. I wasn't supposed to be laughing. We would all catch ourselves, like something scalding had spilled from our lips. A gasp. A hum. Then we'd sit silently. I think Pete was waiting for him to come cycling past. Doing his rounds. Watching for a ghost.

Billy died of smoke inhalation. I think that was a relief to Pete. And to us all. That he was already dead when the flames began to lick away at him. Even though his body had to be officially identified by his teeth. His iron bike with the spindly spokes was propped up against the wall. Remnants of his bat-like coat glued to his melted flesh.

And life, the cruel bitch, went on. But Pete never recovered. Not fully.

Everyone in the village had gone to his funeral at the church and Andy's dad did some sandwiches at the pub. Just ham and some Scotch eggs. And everyone chucked in a couple of quid. Pete sneered at those outside the church. Grief tourists, he called them, then slagged everyone off loudly for taking the piss all these years and then rocking up to his funeral like he was their best mate. Hypocrites. The lot of them.

Later at the pub, everyone did karaoke. Billy's favourites. Even Pete got up and sang 'Maggie May'. Billy's dad didn't stay. I thought of him going home, to that hovel, and my heart just couldn't bear it. Neither, it seemed, could his.

He died less than a month later. Someone once told me that peacocks pair for life. But when one of them dies, the other will die from an empty heart.

That fire took two lives that night. And still the world turned.

That massive leisure centre company pulled out. They said it was not financially viable or some bollocks. There had been rumours they'd had cold feet at the planning stage, but the fire, the devastation, the death was the final nail in the coffin. So to speak.

All those jobs. All that promise. That hope. It all faded away and the carcass of the steelworks, the crumbling mill, they both rotted around us. The sky was always grey. The cobbles were never polished. The village hall stopped its coffee mornings. Even the toddler group packed in because there was no one to be on the committee. It was as if a horrible spell had cursed the village, like when Sleeping Beauty pricked her finger and all the castle fell to sleep.

Like that. But not sleep. Depression.

The little spark, that golden promise of Jamie, of being wanted, needed, I snuffed out immediately. He did try to start. Knocked for me once or twice. An impassioned plea at the church gate. A stolen kiss that made my lips tingle. But I couldn't. I couldn't look at the pain in Pete's eyes and feel like anything good had come out of that night. It was right that it was silenced. Filed away forever.

I didn't bother with A levels. I wasn't going away to university so what was the point? Joni scraped onto a

BTEC at the college in performing arts. She would see Jamie in the corridors. He was doing his A levels, of course. Politics. English. Business studies. I answered a job ad in the newsagent's window and started work in the florist's in Holmfirth as a junior. Sweeping the floors. Trimming thorns. Permanently pricked fingers. I barely earned enough to cover my bus fare, but it was still more than I'd ever had before.

Kit and Tom went to work for their dads. Pete had a go, tried doing a foundation course in art, but, never one for the system, he dropped out after a month. Managed to get his old job back at Woolworths. Lasted another month before getting fired again. Damn those pick 'n' mix. Ended up doing odd jobs with Tom and Kit, floating around. Still drawing. I saw one once. In his garage. He threw an old dust sheet over it when he saw me coming, but when he went inside to get us a drink, I peeked. It was, of course, charcoal. The fire. Even in black and grey, I could see the colours of the flames. I could feel the heat. The paper almost crackled.

Then, one brisk October morning, when the sky was the coldest kind of blue, the wheel of fortune started to turn. Pete's mum decided to move to Leeds with her new man, which was horrific at first, but then Tom's gran offered Pete the spare room. He moved in with Tom and in the space of six weeks put on a stone in weight. The shadows under his eyes started to fade. Andy's mum offered him a kitchen job in the pub, where they didn't mind if he scoffed the odd chicken wing or cube of cheese. After a while, he got the band to come in and start playing again. No Jamie anymore. He was never around. So it became Joni and the Slaughterhouse Boys. He started running the karaoke. Dedicated 'Maggie May' to Billy every Thursday night.

Even though in the months after the fire we seemed to

part, we then slowly began to come back together again. It was as if our shared guilt both repelled us, but drew us back together. I remembered what Joni had said – that you couldn't have good without evil. Maybe we needed each other to remind ourselves who we'd been before. And with money in our pockets now, it was as if we could rule the world, even after we'd shelled out board to our mums and paid the weekly bus fare. We could afford a couple of beers. We'd started being served. We all went to watch Joni in *Blitz!* at the local theatre, now able to afford the tickets. Not that they were much for a college production. We started laughing again.

But we never walked past what was left of the steelworks. We never ventured south of the village. Pete and Joni started getting off with each other occasionally. Pete seemed to like having someone to hold on tight to. Joni was just bored. Tom just looked on in pain. And me? Every night I'd think about Jamie. The way his hand had felt on my hip. The way he'd kissed my neck. For everything that could have been. I could have had a boyfriend. I could have been in love. I could have been loved. I could have been visible.

I didn't see Jamie again for a few months. It was easy back then to lose touch when mobile phones and social media weren't a thing. Our landline had been cut off again and my meagre wages couldn't afford the reconnection fee. I didn't go to college and Jamie didn't live in the village. It was as simple as that.

And then, by the time I saw him again, I had somehow, along the way, become the property of Kit. Even I couldn't tell you how it had come about. One day we were all drinking Newkie Brown and Smirnoff Ices at the pub, the next minute he was walking me home and kissing me goodbye at the door. It was as if it had always been like that. No asking out. No, 'I like you, do you like me?' It was as if there had been a huge, catastrophic shift in the group, like a deck of cards that had been thrown up in the air and shuffled back into the wrong places.

I was Kit's girlfriend and no one thought to mention it to me. Not even Kit. I should have been the happiest I had ever been. All my dreams had come true. Kit walked with his arm slung around my neck; once bony, he had now developed muscles from lugging buckets and tools for his dad all day. Celtic tribal band tattoo around his bicep. Song lyrics meant for me. Kit and Cass. Twos on cigarettes. I wore his Nirvana T-shirt to bed. We'd spend hours on his bed, or mine, kissing roughly until my chin was raw from his attempts to grow stubble and his balls, he claimed, were blue from my reluctance to take things any further than third base. And even that was testing. I had to ask Joni about it as I was sure it was meant to be feeling better than it did.

'Three? Oh, for God's sake, you're not a bloody jar of peanut butter. Tell him two, max. What is it with boys? Why do they always think it's some kind of triumph to get as many fingers in as possible? Babe, you need a man, not a boy.'

Pete ended up getting on a food tech apprentice course that Andy's mum put him forward for. The government paid his wages, so it was win-win.

A planning application was in to bulldoze the rest of the steelworks and put up apartments in an old mill character conversion-type thing. Not exactly a leisure centre, but it would provide jobs.

The morning they broke the ground, I stood and watched, pulling my jumper around myself tight.

And, for some reason, I thought about that little mouse we called Mickey.

27

Now

Something happens.

Tom calls just after 7 a.m. to say the vans were up by Joni's and I have never run so fast in my life.

There've been little white tents and men in those beekeeper-type suits in the fields all morning. The rain is thrashing down, and I am soaked to the skin. I didn't bother with a coat and my jumper is sticking to me and my hair is plastered to my head.

And no one will tell me anything. The policewoman blocking the entrance to the field won't let me near or answer a single question, and just keeps trying to get me to go home. Tells me that she doesn't know anything and at the moment it's just a response to a call. No, she doesn't know what in relation to. No, she doesn't know if it's anything to do with Joni.

Lying bitch.

Eventually, Stella takes me into her house and tries to calm me down with a custard cream. I stand vigil at her living-room window, all her little china dogs in a row on the sill, staring up at me, for what seems like hours. But they don't bring anything that looks like a body out.

If the weather was better, I'm sure there'd be a crowd.

I try Millie again and again, but it just keeps going to

voicemail. The boys come up for a bit and Stella puts the kettle on with delight, but eventually they get fed up too. There is literally nothing to see. When she starts fidgeting and muttering about getting her stewing steak on, I give up the ghost and head home, after making her promise she will call with any news.

The rain is relentless.

'Mum?'

The door slams so hard, I hear the glass panel rattle. I've been sitting on the edge of my bed for what feels like hours, although it could well have just been seconds. Kit is still sleeping downstairs, of course. The room is all mine. But it feels cold and sterile somehow. I've been staring at the walls, like I'm in some kind of padded cell. I can't see any colour anywhere and my mouth feels dry.

'In here.' I stand and pull Joni's old cardigan around me. She left it here because she always said my house was cold. Knee-length and hand-knitted, swirls and patches, and all very Joni. It still smells of her.

I assume Millie has heard about the police in the fields, so I go onto the landing. She looks frazzled. Her coat is half hanging off her shoulder and her hair is in some weird top-knot with stray strands everywhere. She looks like Medusa. Especially in the eyes.

'You OK?' I take a deep breath. 'Did you hear?'

'I've found something.' Millie stands firmly and drops her bag on the floor with a thud.

'What? What have you found?' I lean against the door frame. My legs are starting to feel jellified.

'Mum, you never said Joni used to live in Nottingham.'

'Well, she didn't really. I think she went there on tour.' I gulp. 'With that band, I think. I think they played at Rock City or something. I don't know. Your dad might,' I throw on at the end.

'No, I got hold of the pubs Dad said to. No one remembers him. Or Joni. Or even the band.'

'Well, fifteen years is a long time ago, Millie, staff change. I'm sorry that—'

'But then someone sent me this.' She cuts me off and holds up her phone. It's a picture. Sent to the Instagram appeal account. An actual picture of a photograph pinned on a corkboard. Joni, Kit and three other young men, all zipped-up anoraks and baggy jeans and bucket hats. God, Kit looks so young. And so moody still. I know what she's looking at, though. I know, but I don't say anything. Just in case.

'Wow, who sent you that? Look at Dad!' The smile does not meet my eyes.

'Someone who saw my posters. They used to be a roadie.'

'I bet Dad will remember them.'

'MUM!'

'What?' I know it's coming.

'Joni's pregnant in this picture!'

I close my eyes. Not now. Not now. Not now.

'Mum ... It *was* Joni's baby, wasn't it? The one that was dug up? Is this her pregnant with that baby?'

I don't know what to say. There's so much racing through my mind. My heart is pounding. I open my eyes and Millie is standing so close to me. She's taller than me now. Suddenly I feel very, very afraid. I need Kit here.

'Did you know, Mum? Did you know Joni was pregnant?'

'Yes,' I say, after a while. 'I did.'

'Well ... why didn't you tell the police?'

I turn and walk into my room and sink onto the edge of my bed, my head in my hands.

'Because it's irrelevant.'

'*How* is it irrelevant? *How*? Some baby bones getting discovered on the day she goes missing? She was pregnant and no one knew?'

Millie grabs hold of the door frame. I can see her world is falling apart. I want to do something, anything, to protect her. But I can't.

'The dates don't add up, honey. Joni was in her late twenties in this picture, twenty-six maybe. The bones, they're ten years older at least.'

'So what happened to the baby? Did she have it? I don't understand. How come no one ever talks about it?'

'Look, Millie, I think we need to give your dad a ring.'

'Why? Oh my God. It's his, isn't it? Did Dad have an affair with Joni?'

The question that had always been on my lips. Ever since we were kids.

'No, of course not. I just . . . I think your dad should be here for this conversation.'

'Why? Mum, you're scaring me.' Millie comes into the bedroom and stands in front of me. She still looks so young behind her cocksure stance, her dropped hip. Those eyes. The puppy fat on her hips. Her plump lips. I don't want to tell her. I can't lose her too.

'The baby was adopted, Millie. Joni couldn't cope with a . . . termination. But she didn't want people to judge her either. For being able to give her away. She just didn't want anyone to know about it all. Then Kit and Joni got the offer of the tour. She'd be gone from the village for a while. It seemed like good timing. She went away for a few months. She had the baby. And came back.'

'Who was the dad?' Millie looks like she can't quite believe what she's hearing.

'No one you know.'

'Who adopted her?

I'm about to sucker punch her.

'I did, sweetheart.'

28

Now

My phone rings and I fumble for it so clumsily, it drops on the tiles and shatters even more. Swearing, I see it's an unrecognised number and for a second my blood runs cold.

'Cass, it's Mark Easton here.'

'Hi… hi,' I say a little breathlessly. 'Any news?'

'I am just ringing to ask you if you wouldn't mind popping down to the station?'

'Is there any news? Oh God, have you found something? I saw the cordons in the field.'

'We do need to talk to you again.'

'What do you mean?' My voice is small.

'Please do bring someone with you, if you need to. Tomorrow? Is 9 a.m. OK?'

'Er… yeah,' I say. I have no idea what day it even is.

We say our goodbyes and hang up. I let myself think about Jamie then. His touch. His kiss. The way he looked into my eyes. Him sitting there, in a cell, being interrogated by the police.

'You're so much better than this. Than him.' That's what Kit had said, clutching a bag of frozen peas to his jaw. The night he left for good.

'I'm not better than anyone,' I had said.

'You are. God, Cass. You are.' He'd climbed into the front

seat of his dad's car and driven away and my heart was breaking. I had wanted to run after him, run down the cobbles, screaming for him to come and take me with him. Take me away.

But I couldn't. The shadows were still keeping me here. They would keep me here forever.

Millie is in her room. Where she's been since the conversation yesterday.

Kit came over, but she wouldn't speak to him either. I keep seeing her horrified face over and over in my mind. The pain in her eyes.

'I'm … not yours?' She looked like she was about to topple down the stairs.

'Yes. Yes. You're mine. You have *always* been mine,' I said and reached for her shoulders. 'But I can't have children, Millie. Joni gave me the best present anyone in the world could. She might have been the woman who gave birth to you, but you're *my* child.'

'I'm adopted? But I don't understand. What about my birth certificate? I've seen it.'

'Not adopted formally. I just brought you home. You haven't seen your real certificate. That was one we printed off the internet. Just until the time was right to tell you.'

'But it must have been illegal. What you did. That's … fraud? I don't know what it is, but that's messed up.'

I started to cry. I couldn't help it. 'I would have done anything for you.'

Millie took two dazed steps backwards and hit the wall with a thump.

'Joni's my mum? All this time?'

'No, Millie, *I'm* your mum. From the second I held you in the hospital. I cut the umbilical cord.' I could barely get the words out, I was sobbing so hard. 'I held you and you looked up at me, and I swear, Millie, you were always meant for me.'

'But ... she didn't want me. She saw me every day. And she still didn't want me. Did I mean so little that she could just give me away? Like ... just, "Here, like, you have it"?' Millie slid down the wall and I jumped up to go and put my arms around her, but she held her palms up to warn me off. I knelt in front of her instead.

'No. Oh God no, Millie. Joni *adored* you. She just wasn't ready. To be a mother. To be a single mother at that. She thought you'd suffer. I think she thought this way would be perfect. She could be your godmother instead and give me everything I ever wanted. Millie, it was her ultimate sacrifice.'

We just sat there for a while. The clock ticked.

'She is dead. Isn't she?' Millie said quietly, when the shadows had grown thick and mossy on the walls.

'I don't know, darling. I can't feel her anymore. That's all I know. Does that make sense?'

Millie didn't say anything.

'But *I'm* your mum, Millie. And I'm here.'

But then she looked at me, her eyes a terrifying pale. 'No. You're dead to me too.'

Then she stood and left, leaving the back door hanging wide open in her wake.

I called Kit in a panic and enjoyed a massive mouthful from him. Who did I think I was? That I had no right to tell her. That I'd ruined their relationship for good. I took it. And I hated myself for it, but there was a sense of relief too. I felt the way you do after a bout of gastroenteritis, when there's nothing left inside. I felt empty, gutted from throat to sternum. And yet the sickness had been purged. In a way, I felt I owed it just as much to Joni. Wherever she was.

Joni never told anyone but me who Millie's dad was. She simply said Kit would be Millie's dad. And that was that. Most assumed she just didn't know. That's what it says on the birth certificate up in the attic. 'Father unknown'.

But when Pete came to visit us all in the hospital, when she was in my arms and not Joni's, he looked appalled. He asked to hold her. But Kit said no, not yet. That was the first time he looked at me in that way. Pure resentment. It wouldn't be the last.

As Millie grew, I would watch her through Joni's eyes. As her fine hair thickened and curled. The freckles across her noise. Those green eyes. But she had Pete's abrasiveness. His scowl. His lanky frame. His height. His compassion for animals. For underdogs. I was relieved.

I used to see him watching her. Not in a grotesque way. Or even with wistful eyes. More with curiosity. Was she a card to be played? Who knows. Did he believe it too? He never asked Joni if he was the father. And she never told him.

It was only a week before Joni was due, and we told Kit's mum we were getting a baby. She – the whole village – assumed we'd adopted. Everyone knew we were struggling to get pregnant. We didn't tell anyone anything different. And no one ever asked. It was as if everyone was just delighted for us. At last. How wonderful. You're going to be such wonderful parents! Was it an easy process? *Very.* Will you tell her when she's older? *We haven't decided.*

Then, it was as if everyone just forgot she wasn't mine to begin with. Including us. That day in the hospital, Joni giving birth. It was like some far-off dream that never really happened. That it was me on the bed, it was Cass cutting the cord. When you believe hard enough, you can rewrite the past so convincingly it's like cleaning the cobwebs off an old painting and finding beauty where there was once grime.

The next morning, I go to the police station. Kit comes with me, but he sits outside. I sit facing Easton and another officer at a cold metal desk, on a scratchy chair, the grey, horrible, plastic and metal sort that they had in school that laddered your tights. I haven't seen this other officer before. She's a bit more sour than Jenny. A bit lizard-faced. Severe features and a long neck. Not the sort of woman I feel particularly comfortable talking about my sex life with.

'Cass. What do you know about the relationship between Joni Blackwood and James Carter?'

'I wasn't aware they had any kind of relationship,' I say softly. 'Not until I saw ... what I saw. On his computer.'

'And what about when you were younger? What then? How would you describe the relationship?'

'We were all friends for a while. I don't know. I don't think anything happened between them.'

'Did she tell you about any sexual relationship she had with Jamie?'

'No. It wasn't really like that between them. And I ... well, Jamie and me, we kind of had a little fling, so I don't think she would have done that to me. You know. Girl code.' I give a weak smile.

'But she did do it to you now, it would appear.' Easton looks at me and taps the end of his pen on his desk. I stare back. He has the start of a sweat patch under his left arm. Pale blue shirts are not forgiving like that.

'Yeah.' I look down. 'Well, we don't really know what

happened there, do we? I mean, maybe. Maybe he ...' I trail off.

'Maybe he what?' The officer sits back in his chair and relaxs his arms. I can definitely smell sweat now.

'I'm sorry. I really don't know. I can't answer anything about that. It was as much of a shock to me. Jamie and I have been back in touch, like I said, for a while. Joni never mentioned anything when I told her. I just ... I still can't understand it. It's all very strange.'

'You must have felt very angry,' the female office says matter-of-factly. 'Betrayed.'

'Well ...' I'm a little flummoxed. 'I mean, of course it hurts. But that's not really the main concern now, is it?'

'So you're not angry with Joni?'

'I have no idea. Maybe, once we know she's OK and home safe, but right now, all I care about is finding her.'

There's a silence. I can tell it's planned and with purpose. Only I'm not quite sure what the purpose of it is.

The detective just looks at me. I look back. The tick of the clock gets louder and louder and my mouth becomes drier and drier.

'Would Joni have told you? If she had been in a sexual relationship with Jamie when you were younger?' he asks.

'She just wouldn't have done it, so it's a moot question,' I reply.

'What if she felt ashamed of herself? For having sex with someone she knew you ... liked?'

'Why does it matter about Jamie and Joni back then anyway? You know it happened now. Surely that's the main point? Who cares about twenty-five years ago? I don't understand.'

'We have done a DNA test,' the detective says. 'The bones

of the baby that were discovered in the graveyard contain the same DNA as Jamie Carter.'

The ticking of the clock becomes so deafening I have to put my hands over my ears.

'What?' The room seems to be getting smaller.

'Did you know Jamie had fathered a child?'

'Of course not.' I press my palms so flat against my ears the air pops inside the canals like someone once told me they did on an aeroplane. 'I don't understand how that can be right.'

He continues as if he hasn't heard me. 'Concealment of the birth, and death, of a child is a criminal offence. If someone had exhumed the baby, it could have given Joni a reason to run away? Or panic? That she would get in trouble.'

'Why Joni? What are you saying?'

'Cass – tell us now. You need to be honest with us. You're not going to get into any trouble. The father of that baby is Jamie Carter. We have strong reason to believe that Joni is the mother.'

'No!' I shout. 'There's no way Joni could have had a baby without me knowing. I was with her every single day. Have you tested for her DNA? How do you know it's hers?'

There's a silence, then Easton looks at the other officer. I can't quite read what's going on.

'We didn't have an uncontaminated sample to test. We haven't been able to get a sample from Joni's house. It would appear she is a very thorough cleaner. Bleach makes it impossible to get a sample.'

'So, how do you know?'

'Cass, I asked you to bring someone with you today because I'm afraid we have some news.'

My nails press into the fleshy part of my palms.

'We have discovered human remains in the field behind Joni's house. A tooth, in fact.'

'A tooth?'

'We have sent it for tests.'

'You think … you think it's Joni's?'

'Yes. We have reason to believe so.'

'Where was it?'

Easton and the lizard woman exchange glances again.

'It was stuffed in the mouth of a scarecrow. The farmer discovered it. Or, rather, a crow pecked it out. It was wrapped in this.'

A plastic bag is placed in front of me. There's a pink, satin-looking ribbon in there. I know what it is without even asking. It's Joni's Gallows Queen sash.

'Why would …?' I trail off. There's no point. 'You think she's dead, don't you?'

'I'm very sorry, Cass.' The woman leans forward. There is a hint of compassion in her reptilian eyes and I hate her for it. 'This is now a murder investigation.'

29

Then – 1996

When we were thirteen, three years earlier, we went on a school trip to Eden Camp. Tom was sick into a paper bag and had to sit next to the teacher on the front seat all the way there.

We had all eaten our sandwiches before we'd got to the motorway and Joni got off with the bus driver while the rest of us went through a re-enactment of the Blitz.

She had to copy the answers on my worksheet afterwards. Joni at thirteen looked pretty much like Joni at eighteen. Tight, crushed purple velvet dress clinging to each and every curve, a lumberjack shirt thrown over the top. Ripped stripy tights and one purple and one black DM. I, of course, wore the other two mismatches. Even though they were a size too small and caused blisters on the soles of my feet that made me howl. But I wore jeans and a shit fake Smiths T-shirt that had once belonged to Joni's dad.

I used to think that these boys, the lads from the waltzers, the roadies lugging amps around the back of the pub from their white vans, the travellers who would set up camp on the fields every summer, it wasn't their fault – she looked older.

They thought she was older. They were stupid. Wasn't Joni

clever, and intoxicating, convincing them she was legal. She was the one with the power over them.

They weren't even all boys. Some of them were men.

But that bus driver – he knew. It was a Year 8 school trip. He must have known, as he looked both ways to make sure no one was watching, then grabbed her arse and kissed her hungrily up against the side of the coaches. He knew. He knew she was a kid.

And I was watching. I was always watching.

From the candyfloss stand at the fair. From behind the beer barrels at the pub. From the exit of the Blitz experience hut.

I was her unofficial protector. I was the scarecrow.

Back then, girls like Joni didn't understand the terms thrown about so confidently now. Self-esteem. Abandonment issues.

We were the generation of girls who used sex as a way to be noticed. We let ourselves be abused – yes, abused, assaulted, by older boys. Consent wasn't a buzzword then, and even if it was, we wouldn't have understood it. Our bodies were not our own.

When we were fourteen, Joni had taken a liking to one of the travellers. A seventeen-year-old boy with an ear piercing and a shit tattoo.

She made me walk past that camp every day. And wait for her as she climbed over the fence and disappeared into his caravan. I would sit and count the minutes on the dead dandelions, their tiny gossamer parachutes floating into the breeze. The smell of cigarettes and dog shit on the wind.

I'd hide behind the long strands of my hair and think about what she was doing.

With her hands. Her mouth. It made me feel sick.

But it made her feel special. It made her glow with happiness. How could it feel so wrong to me?

One afternoon, when I was sat on the fence, listening to her Walkman that she'd let me use, the batteries died. A couple of the lads walked past me, sniggering and nodding in the direction of the caravan.

'You heard about that? How old she is?' one of them said. My ears pricked up.

'Fourteen, right? I mean, he did say she tasted fresh. Lucky bastard.'

I felt my tuna butty rise in the back of my throat. I wanted to run after them. Scream at them. Make them go in and rescue my precious friend. Drag her out and punch their mate in the face for doing God knows what to a child.

But I didn't. I just sat there, on the fence, the empty silence in my headphones.

When Joni came out, she looked less smug than usual. Her denim shorts rode high as she made her way through the grass. I didn't get a glimpse of him. I suspected he hadn't even bothered to get out of bed.

'You OK?' I asked as she clambered over to my side of the fence, with a slight wince.

'Yeah. God. You won't believe what he did,' she said with a scowl.

'What?' I asked nervously. I knew her virginity was still intact and I was praying that was how it remained.

'He ... you know ... in my mouth.'

Her hands flew up to her lips and she looked as if she was about to retch.

I felt as if the world was dropping out of my stomach, and for the first time, I felt anger bubble up inside me. Anger at her.

I couldn't bear to look at her.

'Your batteries died,' I said and tore off the headphones, and thrust it into her hands. I didn't even wait to see if she had grasped it properly before I let go and took a perverse delight in watching her fumble to stop it tumbling onto the gravel path.

'Hey, careful,' she said. 'What's the matter?'

'Nothing,' I shrugged. 'So, do you like him?'

'Yeah, I mean, he's seventeen. And he's fit. He plays guitar as well.'

'But what do you talk about?'

'We don't talk really. Look...' She pushed up her sleeve. 'He signed my arm.'

I glanced down to see a purple felt-tip scrawl on her forearm. Crazy Davey.

'What's that about?' I screwed my face up.

'I dunno. Thought it was funny though.'

'That he signed you? Like his property?'

'Cass.' Joni stopped on the track and got hold of my arm. 'What's the matter?'

'Nothing.' I stared over her head at the archway of bark and birch leaves. 'Just... doesn't it... I mean, do you like it?'

'Like what?'

'Doing... that.'

'Yeah, I wouldn't do it otherwise.' Joni smiled.

'But do you enjoy doing it?'

'Well yeah. He likes it, so I like it.'

'But you don't actually like it, do you? Do you actually like putting it in your mouth?' I couldn't believe what I was saying.

'I told you. The look on his face, it makes me feel powerful. I like it.'

'It's disgusting!' I shouted. I couldn't help it. My voice rang out and broke through the branches and a cluster of swallows broke from the trees.

'It's normal!' Joni shouted back. 'Why are you making me feel bad for this?'

'Because it's not normal.' Anger burned through the tears threatening to spill over. 'It's not normal.'

'Cass, of course it is. Everyone has sex. Everyone.'

'You're only fourteen!' I yelled back.

'Well ... I'm not having actual sex, am I?' Joni shook her head. 'Not that it would be any of your business if I was. Just because I don't have a mum, don't act like you are one.'

She might as well have slapped me. I felt the burn and the heat in my cheeks as if my face was ringing.

I stood there, mouth falling open, and she looked me up and down, slowly, sneeringly.

'You'll die a virgin, you're so frigid.'

'Joni ...' My mouth felt like it was filling with maggots, the squirm of my stomach. She was all I had. Everything I had. I was about to lose her. But I couldn't let her think it was OK. She was ruining herself. She was ruining me. My head felt like it was filling with straw.

'You know, there's life outside of this village, Cass. There's a whole world out there. It doesn't begin at the mill and end at the steelworks.' Joni was shaking her head. 'As soon as I'm eighteen, I'm out of here. And you'll still be here. With your shopping and your children and your small little life. And you know what ... that's what's disgusting.'

She turned and stomped up the track, and I lost the last shred of dignity I had left by running after her. But she simply shook me off. I slumped down at the crossroads and sat cross-legged in the dirt.

Years later, when Jamie said those words to me, *you could be so much more*, I thought of this moment. When being who I was right here, right now, wasn't good enough for anyone. It wasn't good enough for Joni that I loved the village, that I adored the fields and the golden corn. That I could walk for miles and there wouldn't be a soul, but the crows and the mice. Foxes screaming at night. The sound was like a lullaby to me. Sometimes I could swear I could hear the drum and whirr, as if the mill was turning, or the fire in the steelworks burning. This village felt more alive to me than any city ever could.

The village has souls.

And scarecrows that laid me gently to sleep under the Gallows Tree.

Joni was still disappearing now and then. Then, one night, she knocked on my door because the phone had been cut off again, and she told me she couldn't watch *My So-Called Life* tonight because she felt like she was coming down with something. I let her lie sweetly to my face while smelling of jasmine oil, noticing she had her best lace-up body on under her army jacket, while telling me she was going back home to bed.

But when I went back up to my bedroom, I turned the lights out, ducked under the windowsill so she couldn't see me watching. I saw her look up to my window to check, then turn left and start walking back in the direction of her house. Hugging my pillow to me, I was still watching as she stopped near the bend, looked back, then crossed over the road, and scooched behind the cars, as flat to the wall on my side of the road as she could be. Wherever she was going, she didn't want me to see.

She slunk along the terraces, then shot a furtive glance at my window. I didn't need to duck. I was crouched so low only my eyes were peering over the sill and it was so dark. I tracked her and she picked up speed past my house, and then ducked down the ginnel at the side of next door. I dashed to the bathroom, turned off the light and stood on the avocado toilet to peep out of the top window I'd had to push open due to the hideous frosting. There she was, the red of her hair and paleness of her skin, by the bins, like a fox, dodging the street lights. You could see her breath in the air as she half jogged to the end of the alley, then she looked behind as she crossed the street and ducked through the hedgerows into the back entrance to the graveyard. The one we used to crawl through when we went to Sunday School to get home quicker to watch *The A-Team*.

I grabbed my mum's black jumper off the banister and followed her out into the cold night. Over the years, generations of kids like us had taken the shortcut, so you no longer had to crawl. In fact, I barely had to stoop now through the hawthorns. The little trodden-down path took you into the back of the churchyard. The graves ran in a circle around the little church like a moat, with steps leading up the hill. I weaved between the old soldier and the teenage girl who died from scarlet fever, and made my way up the steps. The bench, where Joni sometimes sat, was empty. There was no light inside the church either, not that I could see from the back. I padded quietly around the side. There was a cellar area down there, something I liked to call the vault. We used to get changed in there for the nativities, donning the same mouldy tea towel headdresses and tunics made from pillowcases that had been stuffed in a bin bag and stored year after year.

245

The steps were dark and slick, the moss slimy and sheeny. I crouched down by the iron bars at the top and tried to see if there was any sign of life behind the thick wooden arched door. I couldn't see any light, but that didn't mean much. Carefully, I held the rails and took the five steps down. I could hear something. Muffled. I leaned my ear against the door but it didn't seem to make any difference. It wasn't coming from inside.

Straightening back up, I realised there was something on the breeze. A sigh. Something inside me felt very wrong all of a sudden. I turned back and slipped in my haste to get away, up the steps and back through the snicket. I didn't like the sound of that sigh. My shin scraped on the harsh edge and I whimpered, biting so hard on my lip to stop me crying out, I imagined I could taste blood.

Scrabbling to the top, I turned to run back the way I had come. But something halted me. I could still hear a muffled noise. Something akin to a groan. I turned around. In my head, the ghosts of the soldiers we had laid wreaths for every Remembrance Day, the victims of the plague believed to have been buried in one mass grave below the vaults of the church, the teenage girl who died from scarlet fever. Billy Miles. Burned. Disfigured. Half his face melted. Like my doll. They would all be there. Arms outreached, eyes rolling.

The scarecrow.

Eyes pecked out. Stuffing from the sack of his head oozing.

Not my scarecrow.

He wouldn't hurt me.

It couldn't hurt me.

Not now.

The breeze lifted my hair as I turned, but there was nothing there.

My feet began to move. I began to walk in the other direction. I reached my fingers out to trail the side of the church. To keep me grounded. To touch something real.

When I turned the corner, I saw the angel before anything else. The moon was catching the curve of her face and she looked as if she was emitting some kind of blue light. I followed her weeping eyes to beneath the statue and what I saw made my stomach heave and my heart plunge.

Joni's head was between his legs, his hands were on the back of her head, his face was leaning back against the statue. Eyes closed. His mouth open and his tongue – God, his tongue – poking obscenely out of the side of his mouth. It was so hard to tell what revolted me most. That, or the grey slug of his penis that Joni was servicing. He was instructing her. Talking to her, in stilted strange sentences as if he was trying to explain to her how to assemble some flat-pack furniture.

The vicar, Reverend Cooper. Still wearing his dog collar. Bile rose up in my mouth and scorched my throat as I swallowed it back down. I couldn't not look. Anger swelled in my gut, but tears started to blur my vision. I was disgusted. I was disgusted by him. But, most of all, I was disgusted by her. And I hated myself for it.

I didn't believe in the reverend's God. The one from Sunday School who left my belly empty and let my mum drink away the child benefit. The God who said if we prayed, it would be OK. The God who took away everyone's jobs, who left families to rot. The God who let my father into my room every night until on my fourth birthday my mother smashed him over the head with a bottle of whisky and held the jagged edge to his neck.

Times were very different then. I believed in a different God.

My father was a church-going man too, I was told. They all deserved to burn in hell.

But Joni was different. I thought back to that day, after we'd been to the travellers' camp, when I called it disgusting. When I called her disgusting.

I didn't mean it. But she was good. She was everything. I couldn't have her making those choices. Taking everything away from what she was. She was choosing to do this. I never had the choice. I screamed.

It rang out like a bullet in the night. Lights began to flicker from the houses. I only caught a glimpse of Joni's shocked face, then I turned and started to run. The ground was wet, and I skidded twice, all I knew was that I needed to run and get away from here. From everything keeping me here in this sick prison. I ran through the main church gates and someone called my name. Not Joni. Not the reverend. I don't know who. But I kept on running. I ran up the black lane lined with fields on one side and the trees on the other that I was usually too terrified to walk down at night. My chest was heaving and my ribs felt like they would burst out of my skin at any moment.

I could hear footsteps pounding behind me – I was too scared to turn and see who it was. The reverend? Running after me, ready to drag me back by my hair. Threaten me. Tell me what happens to girls who don't keep secrets.

Not Joni. No. no. no. no.

I got to the stile for the field and hoisted myself over it, running so fast I couldn't keep my pace with the steepness of the field and my legs buckled underneath me. I landed awkwardly and tumbled over again and again, the way we used to roll when we were kids, screaming with delight. When my body finally came to a stop, I just lay there. The stars were in the sky, so clear and crisp. The grass was damp underneath me. The moon was hanging high.

I closed my eyes and waited. I longed to feel strong arms underneath me. The scarecrow that carried me to the Gallows Tree. Be six years old again. For none of this to be real.

But he didn't come.

I rolled onto my front and started to heave; dry, agonising sobs, deep into the earth, like roots shooting from my mouth and harnessing me. Holding me. Becoming me.

'CASS!' I heard her shout. 'CASS! WHERE ARE YOU?'

I turned onto my side, knowing she couldn't see me in the dark, at the bottom of the field, and hugged my knees to my chest.

'CASS! CASS! ANSWER ME!'

I wondered what they would tell everyone. Poor Cass. Sleepwalked into the graveyard. Must have had a terrible nightmare and woke up. What a massive scare that must have been. Did you hear her scream? Could have woken the dead.

The dead.

Eventually, I must have cried myself to sleep. When I awoke, the fingers of the dawn had stroked the sky and the morning dew was cold and wet against my cheek. When I opened my eyes, a toad was crawling past me. Grey and warty. I sat bolt upright before I remembered toads were not the leaping kind. It shuffled its way down the field, towards the beck over the drystone wall.

My watch said it was just before 5 a.m. My bones were cold and my head was thick and heavy when I lifted it off the ground. I must have been clenching my jaw in my sleep because it practically came off its hinges when I tried to open my mouth. I staggered to my feet and set off for home, shivering so much I could barely make it over the stile. A god, whichever kind, had left a pint of milk and some eggs on the doorstep to the vicarage, I noted, as I stumbled past. I barely gave it a second thought before swiping them both.

The house was unlocked, which meant that my mum hadn't woken up to lock it. Nor had she realised I wasn't there. I popped the milk in the fridge and left the eggs on the side. I'd eat the evidence of my crime once I'd managed to warm up a little.

Knowing there would be no hot water at this time, I went to my room and stripped off my damp, wet clothes, then pulled on clean pyjamas. It was only when I went to climb under my duvet and cocoon myself in warmth that I saw the letter on my pillow.

> *Dear Cass,*
> *I have been looking for you, but, like me, I know when you don't want to be found.*
> *I don't blame you for being angry with me. Disgusted even, I am sure . . .*
> *But you need to understand . . .*

I crumpled it up before I got any further, and tossed it into the bin under my desk. It went into the basket first go, and for no reason at all, I did a little cheer to myself. Then I plumped up my pillow, lay down my head and went to sleep.

It was a surprise when I was woken by Joni roughly yanking my shoulder two hours later.

'Oh my God, Cass. Where were you? I've been worried sick.'

I turned away from her and closed my eyes tight.

'Don't ignore me.' She pulled me onto my back, or at least tried to, but I resisted. 'Did you read my letter?'

'No.' I opened my eyes. 'I don't want to hear it, Joni.'

'Cass. Please.' I noticed she was still wearing the same clothes she had been the night before. Her hair was wild and her eyes were panda chic. She still smelled of jasmine, though. 'It's not like that. It's not what you think.'

'What do you mean? What exactly did you think you were doing? Get off me.' I shook her hand off my shoulder. 'How could you?'

'Come on.' Joni stood up. 'Get dressed. Let's go for a walk.'

'No,' I said. 'Leave me alone. I just want to sleep. I was in a field all fucking night because of you.'

'No, Cass.' Joni shook her head. 'Not because of me. Because of you.'

'What's that supposed to mean?' I threw the covers back and jumped out of bed.

'It's time you stopped judging me, Cass. You judge me for every little thing. And I understand why.' She reached her hands out and placed them on my shoulders. 'I do. I know why. But this one. This one is different. You have to hear me out.'

We both knew I would end up going with her.

It was still early enough for the village to only be stirring. It wasn't that cold out, not really, but after my al fresco autumn camp-out, I couldn't get warm. I'd nicked my mum's woollen kaftan as well as her thick scarf. I looked like Joni.

We walked up past Joni's in silence and over through the woods into the cornfields. My eyes scavenged for the scarecrow. But he wasn't there.

'I ... I started doing it a couple of years ago,' Joni said.

The dawn had given way to early morning and the dew was drying off. The bark still smelled of the morning air, though, and the corn and wheat were crisp. The sky was turning from grey to lilac.

'A couple of years ago?' I slowed my pace.

'Don't, Cass, otherwise I'm not going to tell you anything.'

I stayed quiet. Although I didn't know what was worse. Knowing or not knowing.

'Sorry,' I said eventually.

'He ... he told me ... if I did, then it could be like atonement. That I could still go to heaven.'

'What? Joni? What?' My mouth dropped open.

'He told me ... I could atone. That God had been watching.'

'Joni – what?'

'He said he'd seen me. He knew what I had been doing. With ... boys'

'Joni, no. That's horrific.'

'He told me ... he told me he watched me. That he needed to save my soul.'

'You believed him?'

'I don't know. I was scared. He said that if I did these things, it would stop him ... stop him having an affair. Stop him from breaking his vows and damning his soul. He said God would forgive me then. Because I was helping a religious man. He said he would tell my dad.'

'Why didn't you tell me?'

'Because I knew you thought I was disgusting. And I couldn't bear you looking at me like that again.'

'Oh God, I'm so sorry.'

Joni looked over my shoulder at the crows settling on the corn, their angry squawks the only sound for miles.

Her eyes seemed empty and glassy and her face tinged with blue, like the angel from the night before.

'Joni, do you still think that? That this will save your soul?'

'No.' She shook her head. 'I started to question it. About a year ago. I believed him to start with. I mean, why would he lie? And you know what he was like. Funny. I liked that he was paying me attention.'

'But, Joni, everyone pays you attention.'

'Not good people.' Her eyes welled with tears. 'It's different for you. Everyone respects you. You talk, and people listen.'

'What? How can you say that? Everyone adores you. They always have.'

'It's not the same as respect. I'm nothing. I'm not going anywhere.'

'Joni! You are, you're going to go and become a famous singer ... with your talent.'

'No, Cass, I'm not. I'm more trapped than you are. You could go. You could have left.'

'I don't want to leave.'

'Cass, listen to me!' Joni grabbed me with sudden vigour and her eyes lit up, but not in a bright, shiny way. More like a warning. 'This place will swallow you whole. Please don't stay with Kit. Go with Jamie. Please. Get out of here. Get away from me.'

I threw her arms off. 'What are you talking about? Stop it! What has this got to do with anything? Why are you saying this?'

'Because there's something wrong with this village. It's cursed. It's dying. It's like the fucking Gallows song. It's rotting around us and it's going to take us with it. Everything here is fucked. Billy. The fire. All of it. Cass, I think it's me.

253

I think I attract bad things.' She whispered this last part. I couldn't say anything. It was as if she was possessed. Her hackles were up, her chin was thrusting, her fingers were clawed. I grabbed her hands.

'You don't, Joni. You're good. You're such a good person.'

'I don't want to go to hell.' Her eyes brimmed with tears. 'He said it would save me.'

'How could you believe him, Joni? That's not the kind of God we were taught about in Sunday School. That kind of God doesn't exist.'

'So what does exist?' Joni said, tears streaming down her face. 'Because this can't be it? Can it? This can't be it?'

She fell to the ground and I went with her, and held her in my arms as she sobbed into my chest.

'I'd do anything to get out of here,' she said. 'But you could go ...'

'Why, Joni? Why would you even want to leave? This is where we grew up. Our lives are here. We can be together here.'

'Because I hate it. I hate everything about this place. I hate the way people look at me. I hate the way I know they're all talking about me. All the time.'

'You said there was only one thing worse than being talked about. Not being talked about.'

'I say all kinds of shit to make myself feel better.'

I gritted my teeth so hard I felt them grind and thought I might have even chipped one. 'Well, leave then, Joni. Once your BTEC is over. Go to uni. Go to drama school. Go to music school, I don't know. There's nothing keeping you here.'

'We both know that's not true,' she said flatly.

Over in the next field, I swear I could see the outline of the scarecrow.

'What's keeping you here?' I whispered.

'You,' she replied.

It was then I decided I would never ever have sex. It was rotten. It was wrong. There was something so dark about it. So unclean.

I wouldn't do it to myself. I would remain pure.

For him.

30

Now

'He's being charged,' I sob down the phone to Kit. 'Jamie's going to be charged.'

'Where are you?' I swear there is relief, almost happiness in his voice.

'At the station. The bones. The baby bones. They have the same DNA as Jamie. And they've found a tooth. Joni's tooth.'

'You're kidding me?'

'No. God, Kit, I don't know what's going on.'

And then I really do start to cry. I cry until I feel as if my throat could bleed.

Kit comes to fetch me from outside the station. We walk to the van and I shiver. My bones are cold. He opens the door for me, something he has not done since I carried Millie out of the hospital. For a minute, I see that lanky boy with the grease-stained Stiff Little Fingers T-shirt and the shaved side undercut.

I smile at him. 'Thanks for coming,' I tell him as I buckle myself in.

'So.' Kit clears his throat. 'Back to ours then?'

'Yeah. Back to ours.'

We drive out of Sheffield and back onto the B-roads, gradually coming into the twists, turns and intestines of the countryside. We haven't spoken much; my feet are up on the

dashboard, but he hasn't done his usual routine of slapping
them down and telling me about how I'll break them if
we're in a crash.

We're not far from the village when I turn to look at his
profile. He has gone now. Kit. The sullen, moody, mad-at-
the-world boy. I've watched him wither and crumple over
the years. When he began to grow out his shaved undercut.
Then the day he picked up the clippers and shaved the lot
off. He was always so proud of his thick, stiff mohawk. When
it started to recede, he couldn't handle it. He couldn't cope
at all. He would rather destroy it all than watch it die slowly.

That's what he said. I understood. Somewhere along the
way, that angry-at-the-world boy just became angry at himself. It was never me. Never angry at me. Ours was a funny
kind of love.

'Pull over,' I tell him softly and he does what he is asked at
the side of the road by the cornfields and turns to me with
wide, frightened eyes. I reach out and stroke his unshaven,
rough cheek. The contrast of colour outside is electric. The
corn and wheat so golden in the field, touching the dark,
rolling clouds of the storm beginning to swell in the sky.

I lean over and kiss Kit deeply. His hands are shaking as he
weaves them into my hair. I clamber over the gearstick and
he reaches down to the lever under the chair and pushes the
seat back. An old routine from our teens. Kneeling astride
him, I allow myself to love the feeling of his strong, rough
hands clasping my waist. Lightning fills the sky and we both
jump, then smile, and carry on into the kiss. I lower myself
down and feel his hardness and it is so familiar, so sweet.
The thunder comes, as I knew it would, a minute later. And
I reach over and open the driver's door.

When we were younger, when the rain would come, Joni

and I would dance in the storm. She would spin in circles, her palms up to the rain and her head thrown back. We would jump and splash in our little wellies. Our macs. And then our Dr. Martens and cardigans. Clinging to us, soaking us to the skin, moulding the layers of clothes to the bone, cheap hair dye running down our foreheads. The boys would shake their heads and pull up their hoods and take shelter in the trees. Or just go home. But Joni would dance and dance and dance and spin me round until I felt my wrists were about to snap.

When Kit and I became more confident at being intimate, one day the heavens opened. We'd been by the riverbank, me making daisy chains and smoking the dog end of a spliff, Kit plucking out 'No Surprises' by Radiohead and trying to explain to me why *OK Computer* needed to be my favourite Radiohead album and not *The Bends*.

I jumped up in the rain and held my hands out for Joni before realising she wasn't there. Kit ran to the viaduct to stash his guitar, and I was there, on my own on the bank, being Joni. My palms raised to the air. I was the one spinning around and around.

He watched as I laughed and called for him to come and join me. But he called me a nutter and started rolling a cigarette instead. The trees were giving me too much shelter, so I ran out of the copse and back into the field, and shouted for him to follow me. Whether he thought I was heading for home, and whether he knew what was about to happen, he followed me without question.

In the middle of the field, the woods hugging us from all sides, I pulled off my dress. It was the first time I had ever undressed in the light in front of him. He pushed his flopping bedraggled hair from his eyes and stood still. Thunder rolled and I took off my bra, feeling the rain running down my chest and over my breasts, my ribs. I leaned my head back, like Joni, and saw the sky grow dark. I tried to touch it with my fingertips, and then I felt Kit's lips and hands everywhere. Somehow he laid me on the ground and moved down my body, and paused at my knickers, looking up at me to see if I was about to stop him doing what he was about to do, like I had – crippled with shyness – every time before.

He eased them down and then, softly, I felt his warm tongue between my thighs and I didn't care. I arched my back in the rain and the grass and felt the earth slide over my skin. My breathing was heavy and my body started to move in ways it never had before. Kit carried on, his hands grabbing onto my thighs so tightly I imagined fingerprints.

I screamed when the lightning struck and I came as the thunder rolled. And finally I knew what Joni had been talking about all these years. Kit lay on top of me and whispered beautiful words into my ears and I watched the sky and rolled my head to see if the scarecrow had been watching.

Now, we half jog, half walk, into the field, where the grasses are at their highest, without words. The rain isn't here yet, but I can sense it in the air. It feels thick with promise. This time, I don't stand and undress. We are not wrapped in the embrace of the trees. This time, I don't scream. I just let myself feel it. I lose myself in the feel of his skin against mine, the hunger of his jaw, the familiar feel of his hands on the curve of my hips to my waist, holding the back of my knee. When the rain comes, this time I close my eyes and smell the water as it hits the ground and patters on my cheeks. Kit moves and I move back, together in an age-old rhythm. After a while, I can't tell if the water burning my face is the rain or my tears. Or his.

'Joni's gone,' I whisper. Because it is true. I know it. I've always known it. I've looked for her. Searched for her in the breeze between the trees, the echoes of the water in the stream. She is nowhere and everywhere. 'She's gone, but I'm back now.'

We walk back to the van in silence. And then Kit drives us home.

And the next day, police charge Jamie, a man who once held my beating heart in his hands, with my best friend's murder.

I'd been out of sorts all day. Kit was grumpy; even though there were jobs going on the construction site, it was over-eighteens only. He and Tom had started drinking early. Joni was at college and I had the day off for working Saturday.

I cleaned the house. Mum wasn't feeling too good, so I tucked her on the sofa under a blanket and scrubbed the bathroom with some Jif that Pete had nicked for me from the pub. I dragged the hoover around half-heartedly. Wiped down in the kitchen for no reason. Mum was meant to drop some forms off at the job centre in Huddersfield, so I said I'd go. Her skin looked like tracing paper.

The bus went slowly and the rain started to patter on the windows, blurring the fields, the roads. The colours became more and more grey as we got closer to the city. My stomach grumbled and I remembered I'd not eaten anything that day and decided to wander to the bakery for a sausage roll.

As I got off the bus, I felt him before I saw him. My knees were already wobbly, but I put it down to anxiety. I never did like coming into town on my own, but it wasn't that. It was Jamie. He was striding down the concourse, laughing with a girl. A pretty girl. Dark hair and lips. Liquid liner and Converse. I froze, both willing him to see me and at the same time ducking behind a pillar. They were chatting about some essay, something about Hardy, and she was giggling up into his face. Her skin was like porcelain.

I peeped out from behind the mounted bus timetable. He had grown up somehow. Maybe not in height, as he was always so tall, but his stature. His shoulders were broader. His jawline unshaved. The way he carried himself was so astute. Aware.

He could have been mine.

I was staring so intently, I didn't notice she had clocked me. As they walked towards their bus, she looked back over her shoulder and whispered something to him. He turned too and I winced, and tried to look away, but it was too late.

'Oh, it's Cass,' I saw him say.

Porcelain girl looked pissed off, but he beamed broadly and started to walk towards me, stretching out his arms. I couldn't help it. I smiled and let him wrap them around me. The smell of his chest, all CK Be. I couldn't see as my face was muffled in his shirt, but he made dismissive platitudes to the girl, who I assumed got on the bus without him.

'What are you doing here?' he asked, holding me at arm's length by my shoulders, as if to get a better look at me.

'I do exist outside of Thistleswaite, you know,' I laughed. 'You don't have the monopoly on Huddersfield bus station.'

'My God. What are you doing now? Do you want to go for a coffee or something?' He looked at me hopefully.

'I . . . I've got to do some stuff for my mum.'

'Well, after that? I can keep you company.' He dug his hands in his pockets. His hair was shorter. More styled.

'Erm, sure. I can't be too long, though,' I smiled ruefully.

'Kit keeping tabs on you?' Jamie said darkly, then quickly apologised.

'No. Well, maybe.' I felt instantly treacherous. 'But it's

All Gallows' Eve tonight. I said I'd help Pete with the feast preparation.'

'You know, I'm gutted I never got to come to one of those,' he said. 'It sounds ... well, maybe not ace. Bit weird. But a laugh.'

'Yeah, it's fun.' I gave him a thin-lipped smile.

'That was a hint.' Jamie raised his eyebrows. 'I mean, I know I'm not Kit's cup of tea really, but hey, he got the girl, didn't he? I'm no threat now, right?'

Got the girl. I was the girl? Really? I felt colour rise to my cheeks and my toes started to tingle.

'I mean ... you know, it would be great to have everyone back together,' I offered. 'I know you still see Joni – at college. But the others haven't seen you, I bet.'

'You think it would be OK?' He smiled.

'Yeah.' I wasn't exactly lying, but even I knew that the honesty wasn't pure. We were to meet at the pub around 6 p.m. But as I walked to the job centre, I began to get the dreaddits in the pit of my stomach. By the time I returned home, the dreaddits had turned into a squirmy, writhing mess. Joni said she'd tell everyone she'd invited him in case Kit kicked off, but then Jamie would say he'd seen me at the bus stop and then everyone would know it was me. Kit's thunderous face. I couldn't bear everyone being cross with me.

'It's not like we fell out,' Joni shrugged. 'You have every right to invite him.' She still grimaced, though. 'Let me deal with it.'

We met Pete later in the afternoon and helped spread cheap margarine on stale bread buns. Watched as the faded bunting was strung up. The wood was gathered for the bon-fire and everyone was piling on broken furniture and crap

263

that had been sitting in people's yards all year. By the time Kit and Tom arrived, we were having something resembling fun.

'Jamie is coming tonight,' Joni threw into conversation. 'I meant to invite him at college, but Cass bumped into him in town. Be cool for us to hang out again.'

'Jamie? Really?' Tom looked nervous. Pete inhaled sharply through his nose and Kit sipped from the free pint Andy had pulled him for helping with the lights.

'What were you doing in town?' He looked at me.

'Job centre. For Mum.' I carried on spreading.

No one said anything and the tension throbbed like a sore thumb. Eventually, Kit put his glass down and sniffed. 'What does he want to come for?'

'He misses us, I reckon,' Joni chirped in. 'Bet he'll buy a round.'

'Fair one,' Pete said.

Kit moved closer to me. 'You should have said. I'd have given you a lift. Been driving around all afternoon.'

'Oh, thanks anyway. Just got the bus.'

'You OK? About him coming then?' Kit dropped his voice. 'I mean, I know he was pestering you that night. I don't want you feeling uncomfortable.'

'Oh God no. That was ages ago. I don't even think about it,' I lied smoothly. 'You know I don't like thinking about that night full stop.'

'Yeah,' he said. And kissed me. 'I do.'

And even though his grip on my wrist was too tight, for a moment, I thought it was all going to be OK.

I thought it was going to be OK even after Jamie turned up. There were a few frosty looks to start, but after he'd bought everyone a couple of drinks, the nostalgia kicked

THE VILLAGE

in. We talked bands. We wandered around the rec, swigging from cans, shared a joint behind the pub. I saw Jamie looking down towards the construction site. But he didn't mention it.

I saw him looking at me too.

It was the night we should have always had to repair the fragility of the group. We teased and drank. We lay on the grass, heads all mushed together. Played 'Never Have I Ever'. As usual, I really had never. I had more confidence in joining in the jokes. Jamie seemed surprised at my candour. And pleased. Proud almost. Kit kept his arm hooked over my neck. Hardly loving, but sending a signal of possession. His bones felt heavy and his elbow sharp. Joni's eyes were flicking between me and Kit. Me and Jamie. Kit and Jamie. Like she was watching a tennis game. It started to make me feel sick. Usually, I could always tell what Joni was thinking. But something seemed off. And I couldn't tell what.

By the time night fell and the streets were packed, the cobbles shining, the fires burning, the nooses hung on the tree, we were all drunk and sloppy. Jamie was starting to make noises about the last bus back. No one offered him a floor to crash on. We weren't quite back there yet.

'I'm going to win the Gallows Queen next year.' Joni laid her head on my shoulder as we sat on the kerb and watched the jars come out. 'You'll vote for me, won't you? I'll be eighteen then and eligible.'

'Don't you have to do something good for the community?' Tom pointed out.

'I do good things for the community!' Joni smacked his shoulder.

'DON'T!' I pointed at Pete just as he opened his mouth.

'I really miss you guys,' Jamie said.

The tiny flecks from the burned-out fireworks gently

swayed down from the blackened sky to the tips of the crowd.

'We miss you too,' I said, without thinking. Kit stiffened at the other side of me, but he didn't say anything, or move to touch me.

A quietness settled over us as we watched the overtired toddlers bomb about with hot dogs in one hand and various-sized weapons forged from sticks in the other. For some reason, it made me feel like crying.

'I'm working tomorrow,' I said. 'I better head home soon.'

'You'll not get to sleep with this carry-on,' Kit pointed out. 'Stay up. Call in sick.'

'I'm not calling in sick after All Gallows' Eve,' I spluttered. 'That's like calling in sick on New Year's Day. Too obvious. I'd be fired. Anyway, I don't get sick pay.'

'One more joint then?' Joni pulled one out of the top pocket of her coat.

'Sounds like a plan. Not by the pub, though. Andy's too intense,' Pete said.

'Graveyard?' Kit offered.

'No,' I said too quickly.

'Railway?' Pete laughed. 'Since we *know* there're no ghosts there now.'

'That place still freaks me out.' Tom shuddered.

'How come?' Jamie asked, while Kit stood up and held his hand out to me to pull me up.

'Let Cass tell you about her ghost children on the way,' Joni said.

'Guys, honestly, I'm not going into that tunnel. I'm paranoid enough.' Tom looked alarmed.

'Not in the tunnel. We'll just sit on the old track,' Kit promised. 'It's getting a bit middle-aged hell here.'

No one could argue with that.

We left the shrieks of the young and the what we perceived as old and nestled down with the nettles and rats where we felt we belonged. With no fire to warm us and no suggestions of making one, we were lit only by the watchful eyes of the houses, the glows beginning to come from the windows as families started to return home. Tom and Pete headed back first. Tom's gran ran that house like a military camp, Pete joked. Even though it was clear he kind of liked it.

Joni hung around for a bit. I wondered if she was trying to get Jamie alone. I knew the last bus would have gone from the village now, and he'd have to trek to the main road. I expected she would ask him to walk her home first. My eyes stung at the thought. Kit's elbow remained sharp and I remembered what it had felt like to be snuggled into Jamie. Sat between his legs, the softness of his jumper, his broad forearms wrapped around me.

But he was never meant to be mine. I'd been claimed. In this village. Where I belonged.

And yet still, I couldn't leave. I didn't want to set off home and leave them together. It wasn't as if she was giving off her usual signals, no tossing of hair, tickling, leaning in, but there was an electricity in the air, a hum of something – anticipation. Change. I feared it.

Kit smoked his last roll-up and Joni was swilling the last of her cider. Jamie offered me one of his Marlboro Lights, and I accepted, even just for the warmth of the amber tip and to justify me still being here. The conversation was drying up and we all knew beds were beckoning. But no one wanted to be the first to go. Including Kit.

'Wow. Look at the moon.' Joni hugged her knees to her

chest as it broke out from behind the navy clouds. 'It's proper yellow.'

We all stared too long. I opened my mouth to say something about the man in the moon, when there was a breaking of a branch and the gentle sound of movement ahead of us in the undergrowth by the tunnel.

'Shit, what's that?' I whispered.

'Sssssh,' Jamie said and held his hand up.

For some reason, I wasn't scared, just curious. We sat still, eyes on the knitted hawthorn branches and the brambles, until a fox slunk out from under the hedgerow. It flattened its back to crawl from its den, then trotted over to the tracks. None of us exhaled.

It looked towards us, yellow eyes piercing in the dark, and paused. I smiled and reached out the palm of my hand. But it turned, not afraid, but uninterested, and trotted towards the gate to the field. Soon, it was just part of the darkness. Engulfed and welcomed.

'I've never seen a fox before.' Jamie turned his head and locked eyes with me. 'That was amazing.'

I felt it too.

'It's a fucking fox, man. They're vermin round here.' Kit cracked his neck, then his knuckles. 'Bedtime, baby.'

I could tell he was trying to give the impression that bed was shared. And for the first time that night, I felt the irritation grow.

'They're not vermin. They're beautiful.'

'They really are,' Jamie agreed and Joni rolled her eyes to herself. Again, I couldn't work out her game plan, but all of a sudden, I just felt very, very tired.

'OK, I'm heading home. You don't have to walk me, it's out of the way,' I said pointedly to Kit.

He frowned. 'You're not walking home alone.'

'The village is still heaving, Kit,' Joni said. Was she on my side? Or hers?

We cut down the ginnel and back out onto the road and stood facing each other.

'Bus stop is that way,' Kit pointed with his thumb behind us. 'You know where you're going?'

'Yeah,' Jamie nodded. 'OK, see you.'

The ease and the closeness had somehow disappeared between the party and the railway. I wanted to reach out and hug him. But I knew better.

'Here,' I said, fishing into my pocket for his cigarette packet. 'Don't forget these.'

'Keep them. There's only a couple left. I've got a fresh pack.' He smiled. 'Have one before bed. See you guys. Let's not leave it so long, yeah?'

We all nodded and watched as he turned, shoved his hands deep down in his pockets, and walked away. Kit made sure he was gone before turning to me.

'OK, well, I guess I'll head off. You OK?'

'Yes, I'm fine.' I gestured up the hill. 'See, there's still people about.'

Joni and I hugged, but she waisn't making any attempt to head left up her road. She was just moving from one foot to the other. I was terrified she was going to run after Jamie. But there was nothing I could do but turn and walk away. Once I did, so did Kit, and we rippled out in our different directions. But when I got to the top of the hill, and I turned, Joni was there, smoking a cigarette at the crossroads. I held my hand up slowly in a wave. And she was looking at me too, because she did the same. Then she threw the cigarette on the floor, and stubbed it out with her boot, turned and walked away.

I pulled out Jamie's packet of cigs to count how many he'd given me, and saw, as I opened it, there was something written on the side.

Come back at midnight.

The church bells began to chime.

32
Now

The next month passes in a painful, slow fog. Like we are all being slowly gassed.

The DNA in the tooth comes back as a match to the baby bones. I knew it would.

Kit is at first furious that I have told Millie, but eventually seems relieved that it wouldn't be him having that horrendous conversation. Millie hasn't asked again who her real dad is. Her biological one, I mean. I think there's a huge part of her that doesn't want to know. She barely speaks to me now. I suppose I should get her some counselling, but I wouldn't know where to start. And I'm selfish and scared of the kind of trouble me and Kit would end up in. It lies there between us, a huge, writhing slug of a secret that someone has poured salt on.

Tom still sits and stares at the Gallows Tree. I think he is waiting for it to sprout again. I can't tell whether he wants something of Kit's to appear or not. Would it make it safer for him if we were all on there? Or worse because that confirms it's someone who knows what we've done. He never forgave himself for lying to us to keep me out of trouble, I'm sure. Although was it a lie? Who knows? I have no idea what's real anymore.

Jamie is pleading not guilty, but they've not given him

bail. I've been warned it will be at least another year, maybe two, before it all comes to trial. I will have to give evidence. A lot of statements have been made. The press have had to drop everything now he has been charged.

They thought it was a crime of passion to start with. But now the baby has been found, well, it's taken a darker turn. That perhaps Joni dug it up out of guilt, and Jamie panicked. Perhaps he tried to silence her. And it all went wrong.

Most women are killed by someone they know.

There's no sign of a body. I can't bear to think of her like that anyway. Rotting. I can't. Sometimes at night, I see her in my mind. Her flesh coming away from the bone. And I cling onto Kit and cry into his back. I feel like something is missing inside me.

I think about him too. In a cell. The moon on the water. *It was always you, Cass.*

There are so many lies around me, I can't unpick the truth anymore. Everything feels like the veil of a dream. My little world is not turning in the same way and never will.

But wherever there is dark, there is light. Without evil, you can't have good.

Kit has picked up his guitar again. Last night, I heard him playing 'Cross Road Blues' and I smiled.

Millie and Chris are officially an item. They sit on the sofa and watch Netflix. No drinking cheap shit outside the pub or smoking dog ends of cigs from the ashtray. They are far too woke and mindful for that. He puts his arm round her and she snuggles in. That tiny little movement makes me so happy. Kit and I are back sleeping in the same bed.

I cling onto crusts. And I wait for something, anything, to happen.

After another few weeks, Millie begins to acknowledge

me. I think it was the day we found out we could have a funeral for Joni. With an empty coffin, of course. Her dad was too far gone to be involved, so it fell to me to decide what to do. I was googling at the kitchen table, tears pouring down my cheeks, when Millie came in from school. There was no way I would ever insult Joni's memory by holding her service in that church. With that man.

'What about a mini festival?' Millie suggested over my head. 'Up at the field. Couple of bands. We could call it Joni-fest.'

'Oh my God, Millie. That's perfect.' I turned and smiled at her and she returned it. I reached for her and she ducked out the way. But later that night she silently handed me her hairbrush. I've never been so grateful.

Now, sat at the kitchen table, Millie lets me plait her hair before school. I can't do it as well as she can, all French braids at the crown like some kind of *Game of Thrones* character. Except we never got to see the last few series. We can't afford Sky.

It's early still. I'm going into work today. I have been for a few days now. It's peaceful. A beautiful juxtaposition to the noise in my head. Yesterday, though, I spent an hour picking off every petal, one by one, of a black magic rose. I didn't even realise I'd done it until I looked down and saw the velvety petals strewn across the counter like bloodshed.

Millie pats her head and tilts her face up at me, and smiles. Those beautiful green eyes. I lean down and kiss her forehead.

'Is that OK?'

'Yeah. Feels tight. Thanks, Mum.'

She pushes her chair back to stand and I realise how much taller she has become. As tall, if not taller, than me and Kit.

She is so beautiful. Gazelle-like. She has no idea. I know she believes she is clunky, awkward. Like me.

'Millie?' I call after her as she shrugs her coat on for school.

'Yeah, Mum?' She looks back over her shoulder and it is pure Pete.

'I love you baby,' I say.

She smiles back and rolls her eyes. 'Love you too.'

Stay with me. Stay with me.

She won't, I hope. I hope so much she is not cursed. She is so much stronger than that.

My phone rings. It's an unknown number, but I answer anyway, as it's normally the police when it's withheld.

'Hello?' I start to clear the breakfast dishes.

There's no reply.

I look back down at my phone to see if the number has magically changed. But it's still withheld.

'Hello?' I say again. Still silent. I hang up, assuming it's a personal injury cold caller. But then the phone vibrates in my hand again.

I answer again. But still there is silence. Or almost silence. I cock my head. There's a noise in the background. It sounds like a baby crying.

'Hello?' I try again. 'I'm sorry, I can't hear you.'

Another noise. A muted wail. Of a newborn.

I hang up. And turn my phone off at the source. The air around me feels tight and squalid and the walls feel as if they have started pulsating along with the blood in my ears.

I start to chew on my nails, when all of sudden there is a loud bang at the window. I scream and jump back. Something is hanging down. Something navy and red. Then I realise the red is hair and a noise comes from within – a rattle, then a whine. Before I know it, I am howling like an animal and clawing at the handle of the door.

Millie. 'MILLIE!' I scream and rush out into the yard. She's there, or something is there. Hanging from a rope, dangling from the guttering. It takes me a few seconds to realise the navy is her school uniform. But the red is straw. The whole body is straw. I turn and retch onto the patio. The smell of lavender and rosemary from the pots by the step overwhelms me for a second and I breathe deeply, once, twice, before I stand up again and try to understand what I am seeing.

Not so much a scarecrow, more an effigy. Straw, twigs, a crown twisted together of metal and hawthorn. Millie's school jumper stuffed with grasses. The hair is made from red ornamental grass. Like the stuff we use in the shop. Exactly the same.

My phone vibrates.

Shaking, I answer. And raise it to my ear. I don't say hello this time.

And the noise is different now. It's not a baby crying.

It's a train.

I don't even turn to shut the kitchen door, or stop to slip shoes onto my feet. I run out into the street, and cut my soles on the sharpness of the gravel. The smashed glass outside the pub. More and more scars. I run past the Gallows Tree and I swear I can almost feel its roots erupting through the tarmac. It is not pleased. I pick up speed and run down the hill, past Tom's house. I catch a glimpse of his haggard face in the window, but I don't stop.

The clouds seem to be parting the sky, almost like Moses and the Red Sea. I am running through the rolled-back waves, past the mill. Past the fields. Across the burned-out works. Up the lane where Billy Miles's house once squatted. Now just decayed. Like the village. Like the hearts.

My arms are scratched from branches and barbed wire by the time I clamber through the thicket, over the wall. I haven't been to the tunnel in years.

It is there, mouth gaping, its teeth mossed and rotten. It is overgrown, of course. But not so much that I couldn't pick my way through it. I stand in the mashed-down footsteps of where someone has trodden before me. My feet are already wet and the stones are slippy. The air inside the tunnel cold and insidious. I hadn't thought to stop to bring a torch, or even my phone.

'Millie?' I call out and listen to her name, her beautiful, precious name, bounce and spin off the wall, as if being tossed around by the ghost children playing catch.

She isn't here. I can't sense her. Unless she is too deep into the tunnel. But there is someone here. Something. I can feel the breath, sense the tunnel inhale. I can almost see its sticky black tarred lungs in the dark ahead.

I walk into the thickness.

'Millie?' I call again.

My heart flutters in my chest and my skin is crawling like I am covered in scales.

It wasn't a scarecrow. It was an effigy. A sacrifice.

I know all about sacrifice.

The sacrifice I had made in here. The sacrifices I am making now.

I carry on. 'Millie?' I call again.

Each step I take, I feel my bones tremble. I'm getting nearer. Nearer to the place. I will never forget it. Even though it was dark, and grey, and monotonous and the bricks look the same. I know. I know where it was.

Sacrifice.

I am still shuffling forward when there is a scuffle and a spark in the darkness. A tall figure steps out into the middle of the tunnel, holding a lit cigarette. It's only when he lifts it up and inhales a deep drag that I can see his face.

33
Then – 1997

Joni squeezed my hand, but it was no use. The vomit lurched up through my guts and burned my throat. I let go of her and placed my palms flat against the slimy walls of the tunnel. It splattered on my boots and horrible joggers, but I didn't care. My waters had broken hours and hours earlier and it felt as if the pain was never going to end.

'Cass, please, let's go to a hospital,' Joni begged, gathering my hair in one hand and stroking my back with the other. 'I don't know what to do.'

'No.' I shook my head. 'No. I can't.'

'Cass, come on. It's OK. No one will be mad.'

'I can't. I can't do that. Kit ... he will be devastated. He won't look at me the same. He thinks I'm a virgin.'

'So what? Who cares? So he breaks up with you. That's the worst that can happen. If we don't go to hospital, Cass, I'm scared. I don't know what to do. I can't do this!'

There were no tears left to cry. I loathed everything about myself. I could barely even look in the mirror anymore. When I did, I saw a sallow, gaunt version. I spent hours sobbing in the foetal position in the fields, lying on my back, silently screaming at the stars. Waiting and waiting. The sky was a cold, cruel dome that stretched on and on, reached out, treacherously beyond the village. I couldn't fathom the end, either of the sky or of me. The guilt grew and grew in my belly. I had become everything I couldn't bear.

The book I'd taken that time, from the shop in Haworth, it spoke of the Malleus Maleficarum. *All witchcraft comes from carnal lust, which is in women insatiable.*

It was burned on my mind. I was being punished.

I didn't even realise until I was too far along. My periods, scattergun at the best of times, had still been making an appearance. My belly had swollen, but so had my hips and breasts. I had assumed I was just developing the womanly figure I had so often envied on Joni. A late bloomer. Having lost so much weight after the fire, when the scales began to creep up, I thought it was normal. That I was recovering. I hadn't even remembered what a normal weight was.

Kit hadn't noticed. Hands always over my shapeless hoodies and nineties fashion for oversized shirts and combats.

I was trimming the thorns at the florist's when I first felt the kick. A little butterfly in the stomach. Soft, gentle, tiny movements. Period pain, I put it down to. Then they started becoming stronger over the next few weeks. One night, I was lying in bed with a book resting on my stomach when I saw it jump. The book moved. I scuttled up and stared in utter astonishment, pulling my T-shirt up, half expecting an alien to burst out of it.

It moved again. Just a flicker. I jumped out of bed and yanked on a jumper, and ran to Joni's. Her dad answered my hammering, but was nonplussed. Not that he didn't care, but he was used to my red puffy eyes. Normally, he would open the door and hug me. Check if I needed help moving Mum. Or some food. He stroked my hair once and I closed my eyes and lay my head on his chest until he coughed and stiffened and I felt like I had done something wrong but didn't know what.

This time, he didn't reach out for me. I think he must have seen the fear in my eyes. Instead, he just shouted for Joni. I thundered up the stairs. Joni was sat cross-legged on her bed dicking about with her tarot. With one hand, I swept them to the floor.

'What? What's happened?' Joni got to her feet.

I lifted up my T-shirt. Her eyes flickered over my body, but she just shook her head.

'What am I looking at?'

'I thought it was weight. I thought I was just getting fat. But, Joni, I swear I felt something kick. I swear I did. Well, I know I did. I saw it.'

'Are you kidding me?' Joni said. 'You lost your virginity and didn't *tell* me?'

'That's not the most important thing right now.'

'Well it is to me. I'm hurt.'

'JONI!'

We both stared at my stomach, but nothing moved. It was the longest minute ever.

'I don't see anything.'

'Well, it's stopped now.' I dropped down onto the floor and sank my head between my knees.

'Well, have you done a test?' Joni sat down next to me, and pulled the crochet blanket off her bed to wrap around us both. I hadn't even realised I was shaking.

'No. I mean, I had no idea.' I looked at her with wide eyes. 'I can't even afford a test. They are, like, almost a fiver.'

'Get Kit to pay.'

'Joni …' I couldn't bring myself to say it.

'Isn't it Kit's?'

My face contorted and pushed into unfamiliar positions. I felt like *The Scream* painting.

Of course I'd gone back that night. That All Gallows' Eve. He was waiting for me. By the tunnel. We didn't even speak. He stroked my cheek and cupped the back of my head in his hand and whispered sweet little lies and promises of forever.

It will always be you, Cass.

I gave him what I could never give Kit. Because then, in that moment, I thought I knew what true love was.

'Joni, please help me.' I buried my head in her lap and let her rock me, her hand on my hair. The touch I always craved. Deep in my gut, I could feel something evil growing.

I sat, day after day, in the front room. Staring blankly at the broken TV screen. Clearing up bottles. Getting the bus to the florist's. Pruning. Clipping. My arrangements were weak. There were times I wanted to plunge the secateurs into my stomach. The new buds going into bloom made me sick. This wasn't supposed to happen. This baby couldn't be mine. I was being punished.

And then, that Thursday morning, when I was awake early, staring dully out of my bedroom window at the crows picking at the guttering, there was a tight, odd pain, which shot across my back. I shifted onto my side and felt something contract and then pop. Warm fluid gushed out of me, thick, fast and completely detached. I threw back the bedclothes and jumped up, watching it splatter aggressively on the floor with force. It was tinged with pink, and smelled sweet. I stared with a mix of horror and relief. I was way, way too early. Adrenaline flooded through me. My thighs were becoming sticky and cold. I stared at the stain on the carpet, on my bed. When I was sure the waters had stopped, I stripped the covers and scrubbed at the mattress. Then I did the same thing with the cheap thin carpet, already thinking what excuses I could give my mum.

Then, after I'd done the best I could to conceal what had come out of me, I went to the phone to call Joni. Disconnected, of course. I was on my last pair of knickers now, so I stuffed them with toilet roll, changed my trousers into my PE joggers, checked on my mum, and set off to Joni's house to tell her I was in labour.

The pain became almost exquisite. At first, the contractions were bearable. I thought I could do it. But after a while, the rise in them had me doubled over and holding my breath. Joni tried to get me to breathe in and out with her, but I couldn't open my mouth for long enough to inhale without screaming.

'Please, Cass,' Joni sounded desperate. 'Let's get you to the hospital. We can give a fake name. God, you can leave the baby there. They'll take care of it. Please, Cass, I'm scared.'

'Don't be scared,' I said weakly. 'I can do this. I know I can. Just not here. People will hear the screams.'

'Well, where, Cass? Where do you want to go. The fields?'

I was in too much pain to reply, so I shook my head and just gasped.

'OK, I know.' Joni put her arm round me and hoisted me up. 'I've got you. Don't let go.'

I had no idea where she was taking me. All I could think of was the pain and the sweet relief between contractions. Joni tried to get me moving in those minutes, almost dragging me. But then the tightening would begin in my belly and I could do nothing but freeze and squeeze my eyes tight and clutch onto her, begging her to make it stop.

'Cass, come on. Hold it together,' Joni muttered as we approached the cobbles and main street into the village.

'I can't,' I rasped. 'The pain. Oh God. I can't move.'

A red Ford Fiesta slowed down as Joni tried to make me stand up straight.

'You girls all right?' Tom's gran wound down her window. The effort made her tricep wobble.

'Fine. Yeah. Cass just has a tummy bug. I'm taking her home,' Joni smiled and tried to make me keep moving, but a fresh contraction ripped across my abdomen. I couldn't help it, I opened my mouth and screamed.

'My goodness. Get in the car, Cass. I'll take you home.' She started to unbuckle her belt and went to open the door, but Joni started to protest.

'I . . . I need the fresh air,' I managed to garble. 'I'm OK.'

We both willed her to keep driving, but she looked at us with concern.

'Honestly, Coral, I'll keep her moving. That's best. Like colic. And horses.' Joni pulled me by my shoulders and dragged me away, Coral staring in the rear-view mirror as she drove away.

'Does she know?' I panted, as we approached the ginnel.

'No. She'll just think you're on drugs.'

'OK, good.' I gripped onto the fencing as another contraction came. 'Where are we going?'

'I'm sorry – you're not going to like it,' Joni said apologetically. 'But it's the only place we can guarantee there'll be no one about.'

For the next few hours, I thrashed and screamed into Joni's lap. I had no idea what my pain barrier had become. I didn't know I could take that level of agony and still survive. Just when I thought I couldn't take it any longer, and was praying for death, Joni moved down. I lay on my back, with my

LISA ROOKES

legs wide and screwed my eyes closed and listened for the
scurry of the rats. The cries of the ghost children.

I gave birth to a baby boy at 2.34 a.m. on a Friday morning on the wet, grey floor of an abandoned railway tunnel.

34
Now

'Where's Millie, Pete?' I say calmly. I suppose a part of me knew this day would come. I knew he would figure it out. He isn't stupid, like Tom. Said with love, of course. Or trusting, like Kit. 'What have you done with my daughter?'

He takes another drag. The exhale of smoke is strange and foggy in the dark.

'She's not your daughter, though, is she?' His eyes are dead.

'Is she OK?' My voice rises and I try to steady it. 'Why would you do this? Why are you here?'

'Why do you think we are here?' Pete asks me back. I can't tell if he is drunk or stoned. His voice is scaring me. So matter-of-fact. So cold.

We stand off. The air feels tight and I pull at my collar. I am both warm and shivering.

'I don't know. I'll ask you again. Why are you here?'

'Because I know your secret,' Pete says and steps towards me. 'I know it was you that hung those nooses on the Gallows Tree.'

I don't say anything.

'Why did you do it to us? You psycho. And what's the deal with this place?' Pete grabs me by the shoulders and I try to shrug out of his grasp, but his fingers are kneading into me, into the tender, thin stretched flesh of my armpits, and I cry out in pain. 'Why did Joni come down here all the time? What happened here?'

'Pete, you're hurting me,' I sob and try to wriggle away. 'Please promise me Millie is safe. Promise me you haven't done anything to her.'

At this point, he lets go and I fall backward and lose my footing. I throw my hands down onto the ground to break my fall and my palm closes over Pete's lit cigarette butt. I scream as it burns into the centre of my palm.

'How can you even ask me that?' He stands over me. 'How could you?'

'How could you threaten me … with Millie? You know how much I love her.'

'You took everything from me.' Pete leans so his hands are clasping his knees and his face is pressed into mine. I try to scuttle back. But I can't. He has grabbed me again. 'You scared the shit out of all of us. How does it feel now?'

'Pete, STOP IT! You don't understand!'

He is shaking his head, and I am now afraid. The look in his eye. The death stare has rolled and there is rage.

'You fucking lying bitch. You got to Kit. You got to Jamie. Tom's so fucking scared, he won't come out of the house. What, were you trying to set me up too? I was nearly fuck-ing arrested.'

'What do you want from me?' I beg.

'I want the truth. I want to know what happened in this tunnel. Why she used to come here. And cry. And I want to know where she is. And I want to know why she gave you her fucking baby. *Our* baby. *My* baby.'

Tears fall down my cheeks and I start to try to pick myself up, but Pete drags me to my feet.

'If you don't tell me, I'm going straight to the police,' he hisses in my ear.

'Pete, you know why Joni gave me Millie. She didn't want a baby...'

'Did she tell you? That Millie was mine? Did you even care? Does Kit know? You made her do it, I know you did. She wouldn't just give her up. Why? Why the nooses? What the fuck kind of game are you playing? Where's Joni, Cass? What have you done?'

I turn my face away from his spittle. I can smell whisky now. And pot. And something else. Something rancid and animalistic.

'I've stopped it all now. I'm sorry,' I sob.

'What?' Pete grabs my jaw and yanks my face towards his. I feel a sickening, wrenching pain in my neck.

'It *was* me. Hanging the nooses. But I swear, I don't know where Joni is. I didn't hang her crown. That one wasn't me. But then, the way it brought us all back together. I just, I wanted it. I needed you all. And you all hated me.'

'You sick bitch. Where did you get it? All that stuff? Where?'

'I've always had it. Me and Joni did, I mean. One day, when we were looking for Christmas lights, we found it. Up in her dad's attic. The charred sleeping bags. My melted doll. Joni panicked at first. We never said anything to her dad. He never said anything to us. He must have known all along, when he was putting out that fire, damping it down. He must have known it was us.'

'You saw the state of Tom. How could you?' Pete pushes me away and I stumble, my hands making a ugly, wet slapping noise against the wall.

'It had gone too far. I'm sorry. I'm so sorry. How ... how did you know it was me?' I splutter.

'I saw you. Well. Not exactly saw you. That night when you said you were going out to call Millie. And then all of sudden Tom's sticks? I had my suspicions. But I didn't know for sure. Until now.'

'Are you going to tell anyone?'

'And upset everyone even more? God, you're so pathetic.' He stands over me. 'All this for attention? When your best friend is missing? When her body is lying somewhere ... probably fucking mutilated ...' Pete's voice cracks. 'I loved her. I loved her. She had my baby.'

Ugly, raw, rasping sobs come up and out of his chest, and I reach for him, but he pushes me away, and runs.

And I fall to my knees and pull at my hair so hard, I hear the strands rip from the scalp.

35

Then — 1997

I couldn't feel pain anymore. It had stopped. Everything had stopped. My scalp could feel every tiny little shard and pebble and rock digging down into me. There was wetness — blood, I assumed — between my thighs. But what was once warm was now cooling.

There was greyness all around me and I couldn't hear anything. Just the rasp of my breath. Joni's shaky inhale.

'Why isn't it crying?' I pulled myself up onto my elbows. A low pain grumbled across the lower part of my stomach.

'I ...' Joni was wrapping it in her jumper. 'I think it's cold.'

'Give it to me.' I opened my arms up, but Joni just clung it to her chest and closed her eyes. 'Is there ... something wrong with it? What is it? Is it ... is it a boy or a girl?' I could barely focus. It took me a while to understand it was over. That the bundle clasped to her chest, belonged to me. It was on the outside. It was real.

'It's a boy,' she whispered, rubbing it hard on its back, the way I once saw her dad do to the runt of her cat's litter when it came out cold.

'Let me hold him,' I croaked. I tried to sit up, but the pain started to come back.

'Cass ...'

I looked in her eyes and in that moment I had never felt

horror in the way I felt it then. Its blackness squeezed my throat, my lungs. All the air seemed to disappear from my body in one giant swoop.

'Is he ... OK?'

Joni passed him over to me. Her eyes were wide and frightened. Like a deer. I looked down into her jumper and, suddenly, there he was.

My son.

I had never loved or been so afraid of anything more.

Joni put him in my arms and I looked at him. I couldn't see his eyes. They were closed. There was a strange snuffling sound. I looked at Joni and saw the tears running down her face.

'What's wrong with him?' I asked again.

'I think ... I think he's just really, really early, Cass,' Joni said, and came to me. To us. His little body was warm and I smelled his head, kissed his tiny blue lips.

'I love you,' I said, willing him to open his eyes. His chest wasn't rising. 'Please breathe,' I said. 'Breathe, little one.'

And then, just like that, he was gone.

I knew the minute his soul left his body. The second his tiny light went out. Like the way they tell you the mothers of soldiers know the second the bullet hits. I held him until his body was limp and his skin was cold.

Joni cut the umbilical cord with Pete's penknife that she had found in her bag.

'I want him to be buried in the church,' I said to Joni. 'He needs to be buried properly.'

She nodded. 'I think once we get to the hospital, they can figure all that out ...'

'No,' I said. 'You don't understand. Now. It needs to be now. Call him. Get him.'

'Cass, why?'

'Because I don't want anyone to know. What's the point now?'

I squeezed him to me as I delivered the afterbirth. Joni wrapped it in an Iceland carrier bag and dumped it in one of the bins outside the houses by the track.

And just like that, I wasn't pregnant anymore.

But I wasn't a mother either.

My legs hardly managed the walk back through the tunnel. Joni held me up the entire way. By the time we were at the churchyard, it was gone two in the morning. The reverend was in his dressing gown. He looked at the bundle in my arms with an expression somewhere between disbelief and disgust. The same way I looked at him.

And before the dawn broke, the reverend, who had proved his alliance with the devil, blessed my dead baby, and we buried him under the night sky in an unmarked grave. The sparrows sang a lullaby when dawn broke.

I didn't return to the spot for twenty-six years, when I got on my hands and knees on All Gallows' Eve, and dug and dug and dug in the driving rain, until the earth and mud streaked my hands and arms like dark brown blood. And my fingers closed round his tiny skull.

I called him Billy.

36

Then — 2008

When we'd got out of Joni's dad's van after that trip to Haworth, I'd kept the book stuffed up my jumper. I hadn't meant to shoplift. Something made me keep hold of it. That night, I'd curled up on my bed after I'd put Mum to bed, and flicked through it.

The song was in it. Of course it was. 'The Gallows Tree and the Scarecrow'. It's in every Yorkshire myths and legends book there is, along with the Beast of Ossett, Mother Shipton, the Cottingley fairies and the Plumpton redcaps. But I didn't know all the history. The theories. They don't teach you about sacrifice at school — they just make you sit cross-legged on carpets and sing Jesus bangers.

At the end of the Black Plague, after a wall was built to keep the infected bricked in, the village did indeed blossom. A new road was built. The inn was built. The farmers were blessed. The mill was constructed and the wool trade breathed life back into our home.

When public hangings were banned on the Gallows Tree in 1868, the poetry came thick and fast. The bloodthirsty ghouls of the village were outraged. A letter was penned to Queen Victoria to beg her to reconsider, stating the need for the crops to grow from the blood of the gallows. But the letter was intercepted, and the bearer strung up through fears that word would reach the Queen that the village was full of witches.

And so the Gallows Tree remained bare and the mill fell dark.

But no matter what has been thrown at Thistleswaite, it survived.

I started thinking. I watched the scarecrows in the fields. Each time they rotted and disintegrated, another would spring back up in its place.

I started thinking a lot about sacrifice after that. The song. The legends.

They got it all wrong in *The Wicker Man*. Sacrifice isn't sacrifice unless you are giving up something you love.

Then, it's just murder.

I could put a pin in the moment things started to fall apart with Kit. I'd come down ready for work for five minutes of blissful peace while Millie had her morning nap, Kit was sat on the sofa, lacing up his work boots. I could tell the moment I opened the door he was in one of his moods. The clenched jaw. The twitchy muscle. Always when he felt humiliated.

'You said you were going to make a doctor's appointment,' he said without even looking up. 'I bet you've not bothered, have you?'

'I just haven't had time,' I started, but he stood up fast and pushed past me into the kitchen.

'That's because you're always looking after her. No wonder you can't get pregnant. You're either working or dealing with your mum. Or with Joni. I don't even think you want our own baby. You're happy with hers. It's sick.'

'Kit...'

'It's embarrassing. At work. With the lads. They say I'm

firing blanks. *Me*. Making jokes about Millie being the milkman's. Do you have any idea what that's like?'

I shouted back, about not having time to even go for a smear test, due to the shifts I was pulling at the florist's to keep the mortgage covered.

I got the usual. How can I keep in work when we're in a recession and no one can afford to have their houses painted? I argued about the contract he turned down at the council flats. He called me a cold bitch. I muttered under my breath that he was an egotistical wanker. He left for work.

I hadn't been over to Mum's since the morning before. That was unusual for me. I went most nights. Made sure she was on her side. Changed the bedding. I couldn't normally get it washed fast enough. But last night, I just didn't have the energy. I'd had a nightmare getting Millie to bed. Even as a baby, she was as defiant as Joni and as stubborn as Pete. It was moments like those, moments when I looked into her eyes, deeply, searching for a shred of me, somewhere, anywhere, even though I knew it was impossible. She was like a jack-in-the-box. Jumping up and rattling the bars of her cot. Way past her bedtime. Eyes wild and overtired. Brain racing. Screaming into my face.

I had closed her bedroom door after what felt like the billionth time and sat on the top stair and cried and cried silent tears into the knees of my jeans. Her sobs and screams were like razors going through me. Leave her to cry it out, that's what Kit kept telling me. I wondered if he would say the same if it was his, really his little girl behind the bars. Eventually, we both fell asleep where we were. Kit came back home from wherever he had been, Tom's probably, and put us both under our duvets. I had briefly thought about going to Mum's, but Kit had shushed it away.

I fell into a deep, dreamless sleep. But I still awoke with a jolt at the sound of Millie's early morning mews. It was barely light. I'd go straight over to Mum's after Millie's nap, I told myself.

After Kit had stormed out, I wiped down the kitchen surface while the kettle boiled, and clocked another red bill propped up behind the coffee tin. The fridge was pretty empty, but I managed to rustle up some porridge for Millie when she woke and left my own stomach growling. Wrestling with the buggy, I eventually managed to get her strapped in, feeling like I was losing a battle with an octopus on speed. The walk to Mum's was hardly long, but it felt like an eternity that morning. I had a gnawing rat-like feeling in my guts as I bumped the buggy too hard over the cobbles and ignored Millie's squeals of delight as she was flung about. I told myself it was just the argument with Kit that had knocked me off my stride. That everything was fine. It was all going to be OK.

The house looked normal. Of course it would. Curtains open because I hadn't been in the night before to draw them. But I left Millie strapped into her buggy in the kitchen, because I could smell it as soon as I'd opened the front door. I knew that smell. Mum was in bed, there was vomit on the pillow, dried and cracked down her face. Diarrhoea in the bed. I smelt it before I pulled back the sheet. Blood this time too. I pulled the sheet back over.

There were pills as well. On the coffee table. I looked at the silver blister packs to work out what they were, but whatever they were, they were too cheap, or too illegal, to have a brand name.

'Mum,' I whispered, and took her face, her chin, in my hand. Her skin looked nicotine-stained and translucent. She was so fragile. Like a baby bird. Like Billy. I wouldn't have been surprised if her head had fallen off in my hands.

She didn't respond.

'Mum?' I said louder. Downstairs, I could hear Millie singing 'Twinkle Twinkle Little Star' in her baby gabble. My heart began to race. I shook the bones of Mum's shoulders and heard her teeth rattle. 'MUM!'

I knew what was happening. I didn't have that air of disbelief. I didn't even get the panic. I suppose, deep down, I had been waiting for this moment since I was fourteen years old. What I felt was ... relief.

'Caaaaa ...' The words were slurred, as if her tongue had swollen like a fat slug in her mouth.

'Mum ...' I fished in my back pocket for my phone, but she grabbed my wrist. The grip was too weak. I could have shaken her off. I could have tried harder. But I didn't.

'Am I alive?' That's what she said. *Am I alive?* The look of utter disappointment, of despair even, in her eyes was too much to bear. I looked again at the blister packs. At the two empty bottles of cheap vodka on the floor. At the one, still rolling on the bed, half full.

I walked downstairs like a zombie. Checked on Millie, found a glass and a spoon. It was smeared and dirty, but what difference did that make? The trudge back up was as if I was in some crazy mirrored funhouse, slipping and sliding, all funny angles and jagged edges. A maniacal laugh ringing in my head. When I got back to the room, my mother's eyes were wide open. She looked at me, beseechingly. The way Millie did when she was a baby and needed milk in the night.

I crushed the rest of the pills up in the glass and then poured the rest of the vodka in, swirling and stirring it until it was all mixed in. She watched and drank it from me as I held her head up.

'That's it. A little more. Good girl,' I said softly.

At the end, I washed the glass down. Then sat by the side of the bed until she fell back asleep. I stroked her hair, once bleached white, now an oddly tainted yellow, until I heard her breathing become shallow and her chest rattle. It was like straw breaking between my fingers. I left the door open so she could hear Millie singing her strange, contorted lullabies.

When I left, there was a small smile on her face and her chest had stopped the rasps. I kissed her on her temple. Then I went downstairs, and took Millie home.

For years, the world was black. The village was dead. My heart was flatlined. Until that message. From Jamie. A spark. A lifeline. Something brought me back to life.

That's when I realised.

Sacrifice doesn't mean death. Billy, I didn't love. The baby, I didn't kill. Mum was an act of mercy.

Sacrifice means something more.

It means being prepared to lose it all.

37

All Gallows' Eve

'Can you hold my phone?' Jamie pulled it from his back pocket. 'I'm going to go down in this tug of war and I don't have a case at the moment. It's new.'

'Sure.' It slithered into my jeans like a fish, all shiny and slippery. 'You don't have to do this, you know.' I nodded over to where Tom was limbering up while Pete smoked a cig and laughed at him.

'Oh but I do ...' Jamie winked at me. 'I can't show my face in this village again if I don't at least attempt to partake in an outdated, alpha male pissing contest.'

'Well, I'm not going to watch,' I lied. 'I'm off to get another drink.'

'Oh thanks. Sending me off to my gallows.' He shook his head with affection and headed up the rec, along the white chalked lines marked out for the kids' relay race.

The sun was just starting to drop and you could see the midges were out by people randomly slapping themselves. I watched him walk away, a strange glow from the falling light around his crown, like a halo.

I knew Tom and Pete wouldn't exactly make him feel welcome. But, equally, I knew why he was doing it.

'Drink?' Joni slung her arm around my neck and held up a bottle of wine. 'You look like you need it. How's it going with your lover then?' She nodded up the rec. 'Fucking hell, is he doing the tug of war?'

'Don't call him my lover, it makes me sound like I'm in a Harlequin romance.'

'Well, you are. Brooding, stormy, estranged husband. Fit, rich man from the past. With a massive—'

'STOP!'

Joni laughed and filled up my glass while I looked back at the gathering teams, Jamie standing awkwardly between sides.

'How do you know anyway?' I scowled.

'You can always tell,' Joni shrugged. 'Why else would I have ever gone there with Pete?'

I shook my head. 'I don't want to watch. I've got a bad feeling Jamie's about to be dragged through the mud.'

'In more ways than one,' Joni agreed. 'Come on, shall we go and rig the voting jar again?'

'You don't need to rig it.' I slapped her arm as we set off down the field towards the cobbles. 'You'll win. When have you ever not got what you want?'

'Erm ... shall we count?'

I just shook my head and smiled.

More and more people were filling the square now that the kids' races were over. Parents had dutifully watched the sack race, dried eyes over the egg and spoon, and were now either up cheering for the tug of war, the annual battle between our pub and the next village's pub, or starting to concentrate on getting as drunk as possible, ready for tomorrow's hog roast, the annual hangover cure.

The thought of Jamie coming home with me was making me tingle. We'd have to be careful. I wouldn't want Millie to see. The feel of his lips on mine, his hands up my top, grabbing my ribcage, my waist. Whispering the promises he said he was aching to make me.

It was as if I'd been at the bottom of a fish tank for so long, asleep in the green and grey sludge. And now, I was swimming to the surface. Now, I could see the sun glistening on the water. I was so close to breaking through.

The village mums swarmed around Joni immediately. She was infectious. At least, they clearly hoped she was. Like kids around a pied piper, begging for one of her stories or anecdotes on her dating life, all hoping some of her effervescence would rub off on them.

I felt like telling them not to bother. It had never worked for me. I smiled wryly and settled on the wall outside the pub, waiting for her to finish enthralling them all about her trip to the GP last week and them accidentally leaving the tannoy on while she went into explicit detail about her thrush.

There was a buzz in my back pocket as I sat down and, for a second, I panicked, thinking I'd broken Jamie's phone. I'd forgotten it was there. I fished it out to check I hadn't cracked the screen.

And there it was. A notification. On the home screen.

At first, I thought it was mine. That I'd taken out the wrong phone. Because the message was from Joni.

I could only see the first line, without getting into the phone itself. And I knew it was protected by Face ID. But it was enough to make me shake.

You need to tell her about us…

I screwed up my forehead. I didn't understand. I looked up and saw Joni popping her phone back in her bag. She'd just sent it. She must have not realised I had his phone.

I felt the burn of the wine bubble up in my throat and the hairs all over my body jerk.

My eyes raised slowly to hers. She wasn't looking at me. Wasn't thinking of me. She was telling the punchline, flicking her hair, accepting another drink from another hanger-on. I let the plastic glass fall from my hand.

'Please. No,' I whispered.

I could feel myself begin to drown. Weeds grabbing my feet and dragging me back to the sludge. My lungs were bursting and my heart began to hum, like the noise in my ears.

The inside of my head started to pulsate. Him. Her. What had happened? Had anything? Was she trying to make it happen? How could she? How could she do this to me? When she knew, she *knew* how much he meant to me. What I'd gone through, what I'd given up.

Everything began to splinter and crack in my head. I could hear the shouts from the tugging men on the hill. The squeals from the women in the square. The blood pounding in my ears.

Would she tell him? Had she told him? About the baby?

I felt the wine spurt up my throat and I ran to the alley behind the pub and let it all come up into the bins, my stomach clenching and my throat squeezing.

'Cass?'

I looked up. Tom was standing at the end of the alley, a can of lager in his hand. I quickly wiped the vomit off my chin.

'Are you OK?' he said, without meeting my eyes.

'Yeah. Sorry. Just too much wine. Is the tug of war over?' I reached out to steady myself against the wall.

'Yeah. We lost.' He turned and started to walk away before

stopping. I waited for him to turn back round. But he didn't. He paused. And then carried on. Leaving me, on my knees in the gutter in despair.

Two hours later, I watched Joni be crowned. And something inside me died.

When we were little, Tom once rescued a rabbit from the jaws of a spaniel. I can't even remember whose dog it was. He brought it to us, in tears. It was twitching and Pete shook his head at Tom.

'It's too late, mate.'

Tom had opened his mouth to protest, but Pete had already taken a rock, and brought it down on its head. I saw the life leave its eyes. Actually saw it.

And that's how I felt now. An empty carcass. Eyes dim. Breath still.

Jamie had gone home. At least that's where he said he was going. But I had to know.

After I left the party, I crept in the front door and cocked my head to listen out for Millie. There was muffled music coming from inside her room, so I popped in and mouthed to her that I was home, before pouring myself the last of the cheap wine. I watched from the kitchen window as the throngs started to disperse. There was no way Joni would leave until the party ended. It took a while.

I finished the wine, then made myself a coffee and dug in the back of the messy drawer in the kitchen until I found a packet of cigs that both Kit and Millie had claimed did not belong to them. I switched off the kitchen light and watched the orange embers burn in the reflection of the window.

After an hour, there were only stragglers.

No one even batted an eyelid when I slipped on an old black hoodie of Kit's and went over the back wall into the fields. I didn't use a torch, just kept an eye on the strung lights illuminating the inner chambers of the village heart. Nipped over the road, hoodie up, straight onto the rec, over the playing fields. I'd been darting in and out of these shadows since I was knee-high to a grasshopper.

Like I said, I haven't knocked on Joni's door since 1991.

I could hear the shower running and wondered for a moment if she was alone or, for a horrendous, gut-twisting, squirming minute, with Jamie. Taking three deep breaths, I started slowly up the stairs. The plan was for her to be in bed. It was going to be so much easier. But these things don't always go to plan and you have to be resourceful. Resilient. It could work even better, I reassured myself. My mouth was dry and my wrists were weak. I paused at the stop of the steps and sank down. Three more deep breaths. Closing my eyes, I started to remember.

Joni having her hair plaited by the teacher. The first time we played hopscotch in the playground. The smell of Matey on her skin. The bust nose Matthew Molloy received for saying freckles were ugly. Riding rickety bikes through the cornfields and having to stop every hundred yards to put my chain back on. Running through the woods and building dens with fallen branches that we were never to sleep in even though we were convinced we would be allowed. The first time I drank a Blastaway and Joni had to hold my hair back as I puked into the gutter. Watching *The Lost Boys* late at night and me secretly swooning over Corey Haim while she lusted after Jason Patric.

Three more breaths.

Sleeping nose-to-nose, like kittens entwined. Her cleaning the vomit off my mum's cheek. Her dad slipping a fiver into my back pocket when he saw the empty fridge. Directions on hair dye. Nag champa. Green eyes. Red hair. Need. Want. Holding hands when we were too old for it. Inhaling Tipp-Ex. Walking for miles down the old tracks just to see where we would end up. Crows overhead. Lying for hours in the fields, scalp to scalp. Not speaking. Breathing in sync.

Two more breaths.

Feeling the heat of her arm next to me down the aisle when I married Kit. Cutting the cord of Millie after she was born.

One more breath.

The railway tunnel.

All Gallows' Eve.

Maybe if she hadn't been crowned, maybe I could have handled it. Maybe I could have coped with the message that flashed up on Jamie's phone while I was holding it during the tug of war. Maybe I could have shared him. Like we shared everything else in our entire lives.

Or maybe not.

Maybe, for once, I wanted something for me.

Maybe, I didn't always have to be second place. In the shadows.

Maybe ... I was meant for more.

The thought of what sacrifice really meant had been niggling at the corner of my brain for months. Years, if I was truly honest. But I never thought I could do it. Until now.

I stood up. The shower was still running. I reached down into the pocket of Kit's hoodie and pulled out the hammer I'd taken from his toolkit. Then, as I walked slowly to the doorway of the bedroom, watching as the steam billowed from the en suite, I closed my eyes one last time and allowed myself to feel all my love for her. It reached from the ends of my toes to my fingertips. I felt it from my crown to my stomach. I was filled with her. Joni. Joni. Joni. My everything.

Then I stepped forward, opened the shower cubicle and brought the hammer down with all the strength I could muster onto the back of her head.

The booze helped. I don't think she knew it was me, although there is part of me that wanted her to know it was. Her body slumped fast to the side. I had to bring the hammer down a few more times until her skull was soft and spongy and peculiar yellow liquid was flowing out. I'd felt her go on the first hit. I knew. It was as if the lights had plummeted into darkness all around me. I felt part of me shift inside. But still I carried on. I let the water run over her body, over her head, washing the blood away. She didn't open her eyes once. When I felt able, I crouched over her and lifted her eyelid. Her eyes no longer seemed green but polluted. There was no light.

I left the shower running, to make it look like an intruder, and managed to drag her naked body down the stairs after I'd towelled her dry and covered her in her favourite body lotion.

And then I opened the front door, and brought in the scarecrow and laid it by her side. Joni's crown was lying on the kitchen table. I placed it on her head for one last time, and kissed her paling lips.

'I love you, Joni.'

It was like dressing a doll. I took off her crown and untied the rope around the scarecrow's neck, pulling out the straw until just the sack remained. It fit perfectly over Joni's head. I padded it out with straw all around her neck and tied it shut, and then unravelled the chicken wire making up the legs and arms. Singing softly, I layered straw over her skin

305

and moulded the frame over her body and limbs, dressing her finally in the pretty white maypole dress and placing the floral garland on her head.

She had never looked more beautiful. I held the sack head in between my palms and kissed the drawn-on bright pink lips with the kind of passion I have only ever felt once before. Then I gingerly and carefully moved her back to her position by the door, checking the eyes of the neighbouring cottages were still dim. I threw the leftover straw to the animals, retrieved a shovel from the shed, and walked back down to the churchyard. No revellers out anymore, but I still stuck to the ginnels and hedgerows. Darting in and out like a fox, like Joni used to.

The ground was soft. It was as if the gods had sent me rain for this very purpose.

I dropped my shovel once I was deep enough and used my hands to dig, fingers clawing through earthworms and bugs until my skin touched his little bones.

I was always good at looking people in the eye and manipulating them into what to believe.

Just ask the boys.

As the sun stretched in warrior pose and the pale light began to infiltrate the darkness, I tied the crown to the noose of the Gallows Tree and went home. The next morning, I played my part. Checked my phone, like I always did. Called Joni, like I always did. My performance had to be flawless.

I'll admit, I was nervous. Even though I had managed to nestle her body in the centre of the bonfire, I didn't know exactly what smell the burning flesh would make, or what would be left. Luckily, as planned, the meaty, suckling aroma of the hog roast covered up whatever foul stench was emanated, and I was there, on hand, with the accelerant, whenever the fire looked like it might not reach the maximum temperature. Damn the dampened wood, I said as I poured.

Bones don't burn, though. This I already knew. But they don't burn to the chalky white you see on skeletons. Black. Misshapen. They blend well with charred plastic and MDF and all the other rubbish that doesn't burn properly that I bagged up. Just doing my village duty at the crack of dawn.

I clean when I'm anxious.

The next morning, I climbed the crumbling drystone wall into the cornfield, the sun rose and the reds and purples lit the sky surpassing any meagre display attempted by the fireworks the nights before.

When I got to the scarecrow, I wrapped my wisdom tooth, the one I'd had removed and saved as a joke for the tooth fairy, in Joni's sash. The tooth they assumed to be Joni's – and matched to baby Billy's bones. The sun smiled down on the crops as I stood, placed my hands either side of the soggy straw-stuffed sack of his face and kissed him.

Then I went home, got into bed, and fell asleep.

After a while, there were times, I swear, I even forgot myself.

It was all so perfect. Everything just fell into place.

It was as if it was always meant to be this way.

And soon, the crops would grow again.

I could have kept him out of it. If I had wanted to. But it made more sense to frame him.

I am Abraham, sacrificing my son Isaac on the mountain. Because God told him to.

But nobody stopped me, just in time.

I have proved my faith.

I expect the trial will be a media sensation. Murdered Gallows Queen. I bet it will bring some visitors back here again. Now the folk legend that seemed to be getting lost has risen from the ashes. The village will flourish.

Yesterday, I went to the railway tunnel and thought about Joni.

I still see her everywhere. She hasn't left this village. She never would. I see her in the cemetery when I go and scatter wildflowers where my baby once lay. I see her in the meadows. Behind the pub. In the alleyways. On the end of my bed at night. Her hand on her hair. I taste her when I breathe.

It was both of them I had to give up.

The village demanded a sacrifice after all. I didn't realise it. I hadn't planned it. I wanted Jamie all for myself. I wanted to feel free. It was always her keeping me in the village. Tethering me. Like my mother had. I was like a tree pulled down by each and every root. It was only when the hammer splintered her skull that I realised this was it. This was true sacrifice. Giving up something you love.

I may not have killed Jamie. But I still sacrificed him. Like a lamb to the slaughter. His life is over. And so is the love we could have had. So are my chances of happiness.

I have never given up more.

After a few months, Millie and I moved into Joni's cottage. It was left to me in her will. It was as if we belonged there. Like it was always meant for us. Kit was disappointed, of course, when I told him we were moving out. I think he thought everything would go back to how it was. But, of course, everything has changed now. He's OK though. In fact, I think he's happier. The band has reformed, and without Joni to front it, he's the lead singer now too. They've changed their name. Getting a few bookings, weddings mostly.

Everyone said that it was too much for our marriage to

survive. No one blames either of us. When the nights are quiet, and I sit and think about him, I don't feel any malice. Or bitterness. For in a way, he tried to kill me too. But I have risen.

I'm saving up now for Millie's university place. The reverend transfers a bit of cash every month in to my savings account. No doubt from the church collection plate. Hush money. Blood money. Call it what you want. I just call it debt.

Today, I walked to the cornfields. Millie was at school. I'm so pleased she changed her mind and stayed on to sixth form. We can afford university now.

I watch her sleep. I need her to leave this village. This curse. I need her to leave me. Because I love her more than anything in this world. She was never mine and Kit's. She was always mine and Joni's. And it scares me what that could mean.

I've taken a day off work. The florist's, excuse the pun, is blooming. The owner asked me if I wanted to buy her out last week. Her arthritis is getting worse and she struggles with the arrangements now. I have a little bit of money. After all, Joni left it all to me. My crops are plentiful.

Andy is opening the pub again now his mum has passed on. I think that's going to really help the village. I saw on Facebook that Pete even asked him if he would bring back karaoke nights. Poor Pete. In his long flapping coat. Always just looking for that place to belong. I hope he finds it there. He's on new medication now. Sometimes I swear I can see a sparkle of the old Pete in his eyes. I saw him having a drink with a woman from the next village last week, and I even saw him laugh. I wonder if, somehow, he's been freed now too.

Tom is still stunned by everything. He would be, of course. Always the most sensitive of souls. But his business seems to be better now. A terrible accident happened in Shelton, about three villages along. The roof collapsed on one of the new-builds, and the scaffolder was impaled by one of his own poles. Dreadful. This is what happens when you try to bring the new into the old. Now Tom's phone is ringing off the hook. He was always the best of us.

The church bells have been fixed and are ringing again on the hour. The village school has had to put in an application to build a Portakabin. This year's enrolment has been unprecedented. Small schools in the country are very fashionable now. Less disease. A return to old-fashioned values, green spaces. Fresh air.

The hay has been baled and it is golden in the fields. I breathe deeply. The sky is so blue. The trees are so tall. I open my arms wide and stretch out my fingertips to feel the birth of summer grazing the fields.

They say the stories really are just fairy tales. Song. Folklores.

You don't have to believe me.

Just believe that I believe it.

Acknowledgments

I am so grateful to Leodora Darlington at Orion and Heather Weatherill, my former agent (who has a fab new job; she didn't sack me), for seeing the sinister magic in my odd little book. It wasn't everyone's cuppa, but these two powerhouse women brought it to life and made my creepy dreams come true.

Working with Team Lisa has been the most amazing experience – as well as Leodora being such an amazing editor, a massive thank you to Sahil Javed, a mega editorial assistant, and my new agent Elizabeth Counsell at Northbank Talent for jumping on board without even taking a breath.

I wrote this novel during a bit of a rocky time in my life, so thank you to my amazing friends who, as always, have reminded me to straighten my crown and keep on going.

So, firstly, the golden circle, Carolynn, Ruth, Kate, Lynette and Sarah – for the laughs, wine, never-ending support, T-Rex, Queenie, King Louis, First Aid and Fingers – we may not live in each other's pockets, but this year you diamonds have always had my back. I am very grateful for you all. And the fairies. And Whitby.

Arlene, Polly, Michelle, Yvonne, Lindsay, Emma – you've all propped me up and championed me when I felt like giving up. Thank you so much for being so ace. Always.

I loved reliving my nineties teenage years while writing this book – which has meant I got to live out my escapades with Lucy and Becky all over again. I felt you both in every word I wrote. Thank you, and Karen, for being the best friends I could ever have – and for always reminding me of the song in my heart when I've forgotten the words. I know. Utter drivel.

Mum, big sister Suzanne, my dad, and stepdad Dave – thank you for your unwavering belief in me. Dad, for the tales of the Lambton Worm at bedtime which made me fall in love with the art of telling stories. Mum, for always being my biggest cheerleader, first reader, and wherever you are – my home.

And, as usual, my biggest thanks go to Mark, Tommy and Oscar. Without you, the words would not come out. Sometimes the words that *do* come out start with F – but, hey, I'm told I'll look back on your teenage years with joy and fondness. I'd better.

I can't wait for your next chapters. Make them amazing.

I love you all so much.

Thank you. Thank you. Thank you.

Credits

Lisa Rookes and Orion Fiction would like to thank everyone at Orion who worked on the publication of *The Village* in the UK.

Editorial
Leodora Darlington
Snigdha Koirala

Copyeditor
Laura Gerrard

Proofreader
Jade Craddock

Contracts
Dan Herron
Ellie Bowker
Oliver Chacón

Marketing
Jen Hope

Design
Tomás Almeida

Audio
Paul Stark
Louise Richardson

Editorial Management
Charlie Panayiotou
Jane Hughes
Bartley Shaw

Finance
Jasdip Nandra
Nick Gibson
Sue Baker

Sales
David Murphy
Esther Waters
Victoria Laws
Rachael Hum
Georgina Cutler

Production
Ruth Sharvell

Publicity
Sian Baldwin

Operations
Jo Jacobs